ROBERT B. PARKER'S
COLORBLIND

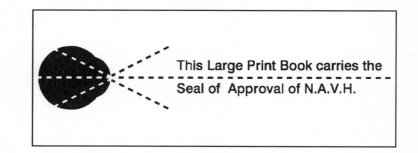
This Large Print Book carries the
Seal of Approval of N.A.V.H.

A JESSE STONE NOVEL

ROBERT B. PARKER'S COLORBLIND

REED FARREL COLEMAN

THORNDIKE PRESS
A part of Gale, a Cengage Company

Farmington Hills, Mich • San Francisco • New York • Waterville, Maine
Meriden, Conn • Mason, Ohio • Chicago

ALL RIGHTS RESERVED

LIBRARY OF CONGRESS CIP DATA ON FILE.
CATALOGUING IN PUBLICATION FOR THIS BOOK
IS AVAILABLE FROM THE LIBRARY OF CONGRESS

ISBN-13: 978-1-4328-5514-7 (hardcover)

Published in 2018 by arrangement with G. P. Putnam's Sons, an imprint of Penguin Publishing Group, a division of Penguin Random House LLC

Printed in the United States of America
1 2 3 4 5 6 7 22 21 20 19 18

FOR ACE ATKINS
AND TOM SCHRECK

It is not flesh and blood, but heart which makes us fathers and sons.

— SCHILLER

1

She thought she might pass out from the ache in her side or that her heart might explode in her chest as she ran barefoot along the dunes. Her beautiful long beaded braids, of which she was rightfully proud, slapped against her shoulders, her face, and fell in front of her eyes. She stopped, trying to catch her breath and to listen for them, for their heavy footfalls, but the low roar of the waves swallowed up all the sounds of the night, much as they had overwhelmed her cries for help.

Too tired to think, she bent over at the waist, sucking in huge gulps of crisp sea air. Her throat was raw from screaming. Sweat rolled down her forehead, stinging her eyes. It covered her dark black skin and soaked through her sports bra, panties, and torn warm-up pants. As her wind returned to her and the stitch in her side subsided, she felt the burn of her sweat seeping into the nicks and cuts around her ankles caused by the brambles and sharp dune grasses. Her jaw was throbbing from where one of them had smashed his fist into her face. And as she pressed her fingers to the swelling, the absurdity of the situation rushed back in like the waves on the beach below. *This can't be happening to me. Things like this happen to other women.*

She reached into her pocket to feel for the cell phone that she knew wasn't there, the image of it on top of the nightstand as clear to her as if she were back in the room at the bed-and-breakfast. Her skin was suddenly gooseflesh, her perspiration turning cold with fear, and she wished she'd listened to Steve and taken her phone, wished she'd been able to hang on to her Harvard hoodie. But the man who'd laid her out with that one punch, the man who'd torn at her pants and climbed on top of her, grunting, pawing her, had clutched it even after she'd kneed him in the groin. It was only when she rolled out from under him and ran, hearing laughter in the night, that she realized the man who'd attacked her wasn't alone. She ran down to the beach, hoping, praying, that she'd come upon another runner or a couple, maybe some kids around a campfire. But there was no one, not in

10

either direction, not as far as she could see.

There were tears in her eyes. She was shaking and her heart was doing a fluttery thing she wasn't sure she had ever felt before. She'd been able to hold it together until then, until she saw that she was very alone on that stretch of Massachusetts beach. She decided to double back and head north along the shore toward the B-and-B in Swan Harbor. She prayed the men chasing her had gone south, trying to get ahead of her to wall her off and pin her in. Besides, she had no idea what was down the beach beyond the edge of darkness. At least she had some sense of the beach in Swan Harbor and knew that at one point the beach became rocky. Maybe there was a cave or a cove she could hide herself in until sunup. The thought of that, of the sun rising over the Atlantic, stopped the tears and filled her with hope. It was short-lived.

There they were, above her, to her left along the dunes. She ran faster, then stopped dead in her tracks at the sight of a shadowy figure thirty yards ahead of her on the beach. She turned the other way, but it was no good. Two of them were there. She ran to the dunes, her churning feet sinking into the cool sand as they came around slowly behind her, their sneering laughter

11

filling the night. One of them yanked her braids so that her head snapped back and she lost her balance, the sand slipping out from under her feet. She fell awkwardly onto her neck and shoulder, landing so hard that pain shot down her whole left side, the jolt of it taking her breath away.

When she came back into the moment a few seconds later, she wished she hadn't. They had her pinned and he was on top of her again. Only this time his knees were on either side of her. She swung her head wildly from side to side, writhed beneath him, fighting to break free of the hands holding her down, but it was no good. He clamped a powerful hand under her chin to force her to look up at him.

"You just had to go and knee me, didn't you?" he said, squeezing her face so hard that her teeth cut into the insides of her cheeks. The taste of copper and iron flashed across her tongue. Her body steadied as much out of exhaustion as anything else. "You made a mistake doing that. A very big mistake. Get her damned pants off. Time to teach her a lesson."

She was at it again, her muscles giving absolutely everything they had left to give, and she screamed for all it was worth. But her voice was nearly gone, as was all of her strength.

"You done now?" he said in a whisper, his lips close to her ear. "Are you done?"

She was crying too fiercely to answer him, and before she could even think what to do next she felt his fist crash into her face again and again. Her body went limp and her mind empty. When she roused, she'd retreated into a peaceful world so deep inside her own head that she wanted to stay there forever. It was strange, she thought, how she could still hear the sea and could feel them dragging her by the feet, the sand and dune grasses tearing at her face. Then, just before she slipped completely away, she remembered that tomorrow was Columbus Day. *The Niña, the Pinta, and the Santa María. The Niña, the Pinta, and the Santa María. The Niña . . .* She could no longer hear the ocean.

2

Everything was completely different, yet just the same. Paradise was as it had always been in the fall, the trees exploding with color, the wind blowing in off the Atlantic biting with sharper teeth. Jesse Stone wasn't a man given to deep philosophical thought. He knew up from down, which base to cover when throws came in from the outfield, and, most important, right from wrong. His sense of right and wrong was like his North Star, guiding him through the wilderness of a world that had lost its way. Yet as he looked at the windblown swirl of reds, yellows, browns, and greens on the trees outside his new condo that morning, he could not help but think it strange that the beauty of the leaves was an expression of their deaths. As far as he could tell, there was only inevitability in human death and not much beauty in it. There was certainly no beauty in murder, the kind of death he was most familiar with.

He didn't waste any more time contemplating the leaves or why the familiar now seemed strange. There was the fact that his house had been sold that summer and that he'd moved into a two-bedroom condo in a development at the edge of the Swap. That wasn't it. He had moved many times in his life without it shaking his foundation. Nor was it that today would be his first day back on the job after two months away. He had to admit that it had taken some getting used to, being away from Paradise. Jesse hadn't taken any real time off since he'd been forced to walk away from baseball and joined the LAPD. That was strange, too, because it felt like it had happened both only yesterday and a million years ago. He knew exactly what it was that was causing him to see the world with new eyes, and he knew he was going to have to spend every day for the rest of his life getting used to it.

Patricia Cooper at the donut shop raised her right eyebrow at the sight of Jesse standing before her. For an old Yankee like Patricia, a raised eyebrow was tantamount to a fainting spell.

"Jeez, Jesse. Been a long time. Got so we were worried Molly would be warming your seat on a permanent basis."

"She would never let that happen."

One corner of Patricia's mouth turned up. "No, I s'pose not. An assorted dozen for you?"

"Better make that two dozen and a large cup of coffee. We've got that machine in the station now, but I've thought about the taste of your coffee every day since I've been gone."

The other corner of her mouth turned up.

Molly was seated at the front desk, not in Jesse's office as he'd expected. They'd spoken a few times since he'd returned, but like everything else since he'd come home, their conversations had been just a bit different. The usual rhythm of their banter seemed out of joint. He'd supposed that was a function of Molly's anger at him for sticking her in a job she never wanted and for staying away a few weeks longer than he'd planned to be gone.

Before he could open his mouth, Molly said, "Don't you ever do that to me again, Jesse Stone. God knows why I love you in the first place, but it won't last two more months of me sitting in that office." She pointed over her shoulder at the door with chief printed in black letters on the pebbled glass.

He placed the donuts in front of her. "Cross my heart, Crane."

"Put them in the break room yourself. Until you walk into that office back there, I'm still acting chief."

"Seems to me you're pretty comfortable with giving orders."

"Seems to me I hated every minute of it."

"How about the extra pay?"

When Molly smiled up at him, he knew things would be all right. Just as his sense of right and wrong had been his internal guide, Molly had long since become the person by whom he could set his watch.

Jesse took two donuts out of the box and left the rest right where they were. "I'm going into my office now, Crane. You can make an executive decision about what to do with the donuts." He turned and walked away.

"Jesse!" she called after him.

"What is it, Molly?"

"It's good to have you back."

"Good to be back. In ten minutes, come in and we'll talk over personnel and what's been going on while I've been gone."

The office was much as he had left it, if neater and a tad less dusty. But the essentials were in place: his worn glove and ball on his desk, the flags in the corner, the photos of the past chiefs on the wall, the slats of the old blinds open on the yacht club and Stiles Island. He sat behind his desk, his eyes immediately turning to the lower right-hand drawer, the drawer in which he had kept a bottle of Johnny Walker Black Label since he first arrived in Paradise. There was no bottle in there now. He was determined that there would never be one there again. He wasn't just playing at not drinking anymore or, as Dix phrased it, holding his breath to prove to the world he didn't need to drink. He'd been to rehab, finally, and had been sober for a few weeks. But he had been warned that the struggles might not begin in earnest until he got back to his familiar surroundings. Seeing the empty space where the bottle used to reside, smelling the scotch that wasn't there, he felt a phantom twinge, as if from a limb that had recently been removed.

3

Molly sat across the desk from him, a small pile of files between them. Jesse picked up the top file, opened it, and scanned the few sheets of paper within.

"How's Suit?"

Molly shook her head. "Even more boring now that he's married."

"Alisha," he said. "How's she doing?"

Molly's expression surprised him.

"What's that face about?"

She said, "I guess Alisha's feeling her oats."

"C'mon, Molly, this isn't *Modern Farmer*. What does that mean?"

"It's just that she's not the shy, quiet, obedient rookie anymore. She questioned the way a few of the older guys handled some things. They didn't like it much."

"Coming from a woman, you mean?"

Molly didn't answer.

"Or from an African American woman?"

Hiring Alisha hadn't been a popular move with the Board of Selectmen. Some of it had to do with her race, though Jesse suspected it had less to do with her gender or the color of her skin than budgetary concerns. They would have preferred he take on a retired big-city cop who already had a pension and medical benefits. But Jesse knew that hiring a retired cop came with baggage. He didn't need a cop who had bad habits or thought he was doing Paradise a favor, someone who could walk away the first time things got rough or he got an order he didn't like. Jesse wanted someone he could train himself, someone who would be committed to Paradise. Jesse recognized that the town was changing, that people from Boston were moving in and commuting. He wanted a more diverse force and for his cops to reflect Paradise's future and not only its past.

"I don't think it's that, Jesse," Molly said. "She's young, and you know how guys set in their ways can get."

"Uh-huh."

"I was going to have to tell you anyway, so I might as well tell you now. For the last few weeks, we've been having some trouble with bikers, mostly in the Swap."

"Bikers as in biker gangs like Satan's

Whores? I can deal with —"

She cut him off. "Not them, Jesse. These were skinhead types, belligerent, real troublemakers. They went into the Scupper and started squawking about how even lily-white places like Paradise were being overrun by 'mud people and inferior races.' "

"I've heard it all before. Same song, different day. We had them when I was a kid in Tucson and in L.A. Free speech comes in ugly forms, too. So what happened?"

"Joey the barman phoned it in to the station when some of the patrons took exception, and Alisha was in that sector. I sent Suit and Gabe as backup . . . just in case."

"Good decision. It's what I would have done."

"But when Suit and Gabe saw what was going on, they pulled seniority on Alisha and got between her and the skinheads. I wasn't there, but Gabe says it was getting pretty heated. Sounded to me like they did the right thing by taking charge."

Jesse asked, "You think I need to have a talk with her or with all three of them?"

"That's up to you. Alisha's had a bit of a chip on her shoulder since, but her work's still excellent."

"I'd have that chip there myself if the same thing happened to me, but I'll keep

21

an eye out. Anybody in the cells?"

"One guy, a twentysomething. Talk about a chip on your shoulder," Molly said. "This guy's got a whole city block on his. Showed up in town a few weeks after you left. Second time we've given him accommodations for the night."

"Drunk?"

"And disorderly."

"You charge him?"

"Not officially."

Jesse smiled at her. He knew he had been right to trust her with his job and his town. And the fact that she hadn't charged the kid only confirmed it. The PPD wasn't about arrests and statistics. It was about keeping the peace and doing right by the people. The truth was that putting someone into the system was a decision not to be made lightly. The justice system was overburdened and it tended to grind up the people locked behind its bars. As far as Jesse could tell, very few people came out the other end of time in prison better citizens for the experience. It wasn't a popular attitude these days, but Jesse believed a good kick in the ass and a little understanding often worked better than time inside.

"I'll go have a talk with him. Name?"

"Cole Slayton."

"We done?"

"You're the chief. Your decision."

"Wiseass," he said, standing. "Time for me to meet Mr. Slayton."

"Good luck with that. Talking with him is like talking to a wall. He's about as charming as you after a bender. Sorry, Jesse, I didn't mean to —"

"It's okay, Molly. No tiptoeing around about this between me and you. I didn't go to rehab because I drank too much Earl Grey."

4

Jesse was surprised at the sight of the kid pacing back and forth behind the bars. He thought he'd find a hipster on a road trip, playing at being cool, or some asocial drifter with dead eyes, but that's not who he found in the cell at all. This kid was scruffy, his black hair a mess and his face unshaven for a week, but he was an athlete. He had the build and the look. Even pacing the ten feet from one side of the cell to the other, he moved with fluidity and grace. Part of Jesse's skill set as a ballplayer was the ability to spot your own kind, picking out the guy on the other team who was just a little quicker on the base paths or the one who could manipulate the bat and hit the ball where he wanted to.

"Cole," he said, standing out of the kid's reach. "I'm Jesse Stone, the chief of police here."

The kid stopped dead, turned to face Jesse

through the bars. He stared at him hard in the eyes. It was an intense, assessing stare, almost as if he was trying to look inside Jesse or through him.

The kid sneered, said, "So you're Jesse Stone, huh?"

Jesse laughed. "I am. Why do you say it like that?"

"Never mind." The kid went back to pacing.

"You want to stop that? We need to talk."

The kid thought about it, hesitated, stopped. "Okay, talk." He gave Jesse a cold look.

Molly was right about this guy. He had a sizable chip on his shoulder and seemed incapable of uttering a word that didn't sound or feel like a challenge.

"Officer Crane tells me this is the second time we've had to put you up for the night since you came into town."

"You going to threaten me now? Tell me I can get out of town or —"

"Easy, kid —"

"I'm not a kid."

"Sorry," Jesse said. "At my age, everyone under thirty is a kid. But no one's threatening anybody." Jesse cleared his throat. "Listen, Cole, I'm going to kick you loose and we're going to forget about the drunk and disorderly charges for now. But I don't want to see you back in here again and I don't want one of my officers to have to give you anything more than a parking ticket."

"Or else, huh?"

Jesse said, "Look, I don't know what your deal is or why you seem to want to provoke me, but all I'm doing for you is a favor."

Slayton glared at him. "You expecting gratitude?"

"From you, probably not. My experience is that people with as much attitude as you don't give thanks, because they think the world owes them something."

"I've got a long list of things I'm owed."

"No doubt." Jesse reached for the cell key. "Remember, I don't want to see you in here again."

Before Jesse could open the cell door, Suit Simpson came into the jail corridor. Suit waved Jesse over. They shook hands and slapped each other on the shoulder. Suit motioned for Jesse to step away from the cells and back into the hallway.

"It's great to see you, Jesse. I missed you. Man, don't ever leave Molly in charge again. She gets really grumpy when you're not around."

"You look good, Suit. You lose some

weight?"

"Yeah," he said, slapping his belly proudly. "Elena feeds me right and makes me go to the gym."

"I knew I liked that woman."

Suit's expression turned serious. "You okay, Jesse? I mean, I know things were rough there after Diana . . . you know. And you were away for a long time. I was worried about you. We all were."

"Thanks, Suit, but I'm fine. So why'd you come in here instead of waiting for me to come out?"

"Molly got a call from the Swan Harbor PD. They got a serious assault there and Chief Forster wants you to have a look. You know those guys over there, they don't like getting their nails dirty."

"Any details?"

"No. They want you to hurry. Lundquist'll meet you at the Swan Memorial Junior-Senior High School parking lot."

"Okay, thanks. Do me a favor, Suit. Cut Mr. Slayton loose."

"You sure about that, Jesse?" he said in a quiet voice. "I'm the one that brought this guy in . . . twice. He started the fight both times. All the witnesses said he was almost begging to get arrested."

"Did he use any weapons? A broken bottle

or anything like that?"

Suit shook his head. "No. It wasn't like that."

"Okay, then. It's his last chance."

"Whatever you say, Jesse."

As Jesse drove his Explorer to Swan Harbor, he thought about Cole Slayton. It had been a long time since he'd run into a character with that much attitude. Cole seemed determined to prove something to the world or to himself. Jesse hoped he'd do it without hurting himself or someone else and that he'd do it in another cop's town.

5

Paradise was a town founded by merchants and fishermen. The town fathers would have also had you believe that whaling was a part of the town's past. Jesse never quite bought the whaling stuff, but it made for a good narrative for the tourists. Mostly it helped local shopkeepers hawk their replica harpoons, oil lamps, and oars. Swan Harbor, the tony town just north of Paradise, was a place that wore its pilgrim roots like a neon sign. Though, of course, neon signs were strictly forbidden within town limits.

Swan Memorial was a picture-postcard old school building of red brick and ivy, with a majestic white bell tower rising up from the center of its sloped gray roof. Jesse followed the curve of Commonwealth Way past the front of the school's granite steps and stone columns, and around to the athletic fields and parking lot beyond. The bucolic New England scene was shattered by the sight of ambulances, police cruisers, and trooper SUVs arranged at odd angles on the knoll outside the lot. All their blue, red, white, and yellow light bars whirled, strobed, and flashed in moot silence. Not even the gorgeous backdrop of turning trees and the ocean beyond could camouflage the tear in the fabric of serenity.

Jesse pulled up onto the knoll alongside Brian Lundquist's unmarked Ford. It was officially Captain Lundquist now that he'd gotten the bump and taken over for Healy as the state's chief homicide investigator.

"Jesse," Lundquist said, offering his hand.

"Brian." Jesse took his hand and shook it. "Congratulations on it being official."

Lundquist, a big man who looked more like a Minnesota farm boy than a cop, nodded his thanks.

"It's not pretty, Jesse. Her face is a mess and there are nasty bruises around her throat. There's some signs of sexual assault. She's unconscious and the EMTs say it doesn't look good. The assault had to take place somewhere else, though, and she was dumped here. Name's Felicity Wileford, thirty-two. She's up here from Boston for the weekend with a boyfriend to see the foliage."

"Boyfriend a suspect?"

Lundquist shrugged. "Can't say."

"Any security footage?"

"The security company says no, but I've got someone over at their headquarters reviewing whatever footage they've got. C'mon, let's go take a look."

As they turned to enter the lot, stepping under the crime scene tape, Jesse asked, "Why am I here, Brian? Not my town, not my jurisdiction. What are you doing here, anyway? This isn't a homicide."

"Not yet," Lundquist said. "But it looks like it will be. Besides, they don't have any detectives on their PD and I was in the area."

"I heard it was the chief who asked me to come have a look."

"It was my idea, but it's not officially my case. I had to cajole the rusty-nuts chief here to invite you over. I'll tell you what, Jesse, the cops in this town are acting like they've never seen this kind of thing before."

"They probably haven't. No shame in that. I wish none of my cops had ever seen one."

"Occupational hazard, I guess, me making assumptions like that. I've already seen too many damaged bodies."

"Me, too. But that's no answer to my question, Brian. Why am I here?"

"Come on, let's hurry up before they move her. You'll see."

That was more of an answer. Jesse understood that there must be something about the appearance of the victim or the crime scene that would spark his memory. Either that or there was something about the victim and the nature of the assault that only an ex–LAPD Robbery Homicide detective would comprehend. But the moment he saw the way Felicity Wileford's brutalized body had been positioned, Jesse knew it was the former.

She was a dark-skinned African American woman with long, beautifully braided hair. Her face was so battered that her eyes were swollen shut. A plastic oxygen mask covered her smashed nose and bloodied mouth. As they rolled the gurney toward the waiting ambulance, Lundquist demanded the EMTs stop and lower the sheet that covered her body from neck to toe. They weren't happy about it, but they did as they were told. The swelling and bruising around her throat was obvious. Someone had written the word *slut* across her belly in lurid red lipstick.

As the EMTs hurried her into the ambulance, Jesse turned to Lundquist and said, "The first murder scene I ever dealt with in

Paradise was very similar to this, but you couldn't have known about that. You were still chasing speeders down on the Mass Pike back then. Who spotted the similarity?"

Lundquist pointed to a uniformed Swan Harbor cop standing with a group of troopers and cops about twenty yards to the other side of the body. "Name's Drake Daniels. Been on the job here for twenty-plus years. He told his chief, the chief told me . . . You know how it works."

"Uh-huh." He knew how it worked, but he didn't like it.

"Brian, I'm going to take a walk over to my Explorer. Send Officer Daniels over without drawing attention. I need to have a talk with that man."

Jesse didn't wait for Lundquist's response. He just turned and walked toward his SUV.

6

The STORE FOR RENT sign still hung in the front window of the old card shop on Main Street two months after the short-term lease had been signed. Main Street in Linz, New York, was no more or less dead than the Main Streets in many of the forgotten lock towns along the Erie Canal: forlorn little burgs whose downtowns were now essentially ghost towns. So nobody took notice of the fact that someone had rented the old card shop. There was hardly anyone around *to* notice.

The front room of the old card shop was still as empty as it was the day the lease had been signed. The display cases were just as dusty and the cobwebs remained untouched. But in one corner of the back room, boxes full of fliers were stacked three deep from floor to ceiling. A rectangular red banner was draped across one wall. At the center of the red flag was a white circle, and within the white circle was a black swastika. The Nazi flag was faded, frayed, and battle-scarred. On the opposite wall hung a like-sized American flag with a white, rounded-edged black swastika at the center. On a third wall was a map of New England and the mid-Atlantic states.

There was a desk, a black office chair, and a card table and some folding chairs. A fleshy man in his sixties, bald, with intense gray eyes, sat in the office chair. He stared across his desk at a man twenty-five years his junior who was standing at ease — legs spread, hands clasped behind his back. The younger man, dressed in jeans, black work boots, a black turtleneck, and a camo vest, looked straight ahead, eyes unfocused.

"See that behind you, son?" asked the man behind the desk, pointing at the old Nazi flag. He didn't wait for an answer. "That flag was rescued from Berlin in April of 1945. A lot of brave Aryan men died defending that flag and what it stood for. We're engaged in a desperate struggle to reclaim, for its righteous owners, the body and soul of our great nation. Do you understand that?"

"Yes, sir."

"Do you understand the concept of winning a battle only to lose the war?"

"Of course I do, sir."

"Then why on earth did you permit to happen what took place last night?"

"I was not directly part of the operation, sir," said the younger man, still looking straight ahead. "But I take full responsibility for the actions of those under my command."

"Under your command!" The fleshy man pounded his desk. "Given what occurred last evening, son, I might choose to use another word than *command.*"

"Yes, sir."

"Did they give you an explanation for their actions?"

"They did, sir."

"I'm waiting."

"The group leader said that the woman kneed and scratched him. Then she ran away and nearly escaped capture. He said he wanted to teach her a lesson."

The older man pounded the desk again, this time jumping out of his chair. "A lesson! He wanted to teach her a lesson! He's not a fucking professor and the lesson to be taught needs to be taught to him."

"Yes, sir."

"Did you explain to those nimrods that they may have dealt a severe blow to our cause?"

"I did, sir."

The older man seemed not to hear, strolling out from behind his desk to straighten a framed black-and-white photograph of a burning cross surrounded by hundreds of white hooded men.

"All they were supposed to do was to shake her up, smack her around a little bit, to serve as a warning of things to come. And because she hurt your man's pride, they nearly beat the bitch to death?"

"Nothing like this will happen again, sir."

"You're goddamned right it won't, son." He reached under his jacket and pulled out a vintage Luger. He walked over to the younger man and pressed the muzzle to his left temple. The younger man didn't flinch. "You take responsibility for what your men did?"

"I do, sir."

"You ready to die for their mistakes?" He put his finger on the trigger.

"I am, sir. They were my responsibility."

The older man holstered his pistol. "When the time comes for sacrifice, you know now who the lamb must be."

Those words made the younger man react in a way not even the threat of being shot in the head could. He winced and stuttered, struggling for the words. "But . . . sir, he . . .

he's —"

The older man shouted, "Son, when the time comes, do you know who the lamb must be?"

"I do, sir."

"Good. Now take two boxes and get the fuck out of my sight. I expect not to have to have any future little talks like this one with you again."

"Yes, sir."

"Now get over there and get those distributed as you've been instructed. The time for the clarion call is almost upon us. Listen for it."

The younger man picked up two boxes and left without looking back.

7

Jesse watched Drake Daniels amble over to where the Explorer was parked. He looked the role of an aging small-town cop. His gray hair was kept neat and short under his brown trooper-style hat. The same couldn't be said of his gut, which had long ago reached critical mass, straining the bottom buttons of his tan uniform shirt and spilling over the edge of his black belt. His ample face was clean shaven and he smelled of too much Old Spice.

"You wanted to see me, Chief?" he said in a clear, strong voice.

Jesse nodded, staring into Daniels's eyes, challenging him. Daniels met the challenge. The cop stared right back at Jesse. His clear blue eyes stood in sharp contrast to his sleepy demeanor. Jesse answered him with more silence. He wanted to see how the cop would react, whether Daniels would fidget or paw at the ground with his shoe. Jesse knew people had tells in life just like in poker and that their tics sometimes said more about them than their words. But Daniels was cool, standing right in front of Jesse, relaxed and looking straight at him. Jesse had to give the guy some credit. He seemed to understand that Jesse was attempting to unnerve him.

Finally, Daniels spoke. "I figure you're pretty curious about how I knew about the similarities between this crime scene and the one at Paradise Junior High all those years ago."

Tammy Portugal was a divorced mother of two who had gone out clubbing. Her naked body was found in the parking lot of Paradise Junior High School just as Jesse was first settling into his job as chief. SLUT had been written across her abdomen in red lipstick. She had been picked up at a local club by a muscle head named Jo Jo Genest. He'd raped and beaten her and broken her neck before dumping her body like so much trash.

"Uh-huh," Jesse said. "I'm curious."

"It's not that complicated, Chief. I was good friends with Anthony deAngelo. We grew up together and I got on the job here a year or two after he got hired in Paradise. He was first on the scene of the Portugal woman's murder and he talked to me about it. It kind of freaked him out a little because he had never seen a murder victim before. Too bad about what happened to him."

Jesse got a sick feeling in his belly, remembering how shaken Anthony was when he showed up at the scene that day long ago. Worse, though, was the fact that Anthony deAngelo was one of Jesse's cops who'd been killed in the line of duty. He'd been working undercover at the mall, trying to catch a thrill-killing couple. The wife shot Anthony in his head as she and her husband fled.

"Anthony was a good cop," Jesse said.

"Good friend, too. I miss him a lot sometimes."

Jesse moved on. "So what was it that made it click for you?"

Daniels knew what Jesse was asking. "Naked woman in a school parking lot with SLUT written on her in lipstick . . . not exactly a common occurrence in these parts, Chief. Thank God our vic was still breathing."

Jesse asked, "You share this observation with anyone except your chief?"

"No, sir."

"Not even with your friends I saw you hanging out with over in the lot?"

Daniels shook his head emphatically.

"Okay, Officer, thanks. I have no jurisdiction here, so I can't demand you keep this between you and your chief, but I'd appreciate it."

"You don't think the cases are related, do you?"

Jesse didn't answer and thanked Daniels again. The Swan Harbor cop turned and went back to the scene. A minute or two later, Lundquist, who'd kept a close eye on the conversation between Jesse and Daniels, walked over to the Explorer.

"So?"

"I don't know," Jesse said. "He gave me the right answers."

"You don't seem happy about it."

"I'm not. Says he knew about the similarities because he was friends with one of my murdered cops, a good guy named Anthony deAngelo."

"Healy told me about that. That was the serial-killing couple."

Jesse said, "That was them."

"What don't you like about what Officer Daniels had to say?"

"How many stories have you read about the volunteer fireman who just happens to be driving by a burning house and rescues a family from the flames? Then it turns out

42

that the hero fireman —"

"Set the fire," Lundquist said, finishing Jesse's sentence. "You think Daniels had something to do with the assault?"

"Not my case, but I'd keep an eye on him is all I'm saying."

"Given her condition, it'll probably be my case soon. This town's chief couldn't win at Clue even if he cheated. I'm heading over to talk to the boyfriend. You want to tag along? I'm interested to hear what you think."

"Sure."

As they drove away from the school in Lundquist's blue Ford, Jesse noticed that the knot in his belly hadn't gone away. It had only grown and gotten tighter.

8

The boyfriend wasn't what Jesse expected. Steven Randisi was a tall white man, maybe thirty years old, with a neatly trimmed crop of prematurely gray hair. He was a handsome man, but one with a grave, deeply etched face and light brown eyes, thousand-yard eyes. His eyes weren't red-rimmed or teary. Randisi stared directly at Lundquist and Jesse, yet he seemed far, far away. Jesse had seen a lot of grieving faces in his time. He'd seen one in the mirror frequently over the last several months since Diana was killed. Still, Jesse thought, there was more than grief in Randisi. This was grief plus. That plus didn't seem like fear or guilt or even confusion. And when Randisi pulled his left hand out of his jacket pocket, Jesse figured he knew what it was.

"Lost it in Afghanistan," Randisi said, tapping the back of his prosthetic hand against the table. "I'm being fitted for a fully functional one. They tell me I should have it in a month or two. Helluva thing, losing a piece of your body."

Lundquist saw an opening. "Having your girlfriend beaten nearly to death is also a hell of a thing."

"She wasn't — isn't my girlfriend."

"What is she, then?"

"We dated a few times and we got along. Felicity said she was coming up here to see the fall foliage and asked if I wanted to tag along."

"You sleeping together?" Lundquist asked.

Randisi nodded.

"Any problems there?"

"I lost my hand and most of my forearm. The rest of me still functions pretty well, and no, we didn't have any problems there. As far as I could tell, we were a good fit in bed."

"How about out of bed?"

He shrugged. "We're still feeling each other out. We are kind of an odd match, I guess. She's studying for her Ph.D. in African and African American studies at Harvard. Me, I was helping out my dad at his auto-parts store and going to Bunker Hill Community College just to keep occupied."

Jesse decided to play the good cop and

asked, "So where'd you guys meet?"

Randisi smiled, remembering. "Legal Seafood in Harvard Square. It was a long wait and we both asked for tables for one. Felicity said that we should just eat together. I think maybe she saw I was looking a little lost and felt sorry for me. I don't know." He held up his prosthetic hand. "You always see in TV commercials and stuff, men and women with prosthetics looking all brave and courageous. Me, I felt like a freak, like all that people could see of me was this. And all I could see was that Felicity was beautiful and kind."

It went on like that for about a half-hour. Lundquist's questions getting more intense, taking on accusatory tones. *Where were you last night? Why weren't you together? Did you fight? Why didn't you go running together? Was she running away from you? Can you account for your whereabouts? When did you alert the local police? Why not sooner? If you didn't beat her, who did? Did you know anyone who wanted to do her harm?* Jesse would mix in questions to ease the tension, turning things back to the more personal. His questions were more about where the relationship might've gone and what kind of future Randisi saw for himself. When they were done with him, Randisi looked pretty shaken.

"One more thing," Jesse said, as they parted. "You said you lost your hand and part of your forearm."

"Yeah. So?"

"How's the strength in the rest of your left arm?"

"The shrapnel fucked up my biceps and shoulder, too, but they were able to put me back together well enough to save my upper arm. I'm never going to win any arm-wrestling tournaments, if that's what you're asking."

"What do you think?" Lundquist asked Jesse as they made their way to his car.

Jesse said, "One look at the bruises around her neck will tell you he didn't do it. She had deep bruising on both sides of her neck."

"Maybe he had help."

"I don't know, Brian. I'd be looking somewhere else."

"I'll check him out anyway. So, if not him . . ."

Jesse said, "Randisi says she went jogging. Should be easy enough to find witnesses. Not many black faces in Swan Harbor. My guess, she ran along the beach. That's where a lot of folks in Paradise do their running."

"Good supposition, Jesse. It *was* the beach. There was what looked to be sand in her hair, under her fingernails, and between her toes. That was only a cursory exam. And, Jesse . . ."

"Uh-huh."

"The word that he wrote on her, let's keep that between us."

"No one's going to hear it from me, but a lot of locals and troopers saw it. I asked Officer Daniels to keep it quiet, but you might have some trouble containing it."

"I know. The whole damned Swan Harbor PD was there." Lundquist shook his head in disgust. "It was like they all came for a peek. I'll be able to keep the troopers quiet, at least. C'mon, let me get you back to your vehicle. Will you please send over the old file on the Portugal woman's murder? I don't know what relevance it will have, but I have to be thorough."

"Sure. Soon as I get back to Paradise. And, Brian, keep me in the loop. I don't have a good feeling about this one. Let me know if she survives."

"A woman was beaten into unconsciousness. What's there to feel good about?"

Jesse had no answer for that.

9

Jesse had made it through rehab pretty easily. He hadn't done it on discipline alone, on his ability to simply shut off his drinking for long periods. For his own sake, he knew he couldn't afford to act the part of cleaning himself up, and that, for lack of a better expression, he had to let it all hang out. He had been open with the shrinks, with the counselors, and with the groups about destroying his career in L.A. and about his tangled and doomed relationships with women. He'd even gotten some laughs from the others in the group when he explained that he'd got the job as chief of police in Paradise not because he'd been a good detective, not in spite of being a drunk, but because he was one.

Until today, Jesse hadn't given much thought to his arrival in Paradise almost two decades ago, but the brutal assault on Felicity Wileford couldn't help but cause him to reflect on those early days. And he had plenty of time for reflection on his drive down to Boston. One of the things he'd been told over and over again while in rehab was that he needed to go to AA meetings every night, that he had to find a sponsor, and to do it sooner rather than later. Dix had made the same point to him when Jesse had called from the road on his way back from rehab.

"You got through this part, Jesse," Dix had said. "Good for you."

That was as close as Dix had ever come to an "Attaboy!" and probably as close as he would ever come, but he didn't stop there.

"It might be more of a challenge once you get home in familiar surroundings. And you can't depend on me for reinforcement. You've got to go to meetings and be with other alcoholics. They're your tribe, Jesse. They're your people and they're the ones you need to rely on. You've got to find a sponsor."

It made sense to Jesse and he felt Dix was right, though the thought of standing up in front of a room of drunks and telling his story gave him pause. It was one thing to be in rehab for a few weeks with complete strangers, people he would likely never have contact with again. It was something else to do it close to home, when there was every chance he could run into these folks during the day. Although his alcoholism wasn't exactly a secret in Paradise, he had, for the most part, limited his public displays of drunkenness, and he had missed work only a few times because of his drinking. Still, he felt he couldn't risk a meeting in Paradise, Swan Harbor, Salem, or any of the other close-by towns. Dix had anticipated Jesse's reaction.

"Your default setting is self-reliance, Jesse. Some people can pull it off by themselves, but it would be a mistake for you. You've tried it that way before and it's never worked. So if you're worried about the discomfort of a meeting in or around your town, drive down to Boston."

There were meetings all over Boston, but Jesse had chosen one in the basement of an Episcopal church in Cambridge. He supposed he'd chosen the meeting there because he used to look at the church steeple from Diana's bedroom window, and just lately he had finally been able to think of her and smile again. Some memories of her were of her and her alone or of their time together, memories free of his grief and guilt over her murder.

He was a few minutes late, but no one did more than give him a cursory glance as he came into the room. To them, he was just another drunk. A guy in his early thirties with a shaved head and a mustacheless beard and wearing a beat-up leather jacket was in the front of the room telling his story. Jesse cringed.

This part of the meetings, the public-confessional stuff, was anathema to him. It was too self-indulgent for his taste. Even when he was in the minors, Jesse hated public displays by other ballplayers meant to draw the crowd's attention to them. He never flipped his bat after a home run or stood at the plate admiring his handiwork. He hustled around the bases as if trying to beat out a bunt. He tried never to pump his fist or to celebrate or pout in front of others. There were several parts of the twelve steps that cut hard against Jesse's self-contained nature, though he had begun to compile the list of people to whom he had done wrong and to whom he would have to apologize. It was a long list. Some were his old partners from his time in Robbery Homicide in L.A. Molly, Suit, and Alisha were on the list, too. Sadly, many of the people on the list were in the ground and beyond his apologies.

Jesse found a folding chair in the next-to-last row between an old-timer and a twentyish woman with cropped brown hair, piercings, and tattoos covering most of her pale white skin. The old-timer had a resigned look on his face. Jesse could tell he'd been listening to fellow drunks tell their stories for many years and he didn't find the current saga of alcohol-fueled misjudgments very engaging or original. *Been there. Done that. Bought the T-shirt.* The woman, on the other hand, was very focused on the guy at the rostrum. Her right leg was shaking like mad and she was doing this thing with her fingers, rubbing them together as fast as she could so that they made a shushing sound.

When the guy up front was done with his story, he got a scattered round of applause. A very attractive woman in her early forties with expensively coiffed auburn hair, dressed in a well-tailored blue business suit, replaced the guy at the front of the room. She thanked him for sharing. She then invited other people up to share. When no one volunteered, she said she had to make a few announcements.

"Bill," the old-timer to Jesse's left said, offering his right hand. "First time here, huh?"

Jesse shook Bill's hand. "First time, period."

"This part gets easier. Don't share if you don't want to tonight. But sharing helps. You'll see."

"Not your first time?" Jesse asked, knowing the answer.

Bill laughed. "Nope. I'm an old hand at this. I go to different meetings. It does me good to move around from time to time, to hear new stories."

When the room got quiet, Bill stood and walked to the front of the room.

"Hi, my name is Bill and I'm an alcoholic."

"Hi, Bill," most of the audience answered back.

Jesse pictured himself up there, saying those words, and his belly knotted for the second time that day.

10

Dressed in matte black outfits and like-colored combat hoods, the men knelt down low in the stand of trees on the other side of the footbridge to the house. Up to this point, the trees, the night, and the thick layer of clouds overhead had supplied them with all the cover they'd needed. Their camo-painted 4×4 Jeep was a half-mile back toward Paradise, parked in a nook in the woods, its front end covered in branches and leaves.

So far, it had all gone off like clockwork, but the older of the two men knew the real challenge would come the second they stepped out of the womb of the trees and crossed to the other side of the thin finger of water separating the woods from their objective. Although this wasn't like a real combat zone and no one was likely to die unless things got completely out of hand, it was always at this juncture when the fog of battle set in, when you lost your control of circumstance and any outside factor could cause things to blow up in your face.

He was good with that. As a soldier, he had made his peace with that risk, carrying out operations in Anbar Province and around Mosul, places where *kill or be killed* wasn't a hypothetical. Problem was, the kid with him was amped up, too amped up. The soldier recognized the signs. The kid's breathing was ragged, as if he couldn't quite catch his breath. And in spite of the raw air, he was sweating through his clothing. Maybe that had been the problem with the woman in Swan Harbor. The kid's adrenaline had gotten the better of him and he and his team had taken things too far.

The soldier hated the thought of carrying out an operation with someone he couldn't trust to keep his cool. He'd wanted to do this thing by himself. It was simple enough, and he liked to operate on his own, made things less complicated. But his orders were crystal clear: The kid had to be a part of this.

"Let the boy have a taste of glory before the sacrifice" is how the commander had put it to him.

He wasn't sure he understood, but he kept his thoughts to himself. He had never questioned orders before, not even when they came down from Heebs, Hajjis, beaners, or niggers, and he wasn't going to start now. But he knew he had to distract the kid, to turn it down a few notches.

"That's funny," he said in a whisper, gently slapping the kid above the left temple.

"Hey." The kid swatted his partner's hand. "What's funny?"

"Nothing," the older man said. "I just felt like slapping you."

The kid was confused, but the soldier didn't care. It had done the trick. The kid's breathing was more normal and his eyes less crazed.

"You know what to do?"

The kid was annoyed. "Yeah, man, we've gone over this like a thousand times."

"That's what you said before you almost killed that woman and ruined everything."

"I know. I know. I said I was sorry."

" 'Sorry' doesn't cut it with me. So let's go over it again."

The kid rolled his eyes and said, "You go across first to check things out. When you're sure it's clear, you'll signal for me to follow and to bring the can. Once I'm across, I keep low to the ground until you give me the sign to pour the kerosene. When I'm done with that, I give you the sign and retreat back to the vehicle. You'll follow, dropping the lighter as you go. We regroup at the vehicle, which I've started."

"Good, but what don't you do?"

The kid was confused. "Don't fuck up? I don't know."

"You don't turn the vehicle's headlights on and you don't clear the brush away from it."

"Yeah, yeah, right."

The soldier checked his watch. He checked the sky, the road, checked the lights that were on in the house. He smiled when the kitchen lights went off and, a few seconds later, the children's bedroom lights went on upstairs.

"Now," he said, and took off. He didn't use the footbridge or the driveway access from the road. Instead he stepped quietly through the water and climbed up onto the grass. He did a quick but careful circuit of the house. When he was done, he signaled to the kid with his flashlight.

The kid came out of the woods in a sprint and tripped over his own feet but somehow managed to hold on to the blue plastic container of kerosene. After the longest fifteen seconds of his life, the kid got up and made his way through the water. He hated the way it felt, the cold water soaking through his black pants, socks, and the tops of his boots. But he got across, kept low, and waited.

In a harsh barked whisper, the soldier said, "Go!" He then removed the .40-caliber from his black nylon holster, aiming it at the front door. He had no intention of shooting anyone, but a few well-placed shots were usually enough to deter even the nosiest SOBs. He swiveled his head back and forth, alternating his gaze between the kid pouring out the kerosene and the front door.

An acrid petroleum tang filled up the night. The kid waved the empty canister at the soldier, who signaled for the kid to go. This time, the kid kept his footing and disappeared into the woods. The soldier waited to see if anyone in the house reacted to the sight or the sound of the kid. After a ten-count, sure no one in the house was aware of what was going on, he holstered his sidearm and removed a cheap lighter from his pocket. He moved to where the kid had laid down the pattern on the grass, flicked the lighter, and, when the flame came up, touched it to the kerosene.

A few seconds later, a little girl looked out her bedroom window and said, "Look, Daddy, a pretty fire."

11

They were standing around the coffee-and-refreshments table now: Bill, the tattooed woman with the cropped hair, and the shaved-head guy with the beard who had been sharing his woes when Jesse came in.

"Jesse," he said to the woman. He stuck out his hand.

She seemed taken aback but took his hand. "Anya."

"First time?"

She nodded.

"Me, too."

She smiled, relieved and happy to not feel alone in her newness. In spite of the severe haircut, the piercings, and the tats, Anya had an angelic face and soft features. "This is Hank," she said, introducing the bald guy with the beard. "He finally got me to come with him."

Hank quickly shook Jesse's hand but wasn't particularly friendly and yanked

Anya toward the stairwell by her elbow. She turned back and shrugged before they vanished behind the exit door.

Bill laughed.

Jesse asked, "Did I miss something funny?"

"The boyfriend probably thought you were Thirteen Stepping."

"What?"

He laughed again. "You know you're not supposed to get romantically involved with people in the group, but it happens. I've been guilty of it myself. It's kind of inevitable, all of us with this thing at the center of our lives, sharing so much in common. But there are predators and prey in all groups."

"Tell me about it."

Bill raised his eyebrow at Jesse's response. "You a cop? I've met a lot of 'em in my time and you sure've got the bearing of one."

Jesse didn't answer.

"So there are guys," Bill said, ignoring Jesse's silence, "usually men who've been in the program for years, who take advantage of vulnerable women like Anya there, women just getting started, looking for anyone or anything to hold on to besides the booze." He shook his head in disgust. "Under the guise of befriending or sponsoring them, these guys work them into their beds." Then he fell silent for a moment. "Sorry, Jesse, that was no way to welcome you."

"That's okay, Bill. It's good to know what to watch out for."

"No, no, I should be telling you all the good this does, how it helped save my life and salvage my relationship with my kids. You know: experience, strength, and hope."

"I heard when you were up front," Jesse said. "Rough."

"Oh, that, that's only a little bit of it. You want to go grab a cup of real coffee?"

Jesse didn't get a chance to answer.

"Hi, Bill. Thanks for sharing." It was the woman who had led the group. "They were a little reluctant tonight."

"I was happy to do it. Callie, this is Jesse."

"Welcome," she said, shaking his hand. "I'm happy to see you here, Jesse."

Callie had lovely green eyes that played perfectly to her auburn hair and lightly freckled skin beneath her makeup. But Jesse was acutely aware of the things Bill had just told him, and in spite of her obvious attractiveness, Jesse decided he had to put his recovery ahead of anything else. He had spent too much time over the last year in a semi-drunken haze. And any attraction he had felt to women had been almost devoid of real feeling. Fortunately, he hadn't acted out and hadn't added to his list of people to whom he would have to beg forgiveness.

"We were just going out for real coffee," Bill said. "Want to join us?"

Callie looked from Bill to Jesse and back again. "Sorry, Bill, no. Jesse, I hope we see you again."

Jesse sat across from Bill at a Starbucks a block from the church. A few of the other people from the meeting were there as well, but there were no group hugs and no one had suggested they all sit together. Jesse was relieved they hadn't. Togetherness wasn't his comfort zone. The meetings were one thing. He didn't like the concept, but he understood the value. He didn't even like press conferences. But Jesse's preference was always one-on-one or solitude.

Bill slid a business card across the table. "That's my cell number on the back. You don't know me from Adam, but just in case you need someone to call before you find a regular sponsor . . . Anytime, day or night, weekend or holiday, you need to talk, you call me. We'll get you through it."

Jesse said, "Thanks."

"Why don't you give me your number?" Bill said. "Just so I can check in on you if I don't see you at a meeting or if I haven't heard from you. It can be easy to slip early on."

Jesse didn't hesitate and wrote his cell number on the back of a napkin. They exchanged some small talk and both seemed happy to get away from talk of alcohol-induced self-destruction. Then Bill U-turned.

"Remember what I said about romance between —"

"I remember. Why do you mention it?"

"Because Callie is a beautiful woman and . . . Just be careful, is all. Now I'll shut up about that."

But before Jesse could say another word, his cell buzzed in his pocket. *Paradise PD* flashed on the screen. He excused himself and walked onto the street. A light rain had started to fall and he turned up his collar.

"Jesse, you there?" It was Gabe Weathers, who was on the desk.

"Uh-huh."

"There's trouble."

"What kind?"

"Your old house . . . someone burned a cross on the front lawn."

"Anybody hurt?"

"No, but the family's pretty badly shaken."

"I'll be there in a half-hour."

Jesse hung up, signaled to Bill through the window that he had to go, and waved good-bye.

12

Nothing but Jesse's temper was burning by the time he got up to Paradise from Boston, though the charred, cross-shaped spot on the small knoll in front of the house was evident as he parked his SUV between Alisha's and Peter Perkins's cruisers. Perkins, using a portable floodlight, was on his hands and knees in the damp grass, collecting samples.

"Hey, Jesse," Perkins said, turning over his shoulder.

"You already get the photos?"

"Done."

Jesse caught an acrid whiff of something lingering in the air. "Smells like burnt jet fuel."

Perkins laughed. "Close enough. Probably kerosene. Chemically, it's a lot like jet fuel. We'll know soon enough."

"Kerosene. That doesn't tell us anything. Half the people around here have kerosene heaters."

"We can still check to see if anyone bought some in town tonight."

Jesse liked that idea. "Call Gabe and tell him to have everyone on patrol stop at the gas stations that are still open in town to ask. We'll check the other places that sell kerosene in the morning. Find anything?"

Perkins made an unhappy face. "Some foot impressions in the grass, but nothing distinct. Unless someone saw something, I doubt we're going to come up with any valuable forensics."

"Okay, Peter, keep working it."

Jesse stepped up to the threshold. He hadn't been back to the house since returning to town, and these certainly weren't the circumstances under which he would have chosen to come see the old place. It felt odd to knock at what used to be his own front door. Jesse recognized Alisha's voice as the one asking who was there.

"It's me, Alisha, Jesse."

When the door pulled back, Alisha was standing there, right hand near her weapon, just in case. She wasn't experienced enough to be blasé or to take things for granted. She still had her edge. It would dull a little with time. Jesse hoped she would never lose it completely. Sometimes an edge was all that stood between a cop and a flag-draped coffin and bag-pipes. She relaxed when she saw that Jesse was alone.

Alisha made the introductions. Ron Patel was a handsome man with rich dark skin and jet-black hair. His eyes were dark as well, but he had a kind face. He was clearly stressed, nervously rubbing his lips with his fingers and breathing rapidly. Jesse knew Patel was a doctor and researcher at Brigham and Women's in Boston. Other than that, he didn't know much else about the man. His wife, Liza, surprised Jesse. He knew she was an architect. He didn't know she was blond and blue-eyed. She actually resembled a younger version of Jesse's ex-wife, Jenn. She wouldn't have been out of place on Malibu. She saw the look in Jesse's eyes.

"I know, Chief, I'm not what you were expecting. We get that a lot," she said, no snark in her voice. She looked at her husband and they actually both laughed. The laughter didn't last long.

"Please call me Jesse. The kids asleep?"

She nodded. "They're a little too young to understand. Please sit, Jesse. Would you like some coffee?"

"No, thanks. I've had all the coffee I can bear for one night. Look, I'm not going to make you go over the details with me again tonight. I'm sure you've given them to Officer Davis."

"Yes, Alisha has been very kind," said Dr. Patel.

"I'm going to leave Officer Davis outside all night. No one is likely to bother you again — not tonight, anyway."

"Thank you, Jesse," Liza Patel said. "I'll feel more secure about the kids, knowing an officer will be here."

"Alisha, head out there now. I'll stop by to talk with you when I leave."

Once the front door closed, the room got quiet and Jesse's expression turned very grave.

He said, "I'm sure Alisha asked you if you know of anyone who might've done this to you or if you know of any reason you were singled out?"

Liza Patel laughed a joyless laugh and put her face next to her husband's. "Apparently, skin tone seems reason enough for some. And no, I don't know of anyone who would do this to us."

"Nor I," said Ron Patel. "So far, we've been treated wonderfully by our neighbors and people in town."

Liza added, "Until tonight."

"About that," Jesse said. "Listen —"

Liza Patel's face turned an angry shade of red. "Is this where you tell us Paradise isn't 'that' kind of town and that it must have been done by someone from outside of Paradise? That you're so sorry and that some of your best friends are from the subcontinent?"

"Look, I know you're upset. You're scared for your kids. You have every right to be."

"Well," she said, "now that we have your permission, that makes it all better."

"Liza!" Ron said. "Let the man speak."

"What I was going to say is that I will leave a car outside your door for as long as you want. I'll do everything in my power to make sure we catch the person or persons who did this, whether they come from Paradise or not."

"Thank you, Chief — Jesse," Ron Patel said.

Jesse had a warning for them. "Be prepared for the press. Once they catch wind of this, they are going to be all over you. You might want to have a talk with your kids about it."

Liza Patel got red-faced again. "Are you trying to intimidate us so we'll cover this up?"

"You don't know me," Jesse said. "I get that, but the only people who I'd intimidate

70

in this situation are the people who did this to you and your family. I was just thinking of your kids. No hidden agenda. Nothing more complicated than that."

She turned away from Jesse. "Ron, I'm going upstairs to check on the kids."

When he was sure his wife was out of earshot, Ron Patel said, "Liza doesn't understand. How can she? I have been the target of this sort of thing for many years. Some of it was hurtful but meant to be harmless, like when my college roommates used to ask me to say 'Would you like a Slurpee with that?' After 9/11, as you can imagine, it was very bad. Jesse, is there any way we can report this as simple vandalism? I don't want to put my children through more trauma and I don't want to give a victory to the morons who did this thing to us."

"What about Liza? She doesn't seem like someone who'll back down."

"You leave the explanation to me. There are hard lessons for us all to learn."

"Are you sure?" Jesse asked. "I can do what you ask and you can make book on the fact that we'll be looking hard for the people who did this to you. But I have to inform the mayor and the selectmen. You understand that once I share it, I can't control who says what. Still, I'm pretty sure no one will want to spread this around."

Ron Patel shook Jesse's hand and wished him good night.

13

As Jesse left the house and made his way to Alisha's cruiser, he asked Peter Perkins to join him.

"You guys did great," Jesse said. "Alisha, like I said inside, I want you out here all night. I'll have someone pick you up some coffee and something to eat. Peter, keep doing what you're doing, but we're going after this quietly."

Perkins nodded and went back to his task without a word. Alisha's reaction was different.

"Quietly! What do you mean, 'we're going after this quietly'?"

"It means Dr. Patel asked me to have you report this as simple vandalism."

"Simple vandalism?" she said, agitated. "A family that just moved into town had a cross burned on their lawn."

"It's their lawn and it's their lives."

"But the law is the law, Jesse."

"Right may be right, but you've been around long enough by now to know better about the law. The law can be pretty flexible, and that's not always a bad thing."

"But —"

"Never mind. The law and how it's enforced and prosecuted is situational. You may not like it. I may not like it, but that's the fact. Alisha, I know what you think is the right thing to do here and it may be the right thing in the end, but they're worried about what the press attention might do to their kids."

"It's not right to sweep this under the carpet."

"That's not what's going on here."

"Isn't it, though?"

Jesse encouraged his cops to speak their minds. He didn't want things left unsaid to fester. But he couldn't help but remember what Molly had reported to him about the incident with the bikers at the Scupper.

"Don't misunderstand me. I said quietly. I didn't say we weren't going to go at this hard," he said. "We're going to pursue this until we find out who did it."

That seemed to break the tension, though Alisha's expression wasn't exactly a cheery one. Jesse took a step toward his Explorer, then turned back. He walked around to the passenger side of the cruiser and let himself in.

Jesse said, "I was going to talk to you about this tomorrow, but now works better. Explain to me what happened at the Scupper between you and those assholes."

"Molly told you?"

"She was acting chief. It was her duty to tell me, but I want to hear it from you."

She bowed her head. "I'm sorry, Jesse."

"I'm not interested in apologies. I'm interested in what happened."

"I stepped between the bikers and several bar patrons. I warned them all not to take their disagreements any further because I would arrest anyone who incited violence or acted in a violent manner. I suggested the bikers should consider leaving."

Jesse half smiled. "Suggested?"

"Strongly suggested."

They both laughed, but when the laughter faded, Jesse continued, "I've been told that when Suit and Gabe showed up, things were pretty heated. True?"

"True."

"I also heard you didn't take kindly to them interceding. True?"

"True."

"They're senior officers, Alisha. From what I can tell, they acted appropriately to defuse the situation."

"I know that now, but . . ." She stopped speaking.

"Finish what you were going to say."

"Is that an order, Jesse?"

"It is."

"One of the bikers called me a nigger and I guess I just lost it."

"People are going to call you a lot of things as long as you wear that uniform and pin that badge to your shirt."

"I know. It won't happen again."

Jesse changed subjects. "Are you still dating that security guy from Stiles Island?"

She snapped her head around. "Huh? You asking about Dylan Taylor? That's my personal life."

He seemed not to hear her. "You know about the assault in Swan Harbor?"

She nodded, though still confused. "What's that got to do with what happened at the Scupper or my personal life?"

"The vic in Swan Harbor was an African American woman and the man she was staying with at the B-and-B was white."

"Holy sh—"

"You see where I'm going with this, Alisha? Somebody's targeting interracial couples."

"I'll be careful, Jesse, and I'll let Dylan know."

"Do that. You're a good cop, Alisha."

Jesse didn't say another word and let himself out of the cruiser.

14

Jesse didn't pretend he could read tea leaves or pick up the scent of trouble blowing in off the Atlantic, but he knew enough not to ignore signs of danger when they were tapping him on the shoulder. And what was going on was more than shoulder tapping. It was a gut punch. Something was wrong. The thing was, how to stop it?

What people misunderstood about police work was that it was reactive. Cops rode the wave or followed the wave onto the beach. It wasn't their job to get ahead of it. Cops were really like the guys who followed the parade with brooms and shovels, cleaning up the mess the horses and the spectators left behind.

Instead of heading straight to his new home from his old one, Jesse drove slowly through the darkened, damp streets of Paradise. It had been a ritual of his almost from the day he arrived in town all those years ago. He particularly enjoyed it on nights like this, when a light rain was falling and the pavement glistened in the street light. He wasn't looking for anything specific, he didn't expect to stop a robbery in progress or help deliver a baby. It was just his way of taking stock of things. Taking stock of his life was also part of the program, and he didn't see why he couldn't do both at the same time.

As the rain plinked the roof of his Explorer, his mind drifted back to the church basement and to the meeting. He thought about how kind Bill had been to him, pictured Bill's business card in his wallet with his cell number written on the back. *Anytime, day or night, weekend or holiday, you need to talk, you call me. We'll get you through it.* He thought about Anya's nervous tics, the lost look in her eyes. Had he ever been that lost? There was no denying his dependence on alcohol, yet it wasn't in his nature to be completely lost. Jesse always had something to anchor him in a storm, but he was damned if he could explain it. And there was a part of him that worried the anchor wouldn't hold quite so well without alcohol in his life. He worried the alcohol was the anchor.

He pushed that thought away, and what

took its place was Callie's face. Jesse wasn't going to beat himself up for seeing beauty in a woman's face, especially after a day so full of violence and hate. When he came back into the present, he realized that two months away had given him back the ability to see Paradise with fresh eyes. He liked that he could once again smell the salt air, a scent he had grown nose-blind to over time. He remembered his first day in town and how he noted that the Pacific and the Atlantic were different in more than name alone.

But as he turned into the Swap, toward his condo, the skies opened up and Jesse saw something ahead of him that got his full attention. Cole Slayton, the kid Jesse had kicked loose earlier in the day, was up the street from the Paradise Tavern, hitching a ride. Jesse drove past him and pulled to a stop.

Cole rushed to the passenger door, opened it, and said, "Thanks, man, I really —" He stopped speaking when he saw who the driver was. "It's you. Never mind."

"Get in."

"Nah, that's okay."

"Don't be an idiot, Cole. Just get in out of the rain."

He hesitated for a second, but the increasingly heavy rain made up his mind. "Okay."

Slayton plopped himself down in the passenger seat. His open UCLA hoodie and white T-shirt beneath were soaked through, as were his jeans and Nikes. He was shivering. Jesse turned up the heat.

"UCLA? You from L.A.?"

Slayton didn't answer, staring straight ahead.

"I was LAPD Robbery Homicide," Jesse said, reaching into the backseat for a towel he carried there just in case. "Here, dry yourself off. You from the city or the valley?"

"Woodland Hills."

"Nice." Jesse smiled, remembering his good days in L.A. He could almost feel the sun on his face, smell the eucalyptus in the air. He had never been a backward-looking man. *Nothing back there except trouble and pain.* Rehab and the process of taking stock had changed that. "I liked that area. Lived there for a while when I first got on the job."

"Why'd you leave if you loved it so damned much? You like raw wind and cold rain, or were you running away from something?"

The smile vanished from Jesse's face. The sun and eucalyptus replaced by the stink of alcohol sweat and the sound of his captain's voice demanding his shield and his gun. *You're done here, Stone.*

"Hitching is illegal inside town limits."

"You going to arrest me for hitching in the rain?"

"No, I'm just letting you know. Where can I drop you off?"

The kid hesitated and then gave him the address of the Benson's B-and-B off Scrimshaw. Jesse had his doubts about that but didn't say anything. He just put the Explorer in drive. Slayton didn't say a word during the ride across town. When Jesse let him out, the kid managed a grudging thank-you. And when he tried to give back the towel, Jesse said, "Keep it. You can drop it off at the station anytime." The kid slammed the door shut and walked toward the bed-and-breakfast's doorway. Jesse drove up the street, clicked his lights off, and parked, watching Cole Slayton in his rearview mirror.

15

As Jesse suspected would happen, the kid never went through the door of Benson's. He'd walked up to the entrance, stayed in the shadows of the overhang, and thirty seconds later emerged back onto the street. When he did, he craned his neck, looking in the direction Jesse had driven. Then, satisfied that Jesse's SUV was gone, he threw his hood up over his head, placed the towel over that, and walked in the opposite direction toward the water.

Jesse circled the block and followed him. He was careful to hang far enough back so the kid wouldn't spot him. It wasn't easy following a walker in a car, especially along empty streets. It helped that Slayton's head was covered, though he did occasionally check behind him. Eventually, Jesse parked his Explorer. The rain that only moments before was coming down in sheets had let up and was now nothing more than mist. It was easier tailing the kid on foot. Jesse could hang back in the shadows, use doorways and parked cars to cover movements.

After a minute of trailing the kid this way, Jesse realized that he wasn't exactly sure why he was bothering. He didn't suspect Slayton of having a connection to Felicity Wileford's assault. He'd been in the Paradise lockup during the attack in Swan Harbor. And he doubted the kid had anything to do with tonight's cross-burning. It would have been a hell of a walk to Jesse's old house and back to the Swap. Besides, the kid didn't seem the type. Sure, Slayton was full of attitude and clearly had demons, but they seemed like personal demons. Jesse knew about those. Maybe that was why he was following the kid, because Jesse was aware that sometimes all people had to hold on to were their demons and that the trick of survival was not letting them hold on to you.

When Slayton crossed Berkshire, MacArthur, and Salter Streets and passed the meetinghouse, Jesse had a pretty good idea of where the kid was headed. This was the oldest part of Paradise, where the founders had built their first houses close to Pilgrim Cove before moving into their big Victorians up on the Bluffs. There was never much of a problem with homelessness in Paradise, but on the rare occasion that his cops would run across someone living rough, they would usually be camping out in Pilgrim Cove. The Paradise side of the cove was rocky and largely hidden from the street. To get down to the little sliver of beach below, you had to either take the one set of stairs on the Stiles Island Bridge side of the cove or climb down the rocks. Jesse caught up to Slayton as he was starting to climb down to the beach.

"Stop right there, Cole," Jesse said with a smile in his voice.

But Slayton, startled by Jesse's voice, lost his grip. Jesse grabbed on to the sleeve of his hoodie and held him long enough to let the kid regain his footing. He then helped pull him back up to the street.

Slayton was anything but thankful. "You following me? What are you following me for?"

"Because this is my town and I'm responsible for the safety of the people in it. That includes you, whether you like it or not."

Slayton didn't like it. "Leave me alone. I'm fine."

"No, you're not. If I go down there, will I find your belongings tucked away in the rocks?"

"So what if they are? Wait, don't tell me. I can get arrested for that, too."

"For living on the beach, that's right," Jesse said. "But I'm not interested in arresting you."

"Just leave me alone."

"That's not going to happen. You've got two options."

"I'm listening."

"You seem determined to end up in our jail, so you can spend the night there again. No arrest, just a place to sleep in out of the rain for one night."

Slayton shook his head. "What's option two?"

Jesse ignored the question. "Go get your stuff and come back up here."

"What's the —"

"Whatever the other option is, it isn't sleeping in Pilgrim Cove. Go get your things."

Five minutes later, Slayton, a backpack strapped around his shoulders and a green duffel bag in hand, was standing in front of Jesse.

"C'mon, my Explorer's a few blocks that way."

Jesse started walking, Cole Slayton followed.

"Why are you here, Cole? What does

Paradise hold for you besides trouble?"

He didn't answer but laughed at that second question.

"Do you mean to stick around?" Jesse asked, then added, "And don't tell me it's none of my business. It is my business."

"I'm staying."

"Then you need to find a job and a place to stay. I can help with that."

"I don't need your help."

"You're going to get it anyway."

That angered Slayton. "Why the fuck should you care?"

Jesse stopped in his tracks and turned to face the kid. "Watch your mouth and lose some of that attitude. Why do I care? I don't know. Maybe because someone who I never met before was generous to me tonight."

He turned and walked ahead. The kid followed and caught up.

"What's that place, a church?" the kid asked, pointing to a large rectangular building with white clapboards and a spire. "Where's the cross?"

"That's the old meetinghouse. It was kind of a church once. Now it's a town landmark because it was part of the Underground Railroad. There was a tunnel built that ran from Pilgrim Cove to a secret room beneath the meetinghouse where runaway slaves stayed on their way up to Canada."

The kid had nothing else to say. It was just as well. Jesse was tired and wet and not really in the mood for history lessons.

16

Mayor Walker would have preferred to be Congresswoman or Senator Walker. Jesse Stone would have preferred that, too. Connie Walker had never been Jesse's biggest fan, nor had Jesse ever felt great love for the mayor, but, for the time being, they were stuck with each other. At least the mayor, in spite of strong opposition, had backed Jesse when he hired Alisha. And Jesse had given Walker political cover and taken the media heat during the whole Terry Jester fiasco.

When the mayor strolled in, Jesse stood up from the booth at Daisy's to greet her. Constance Walker didn't look pleased. She was never pleased when she was summoned by Jesse to one of these meetings away from town hall. Connie was a handsome woman, but when she was unhappy, *stern-looking* didn't quite do her expression justice.

"Okay, Jesse, what's wrong this time?" she asked, sliding into the booth, a cup of coffee waiting for her. "It's never good news when we have to meet at seven in the morning. And Daisy's whole-wheat pancakes don't soften the blow as much as you think they do."

As if on cue, Daisy arrived with the mayor's pancakes and Jesse's scrambled eggs and bacon.

"Enjoy." Daisy dropped the plates and left.

Connie asked, "What's up with Daisy?"

"The look on your face. She knows to keep her distance."

The mayor sipped her black coffee, put butter and syrup on her pancakes, took a bite, and made a happy face in spite of herself. It didn't last.

"I asked you a question, Jesse."

"You heard about the assault in Swan Harbor?"

"Horrible. Horrible." She took another bite. "A Harvard prof."

"Not exactly. Her name's Felicity Wileford and she's studying for her Ph.D. at Harvard. She's black and the man she was staying with is white."

Confused, the mayor tilted her head. "Is that significant?"

"What I tell you now is off the record and between us. The word *slut* was written across her abdomen in red lipstick."

The pancakes seemed to turn to sawdust in her mouth. "Oh my God. But still, that was in Swan Harbor."

"Last time I looked, there was no wall separating us from Swan Harbor." Then Jesse explained about the Tammy Portugal murder.

Connie said, "I was living in New York during those years, but that was the whole mess with Hasty Hathaway and his lunatic militiamen. That was a long, long time ago, Jesse. All those people are either dead or in prison."

Jesse nodded.

"Then why was it necessary to summon me here? As horrifying as the assault was —"

"Someone burned a cross on the Patels' lawn last night."

The mayor's face went blank. She immediately understood. "Dr. Patel is Indian and his wife is . . ." Her voice trailed off. "I will go see them today. But that's your old house. Could it have been meant for you?"

"C'mon, Connie. If it had been a brick through the window or if the word *pig* had been spray-painted across the front door, maybe I'd buy it. But a cross burned into their lawn with kerosene wasn't meant for me. And Molly tells me there were some skinhead bikers in town a few weeks back."

"She told me about that after it happened, but I didn't think anything of it."

"Nothing happens in a vacuum."

"So what are you telling me, Jesse? Something wicked this way comes?"

"No."

"Then what?"

"That it's already here."

"What am I supposed to do with that?"

"I don't know, Connie. I thought it was my duty to tell you. And in case you're wondering, the cross-burning is being reported as simple vandalism. The Patels don't want their kids to have to deal with the press."

"Thank heavens for small mercies."

"I don't think this is over."

"You don't think whoever is behind this stuff will just move on?"

"Lamb's blood over the threshold only works in the Old Testament."

"Now I *am* worried," she said, trying and failing to smile.

"Why's that?"

"When you start citing the Old Testament, I know we're in for it." She slid out of the booth, reached for her coffee, and finished it in a single gulp. "Thank Daisy for me. Tell her the coffee and pancakes were wonderful as always. Keep me apprised."

Connie Walker turned and left, her heels clacking against the tile floor as she went. A couple seconds later, Daisy came over to talk to Jesse and refill his cup.

"What's up with Mayor Hottie? That woman is godawful attractive, but she wears tension like too much perfume."

Jesse laughed. "Maybe you could offer her some relief."

Sounding as wistful as he'd ever heard her, Daisy said, "Some things, Jesse Stone, are just not meant to be."

Jesse thought there was no arguing that.

17

Jesse parked his Explorer out in front of the Paradise Hotel and headed down to the video office to speak to Connor Cavanaugh. Cavanaugh, Suit's old high school football buddy, was head of security and played on the PPD's softball team. Like Suit, Cavanaugh was a big, friendly guy, though he didn't have a new wife to watch his diet. Jesse laughed to himself when he stepped into the video room and saw Connor finishing an egg sandwich and reaching for a thick slab of pumpkin bread. Cavanaugh smiled at Jesse, seeming to read his mind.

"Well, Jesse, Halloween's coming, got to do something with all that pumpkin."

"Better take some of that spare tire off before softball season."

Cavanaugh slapped his gut. "I know. If I get any bigger, I'll be able to play two positions at once."

They both laughed at that.

Cavanaugh asked, "You here to collect your friend?"

"I wouldn't call him my friend. He give you any trouble?"

Cavanaugh shook his head. "Nope. Quiet."

"I appreciate you giving him the room."

"No sweat, Jesse. We always have a few spare rooms for emergencies, even during this time of year, when folks come up to see the foliage. One of my perks is that I can use them now and then. I can let him have it for another few days, but this coming weekend we're full and —"

"No need to explain. I appreciate it, Connor. The kid will make good on it."

Cavanaugh shook his head. "That's unnecessary. I owe you and Suit a hundred favors."

"Okay, we'll talk about it when the time comes."

"He's in one-twelve."

Jesse walked over to where Cavanaugh was sitting and leaned against the table. That got Connor's attention, but the serious expression on Jesse's face is really what did it.

He bit into the pumpkin bread and asked, "Something wrong, Jesse?"

"I'm going to ask you a question that may

seem inappropriate."

"Shoot."

"Do you know if any interracial couples are registered here?"

For the first time since they'd met, Connor gave Jesse a wary look. "I don't know about this, Jesse. I'm uncomfortable answering —"

Jesse explained what had happened to Felicity Wileford and about the incident at the Patels' house and said, "So you understand why I'm asking. I'm trying to prevent anything else like that from happening again."

Cavanaugh exhaled and put the pumpkin bread down. He seemed to have lost his appetite. "Yeah, I understand. So you think this is only the beginning of the trouble?"

"I can't afford not to think that."

"I wouldn't want your job, Jesse, not in a million years. As far as interracial couples go . . . I can't remember any. But I guess I don't usually pay attention to that kind of stuff. If I notice any, what should I do? Should I say something?"

"No. Just keep an eye out and let me know. I can have the officer patrolling this sector pay some extra attention to the hotel and surrounding streets."

"And I guess you can't panic people or chase them out of town."

"I don't think the mayor would be a fan of that idea, but if we have any more trouble, there won't be a choice. And, Connor . . ."

"Yeah, Jesse."

"For now," he said, shaking Cavanaugh's big hand, "this is just between us."

"You got it."

Slayton answered the door, hair wet, but dressed in a ragged San Francisco Giants T-shirt, jeans, and his duct-taped Nikes. Although he didn't exactly jump for joy, his expression was less challenging to Jesse than it had been previously. He even asked Jesse to come in.

Slayton said, "That Connor guy is all right. He even got the hotel to wash my clothes."

"He's a good man. He says you can stay in the room for a few more days."

"I'll think about it."

What Jesse couldn't help but notice was the tidiness of the room. Except for the bed quilt being folded over, it would have been hard to tell the place had been slept in. Jesse had been the same way. Still was. He'd attributed it to his minor-league travels, having to pack efficiently for long road trips on buses and stays in cheap hotels. But he guessed he was always pretty neat. It was part of that self-contained thing.

"You play baseball?" Jesse said, pointing at Slayton's T-shirt.

"Right field and relief pitcher for my high school. Made all-city my senior year as an outfielder."

"Why didn't you pursue it?"

"Didn't love it enough."

"Giants shirt. I thought you were from L.A."

The kid's attitude came back in full force. "Fu— screw the Dodgers."

"I used to play in their minor-league system."

But if he thought the kid would ask him about his time as the best shortstop prospect in the Dodgers' system, he was wrong. What he got from Slayton was a full dose of attitude.

"Minor-league ballplayer. Minor-league cop in a minor-league town."

"Let's go," Jesse said, ignoring the comment. "I've got to drop you off before I get to the station."

Slayton furrowed his brow. "Drop me off? Where?"

"At your job."

"Job?"

"You got trouble with strong women?"

Slayton's chest puffed out and his attitude

turned to anger. "No. My mom was the strongest woman I ever met."

"Was?"

"She died about six months ago. She raised me pretty much on her own."

"Sorry to hear that."

"Sure you are. Everybody's sorry. What does that even mean?"

"Good question." Jesse nodded, remembering how people reacted to Diana's murder. "You said your mom raised you pretty much on her own."

"Yeah, I had an asshole stepfather for a while."

"What happened?"

"When I got big enough to kick his butt, I told him if he ever raised his hand to me or my mom again, I'd kill him. He didn't stay too long after that." Slayton seemed to calm down once he got that off his chest. "So why'd you ask me about strong women?"

"When you meet your new boss, you'll understand."

18

Back at the station, Jesse was waiting for Lundquist when Molly walked into his office.

"I know this was your office until a few days ago, but knocking is traditional. Besides, what are you even doing here? Aren't you off today?"

But Molly wasn't laughing. In fact, she seemed close to tears. That shook Jesse, because it took a lot to rattle Molly.

"What is it?" Jesse jumped out of his chair and came around his desk. "Is it your kids?"

She took a folded piece of paper out of her back pocket and handed it to him. "My husband found that on his windshield this morning when he was heading to work."

The slickly produced flier was done in multicolored ink. The logo at the top was an American flag, a rounded-edged swastika superimposed on it. At each corner of the flier was a Confederate flag with an arm raised in the fascist salute superimposed on it.

Think of your town twenty years ago. It was a peaceful place, a place safe to raise your children with their own kind, a place where you understood what marriage meant and where Sunday still belonged to the one true and Christian God. Remember when your town was a place where you could trust your neighbors and where you could leave your front door open without fear. Is that the town you live in today?

No. Today your town is overrun with violence and fear. Your town has been invaded and despoiled while you slept. It has been taken from you by greedy bankers and politicians who have sold your beautiful, peaceful town out from under you for thirty pieces of silver. They have opened the sewer gates of the city and let the muck flow into your streets, neighborhoods, and houses. Do you know your neighbors? Would you trust them with your children? Is their god your God? Do they even believe? Are they sodomites and defilers enabled by atheist liberal conspirators whose mission it is to rob America of its supremacy and destiny?

The Revolution is coming. The time to take back your town, your country, your destiny is almost upon you. The warning shots have already been fired and soon the time will come for you to take up arms against the dark and usurious forces of liberalism, feminism, atheism, socialism, and the corrupt government that wants to take away your guns, a government that takes sides against the people who stand between you and the jungle, a government that supports free immigration and globalization. Listen carefully. The fuse has been lit. When you hear the explosion, take to the streets and take back this nation one town at a time.

The Saviors of Society

As Jesse had told Molly the day he came back to work, he had run across groups like this in Tucson and L.A. There were even some members of the LAPD who'd gotten jammed up for their involvement with fringe groups and militias whose philosophies and agendas strayed pretty close to out-and-out fascism and white supremacy.

Jesse asked, "Do you know if your neighbors got these?"

"I don't know. My husband had to get to

work and I had to get the girls off to the bus."

"That's okay. We'll know soon enough." He shook his head in disgust. "I don't like it."

"Of course you don't."

"These groups are one thing, but this flier . . . it's different than the ones I've seen in the past. It's not the usual crude, simplistic hate speech you usually get. The language is more nuanced than it usually is with these things."

"Why does that matter?"

"Because the writer was smart enough to appeal to people's fear while steering clear of the automatically inflammatory words. Most of the hate here is sheathed in allusion and euphemism, and that makes these people more dangerous. And there's just enough truth in here to get some traction. The nature of Paradise *has* changed in the last twenty years. People from the city *are* moving into town. The nature of the crime is different now."

"But this is a good place with good people. You know these people. I know these people, Jesse. I am these people."

"We're never who we think we are, Molly, good or bad."

"But they're talking about shots, fuses,

explosions, and revolution."

"Uh-huh. Like I said before, free speech cuts in different directions."

Molly opened her mouth to say something, but that's when the station phones started ringing off the hook. They walked through the office door and listened to Gabe answering the phones.

"I think I have my answer about those fliers getting into other people's hands," Jesse said. "You want an hour of overtime helping me handle these calls?"

"Forget the overtime," Molly said, pulling up a chair next to Gabe. "This is my town, Jesse."

19

Lundquist walked into Jesse's office half an hour after the torrent of phone calls had begun. Things had slowed some by then, though calls were still coming in. Jesse had already spoken to the mayor about it and had called Suit in from patrol. After making a copy of the flier for Suit, Jesse sent him over to Molly's street to get a sense of just how many of the fliers had been distributed and to see if he could determine how big an area of the town had been covered.

"Jesse, these things could be all over the place," Suit had said.

"I don't think so. These types operate under cover of darkness. They're not ready to be seen — not yet, anyway."

"Not yet. What are they waiting for?"

"That's the million-dollar question."

Jesse hadn't wanted to get into it with Suit about what he thought might make the Saviors of Society step out into the light of day. He didn't think he'd have that luxury with Lundquist.

"Have a seat, Brian."

Before sitting, Lundquist placed a file on Jesse's desk.

"That's the initial forensics and medical report on Felicity Wileford."

Jesse asked, "Anything unexpected?"

Lundquist didn't answer directly. "She's in bad shape. Broken jaw. Broken ribs. Punctured lung. And they brutalized her."

"What do you mean, 'brutalized'? Was she raped?"

Lundquist made a sick face. "In a way. It's all there in the file. That's not even the worst of it. The doctors have put her in a medically induced coma, but they're not hopeful."

"Any brain function?"

"Some."

"I don't get why whoever did this tried to make it look like the Tammy Portugal crime scene."

"Me, either, though I've got to admit they did go out of their way to make it look that way."

" 'They'?"

"It's all there." Lundquist pointed at the file. "From the injuries, it looks like there was at least two, maybe three, different attackers. Animals."

"Any hits?"

"None so far. The lipstick they used to write on the body was a cheap brand you could pick up anywhere."

"You eliminate the boyfriend, Randisi?"

"Can't yet."

Jesse nodded. "Because of there being more than one assailant."

"Exactly. I don't think he's involved, but I can't be sure. Anyway, he says he's going to stick around until Wileford comes out of her coma."

"Anything else?"

"We found some strands of a black polyester-and-spandex blend."

"That lead anywhere?"

"Pretty common stuff. The lab thinks it might come from athletic wear. You know, the kind of material football players wear under their equipment or runners wear in cold weather. Like I said, it's all there." Lundquist turned in his chair, facing the office door. "What's going on out there? I've never seen two of your people handling calls before. You guys have a blackout in town or a flood or something?"

"Or something," Jesse said. "Here."

Lundquist barely reacted as he read the flier.

Jesse said, "You've seen it before."

"The SS," he said, nodding. "I have, but not this far south. Mostly up along the border with New Hampshire or out west along the New York border."

"What can you tell me about them?"

Lundquist held up the flier and turned it to face Jesse. "What could I tell you about them that this doesn't tell you? I mean, they're called the SS for short."

"You know anything about their leadership or how they operate?"

"Sorry, Jesse. I've just run across these fliers before. I've got no idea who they really are or how they operate. Why, you think there's a connection between Felicity Wileford's assault and this?"

"We had a cross-burning last night while these fliers were being stuck on car windshields across town. Happened to be the people who bought my old house. The husband's a doctor of Indian descent. The wife is blond and blue-eyed and they've got two little kids."

"Shit. Interracial couples."

"Uh-huh."

"Okay, I know some people who work with Homeland Security who monitor potential homegrown terrorist groups and people at the Boston PD in intelligence. I'll see if I can't get them to get in touch with you about this."

"I'd appreciate it, Brian."

Lundquist stood up and shook Jesse's hand. "Then let me get to it."

Before he left, Jesse asked, "Hear anything about the Swan Harbor cop, Daniels?"

Lundquist shrugged. "Service record is pretty clean. Let's face it, Jesse, Swan Harbor's even smaller than Paradise. There's not much trouble for a cop to get into there."

When he was sure he was alone, Jesse reached over to his right and opened the drawer in which he used to keep his office bottle. He didn't even realize what he was doing until he stopped himself from reaching for the bottle that was no longer there. Strange how intensely he wanted a drink and how the meeting he'd been to only last night already felt like a distant memory. He slammed the drawer shut and instead of grabbing his old baseball glove, he pulled a business card out of his wallet.

20

Jesse sat there for several minutes, phone pinched between his cheek and shoulder. He had raised his index finger to punch in the number three or four times before backing off. It was still hard for him to admit weakness or ask for help. Then his finger was tapping in the area code.

"Bill here," said the man on the other end of the line.

"It's Jesse, the guy from —"

"I remember. I don't suppose you're calling to say you had a lovely evening and wanted to see how I was doing."

"You're a smart man."

"Not so smart, just experienced. You jonesing?"

"Just reached into my desk drawer for the office bottle."

"Did you drink?"

"If the bottle was still there, I think I would've."

"The bottle's gone. That's good."

"More lucky than good. Someone else got rid of it."

"Lucky works, Jesse. What matters is that you called instead of going somewhere to get a drink."

"I used to be able to will myself not to drink for weeks or months. Now if I'm not preoccupied, I can't go thirty seconds without thinking about it."

Bill laughed.

Jesse asked, "I say something funny?"

"Not funny, exactly. Ironic."

"Ironic?"

"In the past, when you went weeks without drinking, did you ever really, I mean in your guts, believe you were never going to drink again?"

"Truth? No, I guess I always knew I would drink again. My shrink says it was a trick I played on myself, that I was like a kid holding his breath. That no matter how long I held my breath I would have to breathe again."

"Shrink, huh?"

"Long story."

"Well, now you're in it, Jesse. You may not ever get to a point where you never want to drink again. I've never gotten there. It's a day-by-day thing. In the end, they add up to not drinking."

"Does it get easier?"

Bill laughed again. "Some days are better than others, but that's true about life, no?"

"I thought the idea was for you to help me out here."

"I won't lie to you about this stuff. I never thought much of people who did drugs when they were growing up and then lied to their kids that they were freakin' saints and never touched a joint or popped a greenie. How does that help a kid who might be struggling?"

"I see your point."

"Look, Jesse, they tell us to keep it simple. Don't drink and go find a meeting. If you can't get to a meeting until later, get the hell out of where you are and get busy doing something else. Can you do that?"

"Uh-huh."

"Good man. I'll be here if you need me. You okay?"

"I'm fine now. Thanks."

"No problem."

Jesse hung up the phone and walked out of his office to get a cup of coffee that he didn't actually want. He had struggled with drinking for a long time, but this felt different. It was one thing to struggle with drinking, because, as he had admitted to Bill, drinking was still part of the equation. Johnnie Walker was always going to be there at the end of the line, welcoming arms spread wide open. It was something else struggling not to drink, to not see that rectangular bottle filled just above its curved neck with amber liquid comfort, its slanted black-and-gold label calling to him. It was also something else for Jesse to so quickly ask for help, especially from a stranger.

"Jesse," Gabe Weathers said, waving a piece of paper in the air. "You better have a look at this."

"What?"

"Gas station convenience store off 1A outside of town sold five gallons of kerosene last night."

"I'm sure a lot of places around here sold kerosene. What's special about this one?"

"Guy says his clerk felt hinky about the kid who bought the stuff."

" 'Hinky'?"

"The owner's word, not mine. Who should I send over to check it out?"

Jesse grabbed the slip of paper out of Gabe's hand. "I'll handle it. All the calls, were they about the fliers?"

Gabe nodded. "Mostly, yeah."

Jesse pointed at Molly, who was busy on a call. "When the calls stop, send her home.

Tell her it's an order."

"Sure thing, Jesse. So what do you make of this?"

"Not important what I make of it. It's what these SOBs do or don't make of it that matters."

Gabe shook his head. "Never thought we'd get this kind of thing come into Paradise."

Jesse didn't want to say what he was thinking, that things don't just materialize out of thin air. Some forms of evil don't just appear in your house. They have to be invited in.

21

Jesse was glad to be out of the station, away from the phantom bottle and the hundreds of memories of drinks shared with Healy or with others in his office, but away from the cop house or not, he knew that wherever he went, the past would always ride shotgun. Right at the moment, he was more concerned with what the near future would hold than his past. He drove his Explorer around the gas pumps and pulled into one of the yellow-lined parking spots outside the convenience store. Slamming his door shut behind him, Jesse stopped, checked out the pumps and the brick building, looking for where the security cameras were positioned. He also took a deep breath and remembered that as a kid he had loved the almost sweet chemical smell of gasoline. He didn't know whether it was his age or a change in formula, but the odor of gas no longer held any romance for him.

"Morning to ya, Chief Stone. Be with you in a second," said the middle-aged man behind the counter, taking a twenty-dollar bill from a nondescript woman. "That's twenty unleaded on pump five." He tapped some keys on a touchscreen in front of him, a cash drawer popped open, and he placed the twenty in the tray and closed the till. "Would you like a receipt?"

She didn't say anything to that, turned, and walked past Jesse as if he wasn't there. When the woman was gone, the counterman stuck his hand out to Jesse.

"Gary Cummings. I own the place. So I guess you're here about the kerosene?"

"Specifically about the kid who bought it. You said your clerk thought the kid was hinky."

"Sorry, Chief, that's my word. My night man isn't the sharpest tool in the shed. He said he felt the kid was too nervous, like a kid buying condoms for the first time or buying vodka with fake ID. He kept looking over his shoulder and looking at the cameras. We had a robbery here two years back. Guy pistol-whipped my counterman and threatened a customer. My guys are trained to get suspicious when they see people checking out where the cameras are."

"Good idea."

"This, too." Cummings pulled up his baggy red, blue, and silver Patriots sweatshirt to reveal an automatic pistol holstered to his right hip. "Smith & Wesson M&P 45 Shield, all the stopping power of a big .45, and it fits neatly into even a small hand. Every one of my people has a Class A permit. Rob me once, shame on you. Rob me twice . . . Just let some asshole come in here and try to get us again."

Jesse wasn't so sure he agreed. It wasn't that Jesse was squeamish about guns or using them. He'd certainly used his, sometimes to deadly effect, but he was well trained. He also understood the feeling of powerlessness and sense of violation victims had to deal with. Rape was the worst and the most traumatic to cope with, but all crime leaves scars. Jesse didn't think that arming everyone was necessarily the way to handle things, though he wasn't here to discuss victim trauma or gun control.

"Do you have footage of the kid?"

Cummings, a graying but fit man an inch or two shorter than Jesse, pulled his sweatshirt back down and flashed a broad white smile. "I never thought you'd ask, Chief. I got it cued up in the back. Just let me get my son to cover me and I'll go back there with you." He picked up the phone and

117

pressed the intercom button. "Junior, come up front."

Junior was the spitting image of his father. There was something else about him that Jesse noticed. The son had attitude, the wrong kind of attitude. He took one look at Jesse's PPD hat and jacket, sneered, and shook his head. It wasn't like the look Cole Slayton had given him. Junior's attitude had more malice in it and he clearly had no love for cops. When he stopped shaking his head, he locked eyes with Jesse. Under other circumstances, Jesse might've laughed at him, but he needed the father's cooperation. Jesse had stared into the eyes of serial killers, stared into the eyes of men who'd slit their own children's throats as they slept. He had even stared into the eyes of the man who had murdered Diana. This guy, as tough as he thought he was, had a lot to learn. Jesse also took note of the neck tattoos peeking out from over the edge of the kid's shirt collar. It seemed most of the people under thirty he ran into these days had tats, but Jesse couldn't help but be curious about these.

Cummings broke the stare down between his son and Jesse. "Okay, stay out here until I can show Chief Stone the footage from last night."

"Fine," Gary Cummings Jr. said with little enthusiasm.

"Right this way, Chief Stone." The father led the way into the office.

"We can cover every inch of the property except the interiors of the restrooms, of course," Cummings said. "But you're not interested in that. Here, look at the monitor on the top right and I'll run the footage of the kid who bought the kerosene. Okay, here we go."

Jesse watched as a short, stocky young man dressed in all black strolled from the right side of the station, walked over to the kerosene pump, and put a plastic fuel container down on the ground. He seemed confused about what to do next. He picked up the container, took a few steps toward the store, then turned back to the pump and put the container down.

"Can your clerk watch this in real time from the counter?" Jesse asked.

"He can, and so can anyone back here."

Eventually, the kid walked into the convenience store and asked to pay for five gallons of kerosene. He reached into his pocket with shaking hands and gave the clerk too much money. He turned and left even as the clerk called to him. The clerk came out from behind the counter, ran after the kid, and caught him at the door. He looked scared and confused until the clerk gave him the change.

Jesse said, "Easy to see why the kid got your clerk's attention."

Then the kid filled up the container. When he was done, he ran as best he could, weighed down by the fuel, back in the direction from which he'd come.

"Two things, Mr. Cummings. Can you generate a still photo from the —"

Before Jesse could finish his question, Cummings reached behind him and handed Jesse a somewhat grainy photo of the kid's face.

"I thought you might want that. It's not perfect, but it's the clearest image I could capture. What's the other thing?"

"Do you have any footage of the vehicle the kid came in?"

"Sorry, Chief. If he came in a vehicle at all, it was parked out of range of our cameras. As you can see, he comes into view out of the darkness on the east side of the station and disappears into it when he's done. For all I know, he came on foot."

Jesse was skeptical about that. He kept his doubts to himself. He watched the video a few more times, thanked Cummings, and left. He could feel Junior's eyes burning a hole through his back as he went, but he was more interested in the time-stamped photo in his pocket. More than that, Jesse couldn't get the video footage out of his head. The kid could not have called more attention to himself had he sprayed the words *Hey, look at me* on his back in Day-Glo paint. Jesse didn't like it. He didn't like it one bit.

22

That night, Jesse found himself back in the basement of the Episcopal church in Cambridge. He couldn't help but smile, thinking that he was going to be spending a lot more time in church than he had ever anticipated he would. He hadn't been to church twice in a week since he was a kid, and those occasions had more to do with playing ball for the local church teams than religion. And he had never been a man to expend much energy contemplating God, but, he supposed, in spite of all the carnage he'd witnessed, he still believed. And from what he knew of AA, a belief in a higher power helped. That remained to be seen. For the moment, other than compiling his list and finding a temporary sponsor, he felt more like an AA observer than a participant.

He was a little early this time. Although most of the seats were empty, he found the same seat he'd sat in the previous night.

He'd never been a front-row type of guy anyway, not in school nor in the police academy. He passed the time checking his phone to see if there had been any messages from anyone in Paradise. He'd had his cops distribute the photo of the kid caught on camera at the gas station. Jesse had stopped by the Patels' on his way down to Boston to check in on them and to see if they might recognize the kid in the photo. But only Liza Patel was home and she swore she had never seen the kid before.

"What's his name? Is he the one who did this to us?" she asked, pointing out the window at where the cross had been burned into the grass. Though a landscaper had already rototilled the soil where the charred grass had been, Jesse could tell the cross was not going to vanish from Liza Patel's memory anytime soon.

"We don't have a name yet," he said. "He bought five gallons of kerosene last night about a half-hour before the incident here, at a gas station not too far out of town. But a lot of people buy kerosene in these parts. I'll let you know if we make an arrest. Meanwhile, I'm leaving a car on your house for at least another few days."

Jesse hadn't expected gratitude. That was good, because he didn't get it, not at first.

"You could put fifty cars out there and I wouldn't feel my kids were safe, but you wouldn't understand, would you, Chief Stone?"

He didn't bother asking her to call him Jesse. "Try me. I might surprise you."

"Do you know what it feels like to be 'other'? Ron thinks I don't get it. Believe me, I get it. I didn't know until we began dating, then I learned in a hurry how it feels. And it wasn't only from ignorant asses giving us dirty looks or cursing at us in the street that I learned. No, the hardest lessons were from my friends and family. I can still hide behind my blond hair and blue eyes, but my children can't hide. They will always be 'other,' and I'm scared to death for them."

"I know you think I can't understand, Mrs. Patel, but I do. I'd feel exactly the same way if I had kids. Look, I can't undo what happened here or make your scars go away. All I can do is try to make sure it doesn't happen again, and I can't even guarantee that."

For the first time, Liza Patel smiled a genuine smile at Jesse. "Thank you for being honest with me, Chief. We've talked about me taking the kids for a couple of weeks and staying with my folks."

"I'd hate for that to happen, but in your shoes, I might do the same."

"You'll promise to leave a car there for a few more days?" she asked.

"Uh-huh. Twenty-four hours a day for as long as you want."

"Okay, then, we won't go anywhere . . . yet."

Then it was Jesse's turn to smile. "Understood."

That was more than an hour ago. When Jesse looked up from his phone, Callie, the woman who had run last night's meeting, was standing in front of him. In spite of Bill's admonition and in spite of himself, Jesse couldn't help but react. There was no denying he was attracted to her and, unless there was something severely wrong with his ability to read people, it seemed she was equally attracted to him.

"It's good to see you here again, Jesse," she said, smiling. She had a great smile. It wasn't neon white like Diana's had been, but it was warm and welcoming.

"I really felt like drinking earlier, and Bill suggested I come to a meeting."

"He was right to suggest that. How do you feel now?"

"Not like drinking."

"I won't get preachy, Jesse. I'm just glad

you're here. We're stronger together." She turned, took a step, then turned back. "And if you all go for coffee tonight, I would love to come along."

Jesse just nodded.

A few minutes later, Anya, the tattooed angel, came and sat down by Jesse.

"Hi, Jesse," she said, her voice brittle. She was doing that nervous thing with her fingers.

"Anya, right?"

"Yep."

"Where's Hank?"

Anya seemed almost to collapse in on herself. "He's . . . um . . . He . . . a . . . He couldn't get away from . . . work. You know how it is."

Jesse knew. What he knew was that she was making excuses for him. He was tempted to push her, but then remembered he wasn't there as a cop. He was there for the same reason Anya and Callie were there: to support one another and not to drink.

"That's okay," he said. "We're here."

She seemed to relax a little after that. "Thanks, Jesse. Sometimes the world just feels like a judgment and punishment machine."

"I think the idea is that we're all safe from that in here."

23

As he drove back to Paradise, Jesse's thoughts turned from the meeting to the fliers that had been put on car windshields on the blocks surrounding Molly's house. Many of Molly's neighbors had been rightfully outraged. Suit told Jesse that some of the people he'd spoken with were in tears that such a thing could happen in Paradise. Jesse was too experienced a cop to think that any place, even a town called Paradise, was insulated from evil. There had been ample evidence of that since the day he'd arrived.

But the thing Jesse couldn't get out of his head was not that people had called the police or the mayor's office about the racist leaflets or that some of them were in tears. He understood those reactions. What concerned Jesse were the neighbors who hadn't called. He was confident most of them were also pretty upset but weren't the type of people to call the police and that some were the type to simply shred the fliers and throw them away. Most people hunker down and hope bad things will just blow over like a nor'easter.

But what concerned Jesse most of all were the people in town who agreed with the sentiments expressed in the flier. As he had said to the mayor, nothing happened in a vacuum. And if Jesse was wondering about this, so were Molly's neighbors. Hate grows best in the soil of distrust, and it was easy to imagine that some of Paradise's citizens were looking at one another with a little less confidence in their character than they had only a day or two ago. But just as it hadn't been Jesse's job to act the cop at the meeting, it wasn't his job to be the thought police. As repugnant to him as those fliers were, people had a right to their hatreds. The only law that had been broken was a town ordinance against posting bills without a permit. Still, between what had happened in Swan Harbor and the cross-burning at the Patels', he could not escape the feeling that the worst was yet to come.

Jesse called Suit's home number as he came into town. Elena picked up.

"Hi, Jesse."

"Elena. Is Luther around?"

"You know it's all right for you to call him Suit. Even when you don't say it, you say it."

"Is he there?"

"Sorry, but he's not home."

"Where is he?"

Elena hesitated on the other end of the line. Jesse could almost hear her brain working on an answer that he would believe.

"Elena, do us both a favor and just tell me the truth. I won't be mad at Suit. I can never stay mad at him, anyway."

"He got really angry when he saw my reaction to those horrible fliers. I guess I lost it a little bit and you know how Luther gets."

"I know."

"Well . . ."

"C'mon, Elena."

"He's staking out the old part of town down by Pilgrim Cove because —"

"Suit thinks that's where the fliers will be put on cars tonight. I was thinking about that myself," he said. "That's why I was calling, to see if he wanted to earn some overtime."

"This isn't about money, Jesse. This is our town."

"I understand. It's mine, too. Thanks."

"What are you going to do?"

"Buy him a cup of coffee and sit with him."

"Good night, Jesse."

Jesse hit the disconnect button on his steering wheel and drove through town. Instead of heading home, he stopped at the Gull and picked up a large coffee. The barman winked at Jesse and asked him if he wanted a little Jameson or Black Label in it as a hedge against the chill. Jesse waved him off, thanking him for the offer. Two months ago, he wouldn't've thought twice about an offer like that or about accepting it. Now all he wanted to do was get to Suit.

24

Suit was parked on MacArthur Street in his Dodge pickup. He was fast asleep behind the wheel, head back, mouth wide open. Jesse could hear him snoring through the glass and rapped his knuckles against the window. Suit startled, lurching forward, then realized what was going on. He lowered the window.

"Hey, Jesse."

Jesse handed him the coffee through the open window. "I think you need this."

"Thanks. How'd you find me?"

Jesse walked around to the passenger side of the cab and got in.

"I called the house to ask you if you wanted to make some overtime doing surveillance when Elena told me you were already out here doing it on your own."

"I'm pissed off about those fliers."

"I know, but this is above and beyond. Thanks, Suit."

"What's happening, Jesse? I know we've had a lot of bad stuff go on in town, but this kind of thing . . . it's just not right."

"Not going to get an argument from me. Spot anything?"

Suit took a gulp of his coffee. "Nothing, but I didn't figure there would be anything to see yet." He pointed at the dashboard clock. "Whoever is doing this is waiting till there's no activity in town. The Gray Gull and the Lobster Claw should be closing about now. They're the last two businesses open on this side of town. I figure it's at least another half-hour or so before there's anything going on."

Two hours later and they still hadn't seen anything move except fallen leaves roiled by the wind. They'd long ago run out of conversation. No one actually enjoys stakeout duty, but like any shared discomfort, there's something about it that binds people together. Jesse rolled down his window to help defog the windshield and let some fresh air into the cab. Two hours' worth of stale, coffee-scented carbon dioxide was no treat for either of them.

Suit tapped Jesse's shoulder and pointed out the windshield at a shadowy figure in a hooded sweatshirt a hundred yards ahead of them. He was moving in the opposite direction, stopping at each car on the street.

"Good work, Suit. I see him."

"How should we handle this?"

"On foot," Jesse said. "But first we have to let him get further away from us so that we don't spook him. Then I'm going to turn right at the corner, head north along Salter to get ahead of him, and come south toward him at Lowell Street. You head north along Berkshire and get behind him at Amherst. I'll run him right to you."

Suit grabbed the door handle. "I think he's far enough away. Let's do this."

Jesse clamped his hand on Suit's big right biceps. "No guns. Whoever he is, he's barely breaking the law. No one's going to get shot over this, no matter how ugly it is."

"Got it, Jesse."

Jesse let go of Suit's arm, and as quietly as the two large men could manage, they slipped out of Suit's pickup. Once he made it to the corner, Jesse took off running. He figured it would be easy to get ahead of their target. After all, he had to stop every few feet, but Jesse didn't want to chance startling the guy. As he had warned Suit, there was no need to make this into anything it didn't need to be.

Two minutes later, shirt glued to his skin by sweat, heart thumping, Jesse took some deep breaths and turned off Lowell onto MacArthur Street. The guy he intended to herd into Suit's waiting arms and handcuffs was less than half a block in front of him on the opposite side of the street. He was a short man and his hood was pulled tight on his head. It was too dark and Jesse was still too far away to make out much else about him. He was carrying a paper shopping bag with the fliers. He stopped at each parked car, reached into the shopping bag, took out a flier, and tucked it under the passenger-side wiper. Every few cars, he stopped, looked behind him, and moved on.

Jesse kept to the opposite side of the street, quietly working his way toward the man. Then, when he was about fifty feet away, he stepped out into the middle of the street, holding his shield in front of him.

"Paradise police. Stop what —"

Before Jesse could finish, the guy dropped the shopping bag, about-faced, and bolted like a scared rabbit. He was fast, faster than Jesse. Jesse chased after him, but without trying to catch up. He wanted to stay just close enough behind the rabbit to distract him, but not so close that he would think about doubling back. Jesse wasn't sure he'd be able to catch him if he did that.

"Stop!" Jesse shouted as he ran, keeping

his steady pace. "Stop!"

But this guy had no intention of stopping. The rabbit had one thing on his mind: escape. As he got close to where Suit was waiting, Jesse shouted at the guy one last time. "Stop!"

The rabbit looked behind him. Big mistake, because when he turned back around, Suitcase Simpson leveled him with a perfect-form tackle that would have earned him a helmet sticker from his old high school football coach. The air went out of the rabbit, who collapsed like he'd been hit by a freight train. Suit frisked him, rolled him onto his stomach, and handcuffed his wrists behind him. The guy didn't resist. He was way too preoccupied with gasping for air.

"Good job, Suit," Jesse said, trying to catch his own breath. "Man, I wouldn't have wanted to be tackled by you."

Suit couldn't help but smile. Jesse's praise still meant the world to him. "Thanks, Jesse."

"Okay, let's stand him up."

25

Using one arm, Suit yanked the handcuffed rabbit to his feet. "Okay, wiseass," Suit said, pulling the hood off the man's head, "let's have a look."

Jesse's eyes got wide. Before Suit could even ask, his question was answered.

"Lo siento. Lo siento," the rabbit said.

"What's he saying, Jesse?"

"He's saying I'm sorry."

Jesse asked, "What's your name?"

The rabbit shrugged and stared blankly into Jesse's face.

"Hablas inglés?"

"No hablo inglés," he said, a frightened, tentative smile on his sweat-covered face.

It was a round face with high, flat cheekbones and rich brown skin beneath a mop of jet-black hair. It was an old man's face on a young man's body, a face that had spent many years exposed to the weather and had seen troubles. Jesse didn't know this particular face, but he had known many like it.

Jesse said, *"Me llamo Jesse Stone. Jefe de Policía. Cómo te llamas?"*

"Miguel," he said, his smile less tentative.

"Miguel, tu apellido?" Jesse turned to Suit. "I asked for his last name."

"Cabrera."

"De dónde eres, Miguel Cabrera?" As he started to translate, Suit cut him off.

"You asked where he was from. I remember some of what I learned in high school besides tackling, Jesse."

Miguel answered, "Jalisco."

"You're a long way from home, Miguel," Jesse said in Spanish.

Miguel nodded. *"Sí, many miles."*

"Why did you come so far, Miguel?"

"Many are dying in the drug wars. You have to choose one side or the other. Either way, you die."

Jesse said, "The cartels."

"Sí. Sí." Miguel was nodding furiously. "Don't send me back. Don't send me back."

Jesse put his hand on Miguel's shoulder. "No one is sending you anywhere." He turned to Suit. "Uncuff him."

Suit didn't usually question Jesse's orders, but his face gave him away.

"Relax. Just do it, Suit." Jesse waved his

137

finger at Miguel. "Don't run."

Miguel placed his right hand on his heart. "I promise."

Suit took the handcuffs off Miguel's wrists.

"Miguel, who paid for you to put the papers on the cars?"

"A Northerner."

Jesse said to Suit, "That's what Mexicans sometimes call Americans." He refocused on Miguel. "Describe this Northerner."

Miguel raised his right hand up high. "He is tall like you, with big shoulders. His hair was short. He was a soldier with cold eyes, dead eyes."

"How did you know he was a soldier?"

"Soldiers fight for the cartels. I have seen many soldiers, too many soldiers."

Jesse asked, "Did the soldier speak Spanish?"

"Not so good as you, *jefe,* but enough for me to understand."

"Where did you meet the soldier?"

"I was doing yardwork in the next town and eating lunch when he walked over to me."

"In Swan Harbor?"

"*Sí,* Swan Harbor, for Garrison's Lawn and Landscaping Company."

"You can't read what is on the papers you

are putting on the cars, can you, Miguel?"

"No."

"How did you get the fliers?"

Miguel pointed back down MacArthur Street in the direction of Suit's pickup. "He gave me the address and said I would find the bag there."

"Do you have those addresses?"

Miguel took a slip of paper out of his pocket and handed it to Jesse.

"Did the soldier write these for you?"

"No, *jefe,* I wrote them down."

"One more question, Miguel, then you can go. How did you get from Swan Harbor to Paradise? Did the soldier drive you?"

Miguel shook his head. "I walked."

"Okay, Miguel, thank you. Go now, but go far away. The soldier may be a dangerous man."

Miguel smiled at Jesse, bowed his head to Suit. "I am an uneducated man, not a stupid one. *Buenas noches.*"

Suit and Jesse watched Miguel disappear into the night.

"C'mon, Suit, let's undo Miguel's handiwork. I don't want anyone waking up to one of these fliers on their windshields tomorrow morning."

"Who do you think this soldier is?"

"I don't know *who* he is, Suit, but I have

139

a pretty good idea *what* he is."

It was nearly two in the morning by the time they finished collecting all the fliers and the shopping bag and made it back to Suit's pickup.

Suit asked, "Where'd you learn to speak Spanish like that?"

"I'm not as good at it as you think. But I am from Tucson, lived in L.A., and about a third of the guys I played ball with were Latinos. You learn out of necessity. There isn't always a translator around when you need one."

"I guess. What next?"

"We go home and get some sleep."

"That's not what I mean, Jesse." Suit held up the shopping bag. "I mean, what do we do about what's going on in town?"

Jesse took the shopping bag. "I've got some ideas, but none that won't keep till the morning. Good night, Suit, and thanks for thinking to do the stakeout even before me. One more thing. Let me borrow your pickup for a day. Take my Explorer."

"Should I ask why?"

"No," Jesse said, flipping his car keys to Suit.

Suit handed Jesse the keys to his Dodge. They shook hands. He watched Suit pull away in the Explorer. Jesse used to love the idea of heading home, used to daydream about it, because he knew his Ozzie Smith poster, his Johnnie Walker, and his drinking rituals were there waiting for him. Now the only things there were Ozzie, forever frozen in midair, and Jesse's empty, neatly made bed. Even if he never drank again, there were things he was going to miss about it.

26

Jesse parked Suit's pickup down the block and across the street from the big Victorian house on Bald Hill in Swan Harbor. There wasn't anything about either the house, lovely as it was, or Bald Hill that held any particular attraction for Jesse. He was there because the two trucks parked in front of the grand Victorian bore the name GARRISON'S LAWN AND LANDSCAPING, the company Miguel Cabrera had been working for when he was approached by the soldier.

Jesse watched as six men performed like a well-coached team. Three of the men were blowing leaves onto a huge blue plastic tarp, then hauling the leaf-laden tarp over to a huge vacuum attached to one of the trucks and then sucking the leaves into the rear of the truck. A fourth man was riding a mower and cutting the grass that was now uncovered by leaves. Two other men worked at edging the lawn and pruning the hedges.

All of the men would have fit Miguel Cabrera's general description: short, black-haired, with brown and prematurely wizened faces. Jesse knew that many of these men had stories to tell that were not unlike Miguel's, though not all were as dramatic, and not all of these men were here illegally. Some were, maybe even most, but Jesse wasn't here to play immigration agent. He was here to see if the soldier might reappear.

It was after noon and this was his third stop in Swan Harbor. He had watched two other Garrison crews do their work, take breaks, and get back to it. All the crews, with one or two exceptions, were like the men he was currently watching, doing their work with precision, barely exchanging a word and making no eye contact with passersby. They acted as if they wished they could be invisible. In some ways, Jesse guessed they were. It was no different in Paradise or Salem: The men acted as if they couldn't be seen and the people in town played along. There'd be no illegal immigration if only one side reaped the benefits.

In another important way, this crew, now breaking for lunch, was like the other two Jesse had watched. Neither had been approached by the soldier. And as far as Jesse had been able to tell, he was nowhere in sight. Maybe, Jesse thought, the soldier hadn't caught wind of what had happened last night with Miguel. Jesse dismissed the thought even as it occurred to him. No, the people behind the cross-burning and the fliers would be alert to the townspeople's reaction. That was the whole idea, or at least part of it. Since there were no fliers to be found on any windshields in Paradise that morning, there would be no reaction. Jesse didn't imagine that would make the SS very happy.

At the moment, Jesse wasn't very happy, either. There still hadn't been any hits on the kid who'd purchased the kerosene and, according to Lundquist, the staties had made no progress on Felicity Wileford's assault. Jesse had asked Peter Perkins to see if he could isolate any fingerprints on the fliers from Miguel's abandoned shopping bag. The other fliers, the ones he and Suit had collected off the car windshields, had been tossed into the furnace at the station house. That's where the others would go when Perkins was done.

Jesse, a patient man, was about fresh out, and he was on the verge of exiting Suit's pickup to talk to the landscaping crew when his cell buzzed in his pocket. The Paradise Hotel number came up.

"Jesse Stone."

"Hey, Jesse, it's Connor."

"Uh-huh."

"Listen, I hate to do this to you, but the kid's got to vacate. The hotel owner's coming into town tomorrow and the manager's on the warpath. It'd be tough for me to explain —"

"Understood, Connor. I appreciate what you've done. Pack his things up for him and leave them in your concierge room. I'll come by later and collect them."

"Will do. What are you going to do with him?"

Jesse laughed. "Good question. Thanks again."

It *was* a good question, but Jesse had bigger questions to deal with at the moment. He stepped out of the Dodge and strode up to three of the work crew eating their lunches on the sidewalk between the two trucks. They sensed Jesse wasn't a curious neighbor there to ask about their rates. Even when Jesse made all the right noises and spoke in Spanish, none of them did more than nod. Jesse had to admit he looked like a cop, in or out of his PPD clothing. When he asked if any of the men knew Miguel Cabrera, they shook their heads and asked Jesse to please let them have their lunches in peace. One of them, the oldest of the men, seemed particularly upset at the mention of Miguel.

Until that point, Jesse had resisted playing the heavy. He had no desire to cause them trouble, but there was stuff going on that needed to be stopped in its tracks, and if that meant he had to get tough, so be it. He reached into his pocket and pulled out his chief's shield. None of the men ran, though it was clear that at least two of them were fighting the urge to take off.

"I'm not here to cause trouble," he said, holding his one empty palm up. "I met Miguel last night in my town and he told me he was approached by a soldier. Have any of you seen this soldier?"

The older man, the one most upset by the mention of Miguel, said in perfect English, "Your Spanish is very good for a Northerner, but please, leave us alone. We don't need any trouble."

"I don't want to give you any. Why don't you give me two minutes over by my pickup and then you and your crew can eat in peace."

The older man stood, said something to the others, and followed behind Jesse to Suit's Dodge.

"I'm Roberto," he said to Jesse. "I'm the

crew chief."

"Did Miguel work on your crew?"

But before Roberto could answer, a GMC Denali with a light bar on the roof and SWAN HARBOR POLICE written across its doors pulled up. Screeching to a stop right behind it was an extended-bed Escalade. Jesse didn't know the red-faced guy who hopped out of the Escalade, but he recognized the man who got out of the Denali. It was Bradley Forster, the Swan Harbor chief of police.

27

The bald man stared across his desk at the soldier. He wasn't saying anything. He didn't have to. The condemnation was writ large in his intense gray eyes, in the folds of his fleshy face, and amplified by the drumming of his fingers on the desktop. The soldier, as was his wont, stood at ease, eyes focused on the past, remembering the ruined bodies of his buddies. The images came back to him without warning, and with them the haunting thought that pieces of their bodies would be forever lost to the soil of a strange and distant land. Pieces of him, too. Invisible pieces that no one but him knew were missing.

Finally, the man behind the desk spoke. "Don't misunderstand me, son. I appreciate the irony of having an illegal do our work for us. I truly do."

"I did it to insulate us, sir, not for the irony."

"Am I hearing things? Did someone in this room give you permission? Did I ask you to speak?"

"No, sir. Sorry, sir."

"As I was saying, I can appreciate the irony of it, and I understand that if the beaner got caught, there wasn't anything he could tell the authorities about us, but it was shortsighted, son."

"Permission to speak, sir."

"Go on."

"How was it shortsighted, sir? The man I chose could neither read nor speak English. All he saw was the money. If he got caught, it would be a dead end, sir."

The fleshy man laughed, shook his head, and stood up from his chair. "The difference between us, son, is that we both want to save this country and we both want to bring down the forces that would stain it and make it unrecognizable, but I understand our enemies. I hate them as you hate them, but I am not blind to them. You're a tactical thinker. I'm a strategic one."

"Pardon me, sir, but —"

"You thought that the Mexican's lack of English would protect us, but did you stop to think that many of our own people have betrayed us by stooping to learn their language? No, you didn't, did you? Apparently, Chief Stone is quite proficient in Spanish."

"Even so, sir, what could he possibly tell the police that would be of any value?"

That set the gray-eyed man off. "He could tell them about you, you idiot!"

"I'm nobody, sir."

"Were that only true, but, God help me, it is not. I need you. The movement needs you and you put yourself at risk. Don't you understand that Paradise is the perfect place for us to knock down the first domino, for the first shot of our revolution to be fired? It's our Lexington. It's a town near the place that began this country on the way to its greatness. We have scouted it for a year. We have members, true believers in place to help us, help you light the fuse that will blow the lid off all the anger and desperation to return this country to what it was meant to be. You have heard of Plymouth Rock and Lexington?"

"Yes, sir," the soldier answered, not wanting to point out that the pilgrims on board the *Mayflower* were themselves immigrants and that one of the men killed during the Lexington Massacre was black. The soldier didn't think he'd bother bringing either thing up just then, irony be damned. No one knew the Colonel's moods or the price of his wrath better than the soldier.

"It's also a town in transition, a town being turned to mud by invaders. Sometimes, son, there is a confluence of perfect places, perfect situations, and perfect moments in time. This is one, and we dare not miss our opportunity. You never know when we'll come across it again."

"No, sir."

"Is everything in place?"

"Yes, sir, but —"

The Colonel's face turned red. "But what?" he shouted. "Are you going to start in on that again? Because I'm not going to hear it. Haven't you ever had to make sacrifices in war?"

"Yes, sir. I've seen a lot of sacrifice in war, but —"

"There's that word again. Do you know about Coventry, son?"

"Coventry, sir?"

"It's a city in England, and during W W Two, Churchill's codebreakers discovered that it was to be bombed. Churchill had a decision to make. He could evacuate the city and ambush the attacking German bombers with RAF Spitfires or he could let Coventry go unprepared, unwarned, thereby allowing German bombers to do their worst. Do you know what choice he made?"

151

The Colonel didn't wait for an answer. "He let Coventry get the shit bombed out of it because he couldn't risk the Germans finding out that his people had broken the German code. Do you see my point?"

"Yes, sir."

"Yes, sir, indeed. If Churchill could sacrifice an entire city in order to win the war, then how can we not be willing to do the same, and at such a small price? Don't you agree, son?"

No! "Yes, sir."

"Go back to Paradise and await my instructions."

"Yes, sir."

The soldier had taken two strides toward the back door when the Colonel called after him.

"Remember, son, Coventry. Coventry."

28

Chief Forster, in his crisp brown uniform, perfectly shined black shoes, and trooper-style hat, walked up to Jesse with his right hand extended.

"Chief Stone, good to see you in our fair town."

Jesse shook his hand. "Good to be here, Brad."

Jesse didn't necessarily dislike Forster. He just didn't think much of him as a cop. He was more a politician than a policeman. That was okay most of the time. Swan Harbor wasn't exactly crime central, and the citizens liked having a man who looked like a Macy's window mannequin as their top cop. It suited the town's image. Problem was that when real crime reared its head, Forster was about as effective as a mannequin. That's why it had always wound up in Healy's lap, and now Lundquist's.

"Anything I can help you with?" Forster asked.

"Not really." Jesse shrugged, keeping his eyes on the man who'd gotten out of the cream-colored Escalade. "Is that Mr. Garrison there?"

"That's right," said the red-faced man, his voice less than friendly. "What are you doing cutting into my men's work? I've got a business to run."

Garrison looked the part. He may have been driving a Cadillac, but he was dressed much like his men: company sweatshirt, jeans, and boots. His was a weathered face, wind-chapped and sun-scarred. The deep smile lines around his mouth and eyes were misnamed. He didn't seem to Jesse the type of man to smile at anything.

"Take it easy, Jim," Chief Forster said, playing the politician. "I'm sure Chief Stone meant no harm."

"That's right," Jesse said. "I wasn't cutting into anybody's work. They were having lunch and I just wanted to ask a few questions."

That got a rise out of Forster's right eyebrow. "Questions? Questions about what?"

Garrison chimed in. "Yeah, about what? My men got a right to eat in peace and get back to work."

The way Garrison said that last part was clearly a message to Roberto. Roberto received it loud and clear and walked away from the pickup. A few seconds later, the whine of leaf blowers and the roar of the mower broke the relative quiet of the street. Lunchtime was over.

"I caught one of Mr. Garrison's men breaking the law in Paradise last night," Jesse said above the din.

"Well, that's between you and Miguel," Garrison said.

Jesse smiled. "I didn't mention his name."

"He didn't show up to work this morning, Stone. Don't have to be a rocket scientist to figure out which one of my men you were talking about. Besides, I'm not responsible for my men after hours."

"Your men," Jesse said. "You keep saying your men. I wonder if I asked Brad to check on your men, how many of them would have green cards?"

That did it. Garrison's red face turned a few shades brighter. Pushing past Forster, he got chest to chest with Jesse. "Who the fuck do you think you are? You got no jurisdiction in this town."

Jesse ignored him, looking over Garrison's head at Chief Forster. "Brad, your friend

155

here is getting awfully close to getting himself in trouble, one way or the other."

"What's that supposed to mean, 'one way or the other'?" Garrison said, his voice almost loud enough to drown out the lawn equipment.

Jesse turned his head down and smiled at Garrison.

"Relax, relax," Chief Forster said, working his way between the two men. "I'm sure Chief Stone meant nothing by it, Jim. Now step back, please, and let me handle this. I'd hate to have to arrest you for assaulting a law enforcement officer. Jim, step back!"

Garrison stepped back and Chief Forster waved him farther away. Jesse was impressed. That was the most forceful thing he'd ever seen Forster do during his brief tenure in Swan Harbor. Now it was Jesse's turn.

"Look, Jesse, Jim's a hothead and an ass, but don't come into my town and threaten our local businessmen. What happened in Paradise, anyway, that was such a big deal that you had to come into town to bug these guys?"

Jesse reached into his back pocket, pulled out one of the fliers, and handed it to Forster. "Given what just happened in your

156

town, I think you can understand my concern."

Forster rubbed his smooth-shaven face. "I see."

"I caught one of Garrison's men papering cars in Paradise with those late last night. The guy said a man who reminded him of a soldier paid him to do the work. I was just asking the crew if they had seen the soldier or if any of them had been approached by him."

Forster looked over at Garrison, who was now far enough away to be out of earshot. "You think Garrison's involved?"

"I don't know. You say he's a hothead, so maybe that's all his reaction is about."

"Maybe." Chief Forster didn't sound convinced. "Listen, let me do the asking after you split and I shoo Garrison away. Garrison will be happy to see you go, and I'll call you later. Deal?"

"Uh-huh. The guy I was speaking to was named Roberto, the oldest man in the crew." Jesse pulled a photo out of his jacket pocket and handed it to Forster. "Ask him if this was the soldier."

Forster looked confused. "Wait a second. I recognize this guy. This is Randisi, Wileford's boyfriend. He's got a plastic arm, for crissakes!"

"Doesn't hurt to eliminate suspects," Jesse said. "Humor me."

Jesse drove Suit's pickup away. As he did, he used the truck's mirrors to watch Chief Forster herd Garrison back into his Escalade.

29

Jesse drove straight over to the Paradise Hotel and picked up Cole's things from the concierge, then headed to Daisy's. Slayton almost smiled at Jesse when he walked in and took a seat. Daisy came over to him before the kid did.

"He's good, Jesse. I think I'll keep him."

"Let's see if he wants to be kept."

"You ever know a man who didn't want to be kept?"

Jesse laughed. "That's a sentence I never expected to hear from you."

"You don't have to be a dog to know dogs or to get fleas."

"Now, there's the diplomatic Daisy we all know and love."

But instead of the crooked smile and wink he expected from Daisy, what he got was a worried expression. It looked as out of place on her as a beard.

"Jesse," she said in a whisper, leaning in

close as she poured his coffee, "what's this I hear about racist fliers turning up in town? I also hear there was a cross-burning. And, jeez, with that poor woman being attacked in Swan Harbor . . . What's going on?"

"Where'd you hear about all that?"

"Nothing goes on in this town I don't hear about, so don't stall or bullshit me, Jesse Stone. We've known each other too long for that. Me, I can take care of myself. Always have. Always will. Don't mean I don't worry or care about other folks."

"I'm trying to track down the source of the fliers. We've got a suspect for the cross-burning but haven't found him yet. The assault wasn't in my jurisdiction, but it's not good, any way you look at it."

"Okay, Jesse, I'll send the kid over."

"Is it okay if he takes a break for five minutes and sits with me?"

Now she gave Jesse that crooked smile and wink. "One of the perks of being chief."

Jesse fixed his coffee and watched as Daisy approached Cole. The smile he'd seen on the kid's face when he walked in vanished when he sat down.

"Yeah, what?" he said, that chip on his shoulder returning with a vengeance. "I'm busy."

"Then I won't keep you long. Daisy says

160

you're good."

"She's pretty wacked out, but she's nice enough," he said, softening a little. "She was good to take me on. I guess I have you to thank for that."

Jesse ignored that. "Listen, your stay at the hotel got cut short."

"Shit!" Cole cursed under his breath. "I better get over there to get my things."

"I've got your stuff."

That set the kid off. "You looked through my things?"

"No. I'm not interested in your belongings. Connor packed your stuff. All I did was pick it up. But that's not the issue."

"What is?"

"Where you're going to stay," Jesse said. "And the beach at Pilgrim Cove isn't an option."

"How about the jail? You said I could spend a night there."

"I did, but what about tomorrow night and the night after that?"

Cole shrugged. "I don't know. Maybe I can get an advance from Daisy."

"That'll get you a night or two somewhere."

"Look, I'm not your problem. Thanks for landing me the job and getting me the room. I'll go get my stuff and then you don't

161

have to lose any sleep over me. I've been on my own for a while now. I got this far without your help."

That was the thing Jesse kept coming back to. *What is this kid even doing in Paradise?* Jesse understood wanderlust. He understood the attraction small-town kids felt for places like L.A., Chicago, San Francisco, and New York. But this kid was from L.A., and as scenic as Paradise was, there didn't seem to be anything here that was a magnet for someone with as much attitude as Cole Slayton.

Jesse held his palms up and faced them at the kid. "You're right. You're not my problem. C'mon, let's get your stuff. I'm parked just down the block."

"Just give me your keys. I'll get my stuff. I promise not to steal your shotgun or anything."

Jesse slid the keys to Suit's pickup across the table. "Your things are in the front seat of the Dodge pickup. Belongs to one of my cops." When the kid left, Jesse waved Daisy back.

"The kid doesn't have a place to stay. You willing to let him stay in the back here for a few days?"

"I suppose. It's not very comfortable, but at least there's a bathroom."

"He was sleeping on the beach across from Pilgrim Cove when I found him, so I don't think he'll complain much."

"Can't be permanent, Jesse. That won't work for me."

"Understood. And don't say it was my idea."

"What's your investment in this kid, anyway? I mean, he's good company and a hard worker, but I don't get it."

"I haven't thought about it much. Just seems the right thing to do."

"I've taken in a few strays myself. I guess I never gave too much thought to it, either."

"You!"

"Don't say it too loud. You'll ruin my street cred," she said. "Can't have people thinking I'm soft."

"No, can't have that," he said, standing to go and dropping a five on the table. "Thanks, Daisy."

He passed Cole Slayton on the way out. Handing the pickup's keys to Jesse, the kid opened his mouth to say something, but no words came out and he retreated into Daisy's without looking back.

30

Molly was grinning her *Cat: 1, Canary: 0* grin when Jesse got back to the station. It was hard for him not to notice.

"What is it, Molly?"

"What's what?"

"That look on your face."

"What look?"

"That grin is about as inconspicuous as the Citgo sign outside Fenway. Let's have it."

"Have what?"

"Is *what* your new vocabulary word for the day?"

"Could be."

"Crane!"

"Peter got a hit on a fingerprint. Report's on your desk."

"Did Chief Forster call?"

Molly tilted her head. "That bag of leaves from Swan Harbor?"

"I might've misjudged him. He acted like

a real cop today."

"*Acted* being the operative word there."

Jesse shook his head. "I don't think so. There might be more to him than I thought."

"He didn't call."

"Thanks."

"Jesse . . ."

"What?"

"Stop stealing my vocabulary words."

"Molly."

She whispered to him, though no one else was around. "How's the not drinking going?"

"Truth?"

"Always."

"Not drinking was easy when it was pretending. Real sobriety is rough."

Molly seemed to understand. "Better get in there and look at that report."

"You're still giving orders like the acting chief."

"Sorry."

Jesse gave a small fist pump and headed into his office. Any time he could get Molly to cave, even a little, was a small victory. But the minute he read the report on his desk, the sweet taste of victory turned rancid in his mouth. He looked back and forth between the photos of the man to whom the fingerprints on the fliers belonged and the accompanying pages.

Leon Oskar Vandercamp, aka the Colonel, aka the Lion, looked nothing like a big cat and more like a loyal patron of Colonel Sanders than a military officer. In his most recent photo he resembled an aging, balding, overweight businessman with jowls and neck skin so loose and expansive it nearly hid his shirt collar. Yet in spite of his girth and fleshy face, Vandercamp didn't strike Jesse as the sort of man to play Santa Claus at the volunteer-firehouse Christmas party. There wasn't an ounce of kindness in his cruel mouth or in his icy gray eyes. Jesse found even less humanity in the man's history.

Jesse worked his way back from Vandercamp's arrest record to the self-serving narcissism of the bio Molly had downloaded from the Saviors of Society website to the far-less-flattering histories she had culled from the Internet. The arrest record was long on misdemeanors — harassment, disorderly conduct, parade without permit, defacement of public property, defacement of private property, et al. — that could have easily been misinterpreted or dismissed as petty nuisances or minor violations, had Jesse not been able to match the arrests to newspaper accounts.

Vandercamp and his followers had shown up at funerals of Hispanic, African American, and Muslim soldiers and harassed the mourners. They'd destroyed Hanukah menorahs in public holiday displays and painted *Arbeit macht frei* on the sidewalks surrounding Jewish cemeteries in small, upstate New York towns. He and his followers had come to several Martin Luther King Day celebrations wearing gorilla masks and waving Confederate flags. They would stand across the street from a hospice in a Pennsylvania town that took in AIDS victims and chant "Burn fags, not flags."

There had been some violence, of course. That was the point. They incited others to violence, but none of the charges against Vandercamp or his followers had them throwing the first punch, tossing the first rock, or hurling the first bottle. It wasn't lost on Jesse that many of the accounts mentioned that fliers had often preceded the public displays and demonstrations. But from what he could discern from Molly's downloads, there had been a long lull in the group's public activities. Jesse went online and searched for accounts of any recent dustups involving the Saviors of Society. There weren't any. The last mention of

Vandercamp dated back fourteen months to a story titled "The Future of Hate" in *Rolling Stone.*

"Our methods have failed to gain the necessary traction to move our righteous cause forward," Vandercamp had admitted to the *Rolling Stone* interviewer. "Sometimes you just got to burn down the house to save it, even if you're still inside. But you can't start a fire with wet matches, son. So we either need to find a way to dry the ones we have or to find new ones."

Vandercamp may have been many things Jesse Stone detested, but he wasn't stupid. That was too bad, Jesse thought, grabbing his old glove off his desk. Stupidity in a criminal was a cop's best friend. As he pounded the ball into the pocket of his glove, Jesse stared out the office window at Stiles Island and wondered about what was coming his way. His phone rang before his wondering got him very far.

31

It was Lundquist on the line.

Jesse said, "I had my hand on the phone to call you."

"It's magic how that works."

"I doubt it."

Lundquist was curious. "You don't believe in magic?"

"I believe in evidence and taking the first pitch."

"I like magic because I don't mind being fooled when there's nothing at stake. Why were you calling me, Jesse?"

"Leon Oskar Vandercamp?"

"Who? Guy sounds like he should be conducting an orchestra."

"You're not far wrong. He's the head of the Saviors of Society. He's a real piece of work. We got a hit on his fingerprints from the fliers."

"No offense, Jesse, but their involvement wasn't exactly a secret. It says it on the damned flier."

"His were the only fingerprints on the fliers."

"So?"

"So I think he's close and that's not good. Nothing good comes with him. You said you'd hook me up with some guy from Homeland Security."

"Sorry, Jesse. I have a lot on my plate. I've got other cases besides Felicity Wileford, but she's why I'm calling."

"What about her?"

"Brain dead. She's about to officially become my responsibility. The parents are on a South Pacific cruise, so it may take them a few days to get here to say goodbye, and to pull the plug. Worst part of the job, dealing with the parents. Does it ever get easier?"

"Gets worse."

"Worse?"

"Knowing what's coming can be more a curse than a blessing."

"You're a cheery bastard, Jesse. Thanks. No wonder you and Healy got along."

"You asked," Jesse said. "Steven Randisi."

"The boyfriend? What about him?"

"Would you say he's about my size?"

"An inch or two shorter. Why?"

"I have a witness says the SS fliers are

connected to a guy he described as looking like a soldier. Says the guy's about my size."

"You think it's Randisi?"

"I'm not sure what I think."

"Jeez, Jesse, the guy's got a prosthetic arm and I've had a few talks with him. He seems genuinely upset over what happened to Wileford."

"So did the mother who drowned her kids and then went on TV and cried about her kids were kidnapped. She seemed genuine, too."

"What's with you? When we first met the guy, you were ready to blow him off as a suspect. Now he's at the top of your most-wanted list."

"I'm just working with what I've got, Brian."

"Fair enough. Let me get on the Homeland Security thing for you."

"Thanks."

Jesse didn't bother putting the phone back in its cradle. He called Chief Forster. Forster's voice was subdued.

"Sorry, Jesse, I meant to call you, but —"

"I heard. I just got off the phone with Lundquist."

"Terrible thing."

"Violent death usually is."

"I don't know how guys like you and

Lundquist do it. I never had the stomach for it. That's why I worked community relations as soon as I got out of uniform."

Jesse suppressed a laugh. "That experience will serve you well. I don't figure your citizens are going to react well to a homicide in Swan Harbor."

"You have no idea."

"You'd be wrong about that. So did you show the photo to Roberto?"

"Randisi's not your man. He said no without hesitation."

"Good."

"Says the guy you're looking for approached his crew only once. The guy was wearing desert camo and boots. He's square-jawed, keeps his blond hair cut real short. He's big through the arms and chest."

Jesse asked, "Anything else?"

"His eyes."

"What about them?"

"*Opaco.* Roberto said he didn't have the American word for it, but I looked it up."

"What was the word?"

"Opaque. He said there was no soul behind the soldier's eyes."

Jesse had mixed feelings about his conversation with Forster. Part of him was glad Randisi wasn't the soldier, but that left him with nothing but Vandercamp's fingerprints and a knot in his belly.

32

Alisha checked herself out in the full-length mirror on the bathroom door. She liked how she looked in her black leather jacket, low-slung sweater, and tight jeans. Though heels would've suited her style better, flats were the smarter choice after eight hours in cop shoes. She returned to the Gray Gull's bar and was finishing her second Jack and Coke when her cell rang. Dylan Taylor, the new head of private security on Stiles Island, was already five minutes late and she wasn't pleased about it at the moment. Nothing was sitting well with her just lately. Her food didn't taste right. Her music didn't sound right. Even the Jack and Coke wasn't going down as smooth and warm as it had in the past. She was worn out.

It wasn't the job that had taken the toll on her as much as the cross-burning and her inability to stop obsessing over what had happened at the Scupper. It had all gone so well up to then, until those asshole bikers rode into town. Everybody from Suit to Gabe to Molly had told her it was no big deal, that they'd all gone through similar troubles early in their careers on the PPD.

"Look, Alisha," Molly said, "during my probationary period, I pulled over one of the selectmen for speeding near the elementary school. If it hadn't been by a school, I think I would've let him go. But by the school, I just couldn't give him a pass. He called me a bitch and made a really crude remark about my menstrual cycle. I didn't like that very much and I lost it. I said some stuff to him that could've cost me my job. It happens to everybody."

Suit and Gabe made it a point to tell her that there were no hard feelings about her pushing back when they showed up at the Scupper that day when she confronted the bikers. Suit told her that he would have been just as mad had their roles been reversed. The thing was, their roles could never be reversed, not really. You couldn't change the color of your skin.

It was amazing what getting called a nigger by some angry, uneducated fool had done to her. Those two syllables had kicked out the legs of her chair. And now she had to struggle not to see the world the way her

175

father did. A hard and cynical man, he had begged her not to take the job in Paradise, but to stay home in New York and join the NYPD like he had.

"You're not Rosa Parks, girl," he'd told her. "Ain't nobody gonna thank you or build you no statues for being the first African American woman on some pissant department in Massachusetts."

More painful than hearing her father's voice in her head like some sadistic earworm was her questioning Jesse's motives for hiring her, doubting her colleagues' acceptance of her, and wondering if Dylan saw her not as a woman he could love but as a prize. *Okay, let's scratch the hot black chick off the list of conquests. Next!* But the worst of it was her self-recrimination, the nights spent beating herself up over her weakness, how easily she had let some stupid remark blow her up. That and her drinking.

She saw it was Dylan on the phone and answered. "You're late."

The soldier sat in the front seat of the Jeep with the kid. The soldier was his usual dead-calm self. At least that was the exterior he showed the kid. Inside, he was churning.

He said, "You know what to do, right?"

"Jeez, man, how many times are you go-

176

ing to ask me that?"

"As many times as it takes until I feel confident you understand the timing of this and to be sure you will do what you have to do."

"Yeah, I know what to do and I'll do it."

"It won't be easy. It's never easy, no matter what you think."

"So you keep saying. Didn't the boys and me handle that thing in Swan Harbor?"

The soldier was tempted to slap the kid across the mouth. But the Colonel would never have stood for that and it was already too late to open the kid's eyes and make him see his folly. Instead, he reminded the kid about what had happened the night of the cross-burning.

"You can't afford to slip and fall like you did the other night," the soldier said. "If you fall, the whole plan will fail. She can't catch up to you too soon."

"I know. It's not raining and I won't be on grass. I won't fall and I'll do what I have to do."

The soldier pointed at the Gray Gull. "Okay. She's in there. When she comes out, make sure she gets a good look at you, a real good look. And remember, run her right past the police station."

"All right! All right! I got it."

The soldier patted the kid on the shoulder. "Go!"

Before Dylan could answer, there was an explosion of sirens and honking horns on Alisha's end of the line. He knew what that was about. That's why he was late. That's why he was calling. Truth was, he was almost happy he wasn't going to be able to make it. Alisha had changed. She was angry and drinking too much. The worst of it, though, was that look in her eyes, like she didn't trust him anymore.

"Lisha, Lisha, can you hear me?" he asked, screaming into the phone.

When the noise died down, Alisha put the phone back up to her ear.

"I hear you. There were sirens," she said. "Fire trucks."

"I heard them, too."

"You're late."

"Those fire trucks are headed over here to Stiles," he said. "The Nolan gatehouse is up in flames. Looks like arson."

"Don't tell me you're not coming."

"I can't come. This is my job."

She clicked off and waved to the barman. "Just Jack this time, a double."

Her phone rang almost as soon as she

178

finished ordering. She silenced it. Finished her Jack and Coke, guzzled the double shot of Jack, and left a twenty and a ten on the bar.

When she stepped outside, she thought she saw deliverance in the face of the suspect in the cross-burning.

33

Jesse was sitting across from Bill at the Starbucks in the same seats they'd sat in the last time. He was glad that Bill and Anya were at the meeting. The three of them sat together once again in the next-to-last row. None of them had shared, and Anya once again turned down an invitation to join them for coffee.

"How's it gone, Jesse . . . since we talked?" Bill asked.

Although the question was vague, Jesse knew what he meant. "Haven't had a drink. Haven't felt like it. The meetings help."

"That they do. For me, they help me feel like I have something to live up to. I spent so much of my life disappointing people that I don't want to let the people who support me down again. At the same time, I know if I did that, they'd still be there for me."

"Like being on a team."

"A team, huh? I was never much of a

joiner or a team player. You?" Bill didn't let Jesse answer. "Stupid question. Being a cop must be like being on a team."

"Sometimes." Jesse was curious. "You said you'd been around a lot of cops."

Bill was laughing.

"I miss the joke?"

"Lots of cops in AA, but that's not why I'm laughing. I know I said I wasn't a team player, but that's not a hundred percent accurate. You might say I used to play for the other team."

Now Jesse was laughing, too. "One of the bad guys?"

Bill looked a little sheepish. "Not so bad, but I did some time when I was younger. I made book, but mostly I handled some goods that crossed my desk. You know, stuff that fell off the truck. Like that."

"A fence."

Bill said, "I liked to think of myself as a middleman, an honest broker. Funny how alcohol helps you escape taking responsibility. It was funny right up until they closed the cell door and I lost my first family. For the longest time I couldn't get my head around why no one else understood none of it was my fault. But not even prison and losing my kids was enough to stop me from drinking. It took me nearly losing my second family to wake up."

"That was your second family you were talking about when you shared."

Bill nodded. "It's still hard for me to talk about the early stuff. Not easy knowing you've got a kid out in the world who thinks you abandoned her. After I got straight, I hired a PI to find my wife and daughter so I could try to make it right, but there are some things you can't fix or undo. I tried. Got the door slammed in my face until I gave up. Finally, I left a long letter apologizing and taking responsibility. I gave them all my contact info."

"Never got in touch?"

"Thirty-three years and counting. You got a family, Jesse?"

"Married once. No kids. We would've been bad parents."

Bill waited for Jesse to continue. Jesse stopped there because the full answer was both very simple and extremely complicated. Jenn and he were always so busy doing their dance that there would have been no room for children. And every time Jesse caught a case involving a child or teenage victim, he felt a tremendous sense of relief that violence could never touch him in that way.

Bill said, "I hope you don't think less of

me now. I know I shouldn't care, but I do."

"I'm not like that. Over the years I've had some questionable . . . friends. No offense, but they make you look like a saint."

"None taken."

They finished their coffees in silence. Jesse barely noticed the conversation had stopped. He was thinking about Gino Fish and Vinnie Morris and some of the deals he'd made to see justice done.

34

Alisha wasn't sure why she was rattled, whether it was her disappointment with Dylan, the alcohol, or the shock of seeing the suspect twenty feet in front of her, but whatever the reason, she couldn't think of what to say. *Stop! Freeze! Halt! Don't move! Get on your knees, hands behind your head!* They all zipped through her head, but by the time she opened her mouth, the suspect took off running.

She ran after him, happy she'd chosen flats instead of heels. "Halt! Paradise Police. Halt!"

Alisha was yelling as loudly as she could. She was sure he heard her, but the suspect wouldn't stop. He was pretty quick, though he couldn't seem to lengthen the distance between them, nor did he try to duck down side streets or head into the marina, where, in the dark, it would have been easier to lose her. In fact, he kept turning back to eye her, almost to make sure she was still following behind him. And then there was the look on his face. She could swear he was smirking at her. It was the kind of smirk a little kid has when he knows something you don't and he thinks that matters.

She couldn't get that look on his face out of her head. *What does he know? Why is he looking at me like that?*

"Paradise Police. Stop!"

He didn't stop.

Alisha hadn't yet reached under her jacket for her off-duty piece. Jesse was very clear about how he expected his cops to act. She could hear his voice in her head. *No gunplay in town. We're not going to get any citizens hurt by ricochets or missed shots going through bedroom windows. You draw your weapon in town only when you feel citizens are under threat or you are in imminent danger.* And neither of those thresholds had been met. Besides, she thought, as the suspect took a surprising turn toward the station house, this guy was only wanted for questioning. All they had on him in terms of evidence was surveillance footage of him acting nervous while purchasing five gallons of kerosene. No, she wasn't going to go for her weapon and put herself in any more hot water than she already was.

That's when things began going sideways. When the suspect looked back at her, the smirk was gone. She wasn't sure what to make of his expression. *Could that be disappointment on his face?* They were almost at the police station when the suspect reached around under his jacket.

"Paradise Police! Don't do it, asshole!" Even she could hear the change in her voice, the level of threat in it ratcheting up. And she was suddenly conscious of her off-duty nine-millimeter in her right hand, its polished steel slide glistening in the ambient streetlight. She felt a wave of relief wash over her as the suspect's hand came out from under his jacket with nothing in it. But her sense of relief was short-lived, because as they ran directly in front of the police station, the guy turned back to look at her. And there it was again, that smirk. *What does he know that I don't? Is he playing me?*

Past the station, the suspect picked up the pace. Alisha picked up her pace in kind. As she did, she felt a strange sense that there was someone else, someone hiding in the shadows, keeping up with the chase. It wasn't that she heard anything or saw anything. It was more a feeling than anything else, but she couldn't afford to divide

186

her attention between the very real suspect ten yards ahead of her and a specter out there in the dark. Just as she was prepared to dismiss the specter, she heard the hollow echo of a plastic garbage can falling to the pavement. Then, as she swung her nine-millimeter around, a gray tabby emerged from the shadows, stared at her, sat on his haunches, and began washing himself.

She smiled in spite of herself, but the smile lasted only long enough for her to realize that her brief hesitation had let the suspect gain a half-block on her. She darted ahead, sprinting as hard as she could. As she closed the gap between them, he changed his tactics. Instead of keeping in a basic straight line as he had from when their eyes met outside the Gull to now, he made a sharp left turn between two parked cars and doubled back past her, pumping his arms, breathing loud enough for her to hear. She turned with him. He turned again and again and again, left then left then right. She matched him. She smelled her own sweat soaking through her clothes. Her throat burned. Her left side ached.

Then the suspect seemed to vanish. Alisha stopped in her tracks, forcing herself to calm her breathing, listening. *There! Footsteps!* She smiled because she knew right where he was. Those last frenzied footsteps she'd heard sounded different from the ones that had come beforehand. These last steps had come from Newton Alley, a narrow dead-end lane inaccessible to cars that, in the nineteenth century, had been home to three small oyster houses. Now the home of art galleries, it was the one place in town where discarded shells had been incorporated into the pavement. Photos of Newton Alley were always included in Chamber of Commerce and tourist promotions for Paradise. Alisha had noticed while patrolling the area how her own footsteps sounded different on the pavement in Newton Alley.

She took her time, collected herself, and moved cautiously toward the entrance to the dead end. Boxed in on three sides, the suspect had nowhere to go. Although the dead end was no more than a hundred yards in length and very narrow, it was unlit, and Alisha knew that cornered humans were much like cornered animals. At the edge of the alley, she tried one last time.

"Surrender now. Let me hear you drop your weapon and kick it toward me." She called to him, calm as she could manage, "Do it now. Right now."

Silence.

With her weapon before her, Alisha spun

to face down the lightless dead end. She could barely make out the suspect's silhouette. Although she couldn't see his face at all, she just knew he was smirking at her.

"Drop your weapon."

The silhouette didn't move. Then it did. There was something in its hand. A flash briefly lit up the night and the light, and Alisha saw that the suspect was smirking at her. She didn't wait for the inevitable bang of the shot before returning fire. This was her life or his now. And before she knew it, the slide of her nine-millimeter locked. She'd emptied her clip at the silhouette.

35

Jesse heard the sirens and knew something was very wrong. His cops were under strict rules about using their sirens and light bars in town. He was giving the voice command to call the station when his phone rang. It was Molly.

"Jesse, where are you?"

"Just pulling into town. What's going on?"

"Get over to Newton Alley. There's been a shooting."

"Civilians?"

"Alisha."

"Is she all right?"

"She's not wounded, but she's not all right."

"No riddles, Molly, please."

"The suspect in the cross-burning is dead. Peter and Suit are over there. I sent Gabe and Gary over to help with crowd control."

"Did you call the staties? They're the ones who'll have to investigate this."

"I figured to let you make that decision."

"Call Lundquist and call Connie."

"Will do. Jesse, there's . . . never mind."

"I'm less than a minute away. Finish what you started saying. I don't want to walk into anything blind."

"The deceased didn't have a weapon."

"What?"

"Suit called and said they couldn't find the suspect's weapon."

Jesse didn't want to curse, but it seemed like the only appropriate response. Instead, he kept it to himself. What he said to Molly was "I'm here. Make those calls."

The new ME was getting out of his car just as Jesse pulled up next to him. Carson Minter was, in nearly every way, the direct opposite of Tamara Elkin, the woman who'd preceded him as ME. Whereas Tamara was long and lean, a former world-class distance runner with a lion's mane of curly brown hair, someone who could go drink for drink with Jesse, the new ME was a prematurely bald, rotund little man of thirty-five. Unlike his predecessor, Minter was reserved, a man of few words and stingy with opinions. This was his first big job. Jesse hadn't had more than a few cursory conversations with the man, but that was about to change.

"Dr. Minter," Jesse said, hurrying to get

next to the ME.

"Chief Stone." Minter stopped, turned to Jesse. "Given the circumstances, I believe it would be best to limit our contact to official channels only."

"Let's not get ahead of ourselves, Doc. Until the state police arrive, this is my crime scene."

"Actually, as far as the victim is concerned, it's mine."

Minter turned away from Jesse and hurried to get under the yellow tape. Newton Alley no longer resembled the quiet, unlit finger of walled-in pavement down which the suspect had retreated and down which Alisha had emptied her weapon. With the swirling colored strobes of light bars atop official vehicles, cruiser headlights, and bank of portable lights, it more resembled Bourbon Street at Mardi Gras. Jesse saw Alisha was seated on the back step of a fire-department ambulance, her head buried in her hands. He would talk to her in a few minutes, but first he needed someone to bring him up to speed. He walked up to Suit, who was manning the crime scene tape.

"Did you talk to Alisha?"

Suit nodded. "She spoke to me and Peter, yeah."

"Tell me everything she said. Don't leave out a single detail," Jesse said.

"According to Alisha, she came out of the Gray Gull, and standing there, no more than twenty feet in front of her, was the suspect in the cross-burning. The suspect —"

Jesse cut him off. "Was she at the Gull eating or drinking?"

Suit hesitated, then said, "Drinking. Two Jack and Cokes, a double of Jack straight up."

Jesse's jaw clenched. "Go on."

Suit described to him the rest of the chase and the shooting as it had been described to him.

"She said he fired at her?"

"She swears he did, Jesse. Alisha says he took the first shot and that's when she returned fire."

"But you found no weapon on or in close proximity to the victim."

Suit shrugged. "I wish we did, but Peter and I looked everywhere. Believe me, Jesse, we searched every inch of the alley. I even went around the corner and checked. No weapon."

"Do we have an ID on the suspect?"

"We just checked him for a pulse. We knew this could be trouble, so we didn't want to disturb the body any more than we had to."

"You did right. When the staties debrief you, you tell them exactly what you told me. Exactly. I don't want you or Perkins to color any answers to help Alisha. It won't help her and it will bury you."

"I got it, Jesse, but —"

"But nothing."

"I believe her. At least I believe she believes she was fired on. She's not lying, Jesse. I'd swear to it."

36

Alisha raised her head out of her hands as Jesse approached her. Her eyes were blood-shot and teary. Her mascara had left black streaks and smears on her cheeks. Jesse noticed the blood on the sleeve of her jacket and on the edge of her white sweater sleeve.

He asked, "Are you hurt?"

She shook her head furiously. "That's the vic— I mean, the suspect's blood. I had to check to see if he was alive. I can't get warm, Jesse. I just can't get warm."

"She's shocky, Chief," said Tommy Simonetti, the EMT who was attending to Alisha. He laid two blankets over her shoulders. "She should be okay in a couple of hours."

"Tommy, can you give us a minute?" When the EMT was out of earshot, Jesse said, "I need you to surrender your badge and weapon. It's department policy. You're suspended with pay until further notice."

She handed Jesse her ID case. "Peter already bagged my weapon. Jesse," she said, grabbing his wrist, "I swear to you he fired on me. I know there's no gun on him, but I swear it."

"Alisha, you're under no obligation to talk to me or anyone else. As chief, I want you to fully cooperate with the investigation, but you've got rights. Get yourself a good lawyer. The town is obliged to cover the costs up to a point, and the system, as screwed as it is, only works if everyone is protected."

"I understand, Jesse."

Jesse turned and waved Tommy back over. When the EMT returned, Jesse said to Alisha, "Are you willing to let the EMT draw blood for the purposes of determining your blood alcohol level? Your contract says that under these circumstances you are required to take a Breathalyzer test, but I can try to get a court order to compel you to —"

"No need, Jesse. He can draw blood. I already told Suit and Peter how much I had at the Gull."

"Listen, Alisha, this is going to be investigated by the state police, so even if I was inclined to give you the benefit of the doubt, I can't help you. Remember what I said before. You're under no obligation to talk to anyone, and get a lawyer."

"I understand, Jesse. I swear, he fired on me."

"If there's a gun to find, Alisha, we'll find it."

"Can you call Dylan for me? I don't want to be alone."

"Sure, I'll call him for you." He turned to the EMT. "Tommy, do me a favor. After you draw the blood, stay here with her until someone comes to be with her."

"I can do that." Tommy motioned for Jesse to meet him around the side of the ambulance.

"What is it?"

"What if the investigators ask me what I overheard between you and her?"

Jesse patted Tommy on the shoulder. "If they ask, you tell them the truth."

"You sure, Chief?"

"Uh-huh."

Jesse walked away, digging his cell phone out of his jacket and punching up Dylan's number.

"What's up, Jesse? You calling about the fire?"

"Fire?"

"Yeah, the gatehouse at the Nolan place. Chief Wilson says it was arson."

"That's not why I'm calling, Dylan. There's been a shooting involving Alisha."

There were a few seconds of stunned silence before Dylan spoke. "Is she . . . all right?"

"I think she's probably in a lot of trouble. She shot a suspect and we can't find the suspect's weapon."

"Oh, shit! Where is she?"

"Newton Alley."

"I'll be there in ten minutes."

"Dylan, before you come, take down this phone number. Do you have something to write on?"

"Go ahead, Jesse."

Jesse recited a ten-digit number with a Boston area code. "Call him."

"Who is he?"

"Monty Bernstein. He's half shark, half lawyer. Do you understand?"

"I do." Dylan clicked off.

Jesse buried his phone back in the pocket of his jacket, gloved up, and ducked under the yellow tape. He supposed he should have done this first, but the dead man was beyond his help and he had just given Alisha all the help he could. At the front end of the alley, he swerved around eight numbered placards and shell casings. At the walled end of the Slip, Dr. Minter was dealing with the body. His back was to Jesse, obscuring Jesse's view of the dead man. All Jesse could see were his feet and the large pool of blood. He noted several bullet scars on the back brick wall.

"What's the word, Doc?"

"Three obvious wounds — one in the chest, one in the lower abdomen, and one in the upper-left thigh — any one of which might have been fatal."

"Any ID on him?"

"I believe he has a wallet in his back-right pocket."

"Would it be okay if I had a look?"

"I'll hand it to you," Minter said, obviously annoyed.

When Jesse flipped open the wallet and saw the name on the New York state driver's license, the knot in his gut nearly snapped.

"Well, Chief Stone," Minter said, "what's the victim's name?"

Jesse thought he heard himself say, "John W. Vandercamp."

37

Jesse was still trying to wrap his head around the dead man's identity when Lundquist, another detective from the state police, and the state forensics team showed up at the scene.

"Jesse, this is Detective Lieutenant Mary Weld. She'll be handling the investigation."

Weld was a sturdy-looking woman with brown eyes and a polite but businesslike manner. She let you know just by her expression that charm and a friendly attitude would bounce off her like paper bullets. She nodded and offered her hand. "Chief Stone."

He didn't bother asking her to call him Jesse. "You want a rundown on the situation?"

She thought about it before she answered. "Sorry, Chief, I prefer you step back. I don't want to come to this with a preconceived notion of the chain of events. What I do need is to speak to the responding officers and Officer Davis. She's the shooter, correct?"

"She is."

"I also need all evidence collected by your department immediately turned over to the state forensics team, and I'd like to look at the scene and the victim."

Jesse pointed down Newton Alley. "The ME is at the dead end with the body. I will send over the two responding officers. Officer Davis is in shock."

Detective Weld gave Jesse a cold stare. "Is that your assessment?"

"According to the EMT."

"Okay, Chief, I understand the impulse to want to protect your cop. I do. Brian here will tell you I'm a good detective and a fair one. But don't try to color events in Officer Davis's favor, and please stay out of the investigation unless I request something from you. By the way, Chief Stone, where were you during the events of this evening?"

Jesse asked, "Is that relevant?"

"I won't know until you answer."

"Boston. I got back into town about twenty minutes ago."

"Do we have an ID on the victim?"

"John W. Vandercamp. Twenty-two. New York state resident. His wallet's been

201

bagged."

Lundquist's eyes got big at the mention of the name Vandercamp, but he didn't say anything.

Weld continued. "Was he known to your department?"

"He was wanted for questioning in connection to a vandalism incident."

That got a rise out of Weld. "Vandalism!"

"There was a cross-burning incident here earlier in the week and the victims asked us not to report it as a hate crime in order to protect their children from the potential fallout and publicity. Mr. Vandercamp was captured on surveillance footage purchasing five gallons of kerosene shortly before the cross-burning and in close proximity to the location of the crime."

Weld shook her head, slipping on gloves. "Okay, Chief, if you'll send your officers over. I'm going to have a look at the scene." She took a few steps, stopped, turned back. "Remember, Chief, stay out of it."

Lundquist waited for Weld to be far enough away. "Vandercamp! You think he's related to what's-his-name, Leon Oskar Vandercamp?"

"Uh-huh. Be a helluva coincidence if he wasn't."

"One in a million."

"Sounds about right."

"I suppose I should clue Weld in," Lundquist said. "The shit's hit the fan, Jesse. Can't imagine how bad it's going to get when the family finds out."

But Jesse had spotted Dylan Taylor's car and had already begun walking his way. Lundquist shrugged and headed toward the tape barrier.

Dylan Taylor was a tall, handsome man, solidly built, with dark blond hair and deep blue eyes. He had taken over as head of security on Stiles Island months ago. Jesse didn't know him very well but liked what he did know about him. Jesse grabbed him by the arm as he was running toward the ambulance.

"Oh, sorry, Jesse, I didn't see you."

"Be calm, Dylan. She needs you to be calm."

"What happened?"

"I'll let her tell you. Did you call the lawyer?"

"Yeah, he's already on the way."

"He's good at his job and he's a good guy . . . in his way."

"He said the same thing about you."

"Listen, Dylan. The state investigator is here and she is going to interview Alisha any minute. What did Monty advise you to do?"

"To tell Alisha not to talk to anyone until — shit!"

"Exactly."

Dylan Taylor took off in a mad sprint.

Jesse found Suit and Peter Perkins, who had shifted duties to crowd control. He hadn't noticed until now that there was a crowd. That was the thing about using sirens in town. It made people curious. Maybe this time, Jesse thought, that curiosity might not be such a bad thing.

"Detective Weld, the statie investigator, wants to talk to both of you. She's over by the scene. Go one at a time. Remember, tell her the truth and just answer her questions. Don't volunteer anything more than what's asked for. It won't help Alisha if the statie doesn't trust you. Suit, you go first."

Jesse looked into the faces of the gawkers, many of whom he knew by name. But at the moment they seemed like people he didn't know at all.

38

The soldier knew that Stone was looking for him and understood it was very risky for him to be there, even far back from the crowd gathered around the police cruisers. The kid was gravely wounded. He was certain of that much, but he had to be sure the kid was dead. And then, when the van finally arrived to take the body away, he knew. The soldier watched the two attendants get out of the van, bored expressions on their faces, one carrying the neatly folded and packaged body bag under his arm like a newspaper. There was no longer any need to take the risk. He turned away from the crowd, holding the cell phone up to his face.

"Is it done?" asked the Colonel.

"It's done, sir."

"Did he suffer?"

Yes, probably. "No, sir. She emptied her clip into him."

"Did you take care of everything?"

"Yes, sir, just as planned."

"Good. I'm going to enjoy watching her fry for this. Let's see what the media makes of it."

"Sir," the soldier said, "they don't do that in this state."

"Don't be impertinent, son. I was speaking figuratively. After we're all done with her, she'll wish they did still bring down the wrath of the state."

"Sorry, sir."

"Never mind me," the Colonel said, his voice suddenly brittle.

"My condolences, sir."

"Thank you, but no death was ever more important. Were it only possible that all of our deaths be as meaningful a sacrifice in a glorious cause as my youngest boy's."

"Yes, sir."

"I will wait for the call and then I will join you."

"Yes, sir."

"It begins. There's no turning back. The battle has been joined, the revolution begun. Hallelujah."

The soldier put the phone back in his pocket. He agreed that something had to be done to save the country, but he didn't think there was any reason to be shouting hallelujah. He had seen too much carnage, seen too many of his comrades perish for no good reason, to think there was any glory in death. As far as he could tell, the dead got nothing for their sacrifice except a short trip to hell. But that was the thing. It took a certain kind of strength and dedication to serve up your own flesh and blood for a cause. The soldier was willing to sacrifice himself readily enough. He just didn't think he could sacrifice his own son the way the Colonel had.

Thinking about his own boy being raised by another man on the other side of the country filled him with feelings that tore him to pieces inside. It filled him with a sadness so deep it made him weak. Yet at the same time, it filled him with rage so powerful he swore he'd choke on it. Sometimes he felt it had a life of its own, separate from him. He pushed both feelings down as far as he could. *That's just what a soldier does,* he told himself. *Pushes feelings down so he can move ahead and do his duty.* The Colonel was right about one thing for sure: There was no turning back.

Jesse returned to his office to make the kind of call he dreaded. Although he had no patience for haters — *How can you hate people you've never met?* — Jesse didn't relish the thought of telling yet another father that his son was dead, regardless of the circumstances. But the circumstances of John Vandercamp's death couldn't be ignored and they weren't going to make the conversation he was about to have any easier.

There had been some debate about who was going to make the call: Weld, Lundquist, or Jesse. But in the end, Weld deferred to Jesse, trying to make it sound as if she was somehow bowing to his authority or doing him a favor.

"No, Chief Stone, it's your jurisdiction. My interest is in the righteousness of the shoot and to see that Mr. Vandercamp's rights were not violated. Notification of the family would still be your responsibility."

"Uh-huh."

Jesse wasn't sure how that worked. How was he supposed to keep his distance from the investigation while handling what promised to be a pretty ugly situation? Weld's largesse didn't end there.

"And, Chief, I'm going to need to use your people to canvass the area and take witness statements. I can't get my people in here until tomorrow morning."

Jesse pulled out the old bottle drawer and

stared into the empty space as he dialed.

Someone picked up on the first ring. "Hello," said the voice on the other end of the line.

"Is this Leon Oskar Vandercamp?"

"Yes."

Jesse hesitated for a second. This wasn't how these conversations went. Usually, people would demand Jesse identify himself or ask if this was a solicitation of some kind. But not Vandercamp.

"My name is Jesse Stone. I am chief of the Paradise, Massachusetts, PD."

"Yes."

"Do you have a son named John W. Vandercamp, aged twenty-two, of Oswego, New York?"

"Yes."

"I'm afraid I have some bad news for you about your son."

"Yes."

There it was again, or, rather, there it wasn't. No questions, no shriek or howl in anticipation, just one chilly syllable. It reminded Jesse of how cops were trained to testify in court: Only answer the questions posed as tersely as possible, never elaborate.

"He was killed this evening in a shooting incident in town. I'm sorry for your loss. We'll need you to —"

The line went dead. When Jesse attempted to call back, he got voicemail. People had a right to react to events however they wanted to, but Jesse couldn't escape the sense that something wasn't right.

39

Jesse slept at the station on a cot. He'd done it before and imagined he would do it again. Suit had once asked him why he didn't just sleep in a cell, because the beds were more comfortable than the cot.

"Not if I have a choice, Suit," he'd said.

He got up before the sun, gave himself a hand shower in the bathroom like he used to do sometimes at gas stations or in restaurant bathrooms on long bus trips between road games. Life was a lot less complicated back then. The biggest disputes for him in those days were with second- or third-base umpires. Nobody's life hung in the balance, only wins and losses, and then not always. Once he toweled himself off, he shaved, brushed his teeth, and changed clothes into the spares he kept in his office.

A very weary-looking Molly Crane was at the desk.

"Alisha was supposed to have the desk,"

she said as Jesse came out of the bathroom. "Don't worry about it. My husband's handling the kids. I'll work doubles until . . ." She didn't finish her sentence, because they both knew what "until" meant.

"Thanks, Molly. The budget's going to get blown up by this anyway."

"How's it look for Alisha?"

"Not so good. I'm not part of the investigation. There's a Detective Lieutenant Mary Weld from the state police in charge. She wanted me to back off."

"Wouldn't look good, you handling things. I get it, but I know Alisha says the suspect fired first."

Jesse didn't ask how Molly knew that. He said, "No gun."

"But —"

"It's Newton Alley, Molly. It's a dead end. Weld had Peter and Suit out all night collecting witness statements."

"Don't you believe her?"

"I believe she believes it."

"That's not the same thing, Jesse."

"Evidence, Crane. Without a gun —"

"But she wouldn't've killed an unarmed suspect. You know that. She's a good cop."

"You can't know what someone will do. You can't test how everyone will react."

"Maybe a witness saw or heard something

that backs Alisha's account."

"The suspect's gun didn't sprout wings."

Molly shook her head. "I won't believe it. I just won't."

"If it was about beliefs of friends and families, we'd have empty prisons. But if it makes you feel better, I don't want to believe it, either."

"I'm sorry, Jesse. I know this is hardest on you. I'm just beat."

"No apologies. Alisha is going to need you. I'm going to get some fresh air and donuts. You want something?"

She shook her head.

At the front door, Jesse turned back to her and half smiled. "One good thing, as far as you're concerned."

"What's that?"

"Alisha's lawyer is Monty Bernstein."

Molly blushed in spite of herself and in spite of her exhaustion. As far as Jesse could tell, there were only two men other than her husband Molly ever had eyes for. One was Crow, the Apache hit man, and the other was Monty Bernstein.

"That's a coincidence," Molly said. "I wonder how, out of all the criminal lawyers in the Commonwealth, she picked him."

"I wonder."

■ ■ ■ ■

When Jesse got back from the donut shop, he noticed the Porsche Cayman parked just to the side of the station house. The curvy two-seater's Guards Red paint job fairly screamed "Look at me!" and, if Jesse were colorblind, the fact that the Porsche was parked illegally would have gotten his intention.

Monty Bernstein was right where Jesse expected to find him, kneeling down before the front desk, chatting up Molly in a raspy whisper. Molly, who regardless of her long night and worries, had a sparkle in her eye that hadn't been there ten minutes earlier. Even Jesse had to admit that Monty was one of those people who lit up the room. He was good-looking, for sure — forty, athletic, black-haired, blue-eyed, with perfect white teeth and an angular jawline — but the real secret was his charm. The kind that worked on both men and women. He was confident without being cocky, interesting but without trying too hard. And, like Vinnie Morris, he dressed the part in the finest clothing. Still, Jesse could tell it had been a long, hard night for the lawyer, too.

That didn't stop Monty from turning it

on when he noticed Jesse standing there, donuts in hand.

"Excuse me, Molly," Monty said, walking up to Jesse. "I'd shake your hand, but your hands seem to be occupied."

Jesse gave him a cold stare. "Your vehicle is parked illegally."

Monty didn't skip a beat. "That should be my worst problem . . . and yours."

Jesse smiled. The lawyer smiled in turn.

Jesse put the donuts down on the front desk. "C'mon into my office."

As the lawyer trailed Jesse to his office, he winked at Molly and gave her a smile. That lifted her spirits for a few seconds. Then she remembered why Monty Bernstein was there in the first place.

40

Jesse shook Monty Bernstein's hand. It was a warm handshake that lasted a long time. Jesse gestured at the chair on the opposite side of the desk.

"Sit."

The lawyer said, "I'm curious, Jesse. How did Officer Davis get my number?"

"Typical lawyer," Jesse said, "asking a question he already knows the answer to."

Monty nodded. "You don't know the answer, don't ask the question."

"This isn't the courtroom, Counselor."

"Hell of a case you got me involved in."

"Last I heard, you were free to turn it down."

Monty half smiled. "This case? No way am I turning it down. I believe in my client and I like the notion of Paradise paying my fees. I won't have to waste time chasing my money down." The lawyer's expression changed, his smile vanishing. "Jesse . . . I heard about . . . you know, Diana. I'm so sorry. Did that monster Mr. Peepers actually get away?"

"Thank you." Jesse held up his palms. "Let's focus on why you're here now."

The lawyer leaned forward, lowered his voice. "I know you're not officially part of the investigation."

"Uh-huh."

"I think Alisha may need all the help she can get."

"What kind of help?"

"Off the record?"

"I'm police chief, Monty, not a journalist. There isn't really an 'off the record' with me."

The lawyer sat back in his chair, dragged his hand across the light stubble of his unshaven cheeks.

"Okay, let's start over. First, I want to tell you that, if need be, I'll be able to get any statements Officer Davis made last night before my arrival thrown out. She was clearly still in shock when I spoke to her and she was in no state to be giving statements to anyone."

Jesse didn't react to that but said, "You mentioned help, Counselor."

"Is Officer Davis — wait, let me rephrase that. Before this incident last night, would you have believed Officer Davis the type of person to shoot an unarmed suspect or to fire her weapon without being fired upon first?"

"If I thought she was, she wouldn't be on the PPD. None of my cops would be. But —"

Bernstein said, "That's all I needed to hear."

"Are you deposing me, Monty?"

"Sorry, Jesse. I'm good at my job, very good."

"Yeah, I saw the Porsche out front."

Monty smiled, but it quickly faded. "The thing is, as it stands, I don't know who could win this case. She says she was fired upon first, but without the other gun . . . Listen, I've dealt with liars my whole career: con men, murderers, crooked gamblers, bent cops, you name it. But I don't think she's lying. I'm sure she's not."

"It comes back to one thing: no gun. There's no way around that."

"I know how this looks, Jesse. Young, legally drunk, inexperienced, female African American police officer shoots an unarmed white man. The only way it could look worse was if Vandercamp had been holding a baby. The press is going to have a field day with this, never mind the politicians, but —"

Jesse cut him off. "It gets worse."

"Worse? How the hell could it get worse?"

Jesse explained about the incident in the Scupper between Alisha and the bikers, the vicious assault in Swan Harbor, and the cross-burning in town.

"And the vic— dead man." Jesse couldn't yet bring himself to call him the victim.

"John Vandercamp. What about him?"

"Alisha didn't tell you?"

"She was pretty scattered last night, but she said she was chasing this guy because he was a suspect in a vandalism case."

"The cross-burning. It was reported as simple vandalism."

"Oh, shit!" Monty's jaw dropped.

Then Jesse handed the SS leaflet to the lawyer. He took his time reading it.

"Okay, Jesse, it's a slightly less obvious, more polished version of the racist, anti-Semitic, homophobic, xenophobic crap I've run across before."

"His father is Leon Oskar Vandercamp, the leader of the Saviors of Society." Jesse checked the Seth Thomas clock on the wall. "And he's coming to town this morning to ID his son."

As the words finished coming out of his

mouth, Molly knocked on the pebbled glass of Jesse's office door. She stuck her head in without waiting for word.

"Mr. Vandercamp's here."

The office door swung back and a heavyset man with a bald head barged past Molly. He had the coldest gray eyes Jesse Stone had ever seen.

41

Monty Bernstein knew his being there was awkward and potentially embarrassing for Jesse. He stood to go. Molly, her face red with anger at the man barging past her, stayed at the office door.

"Thank you, Chief Stone," said the lawyer. "I'll be in touch."

Jesse nodded to him and waved at Molly to shut the door. "Go on, I can handle this."

The heavyset man stood perfectly still at the center of the office, watching, listening.

"Mr. Vandercamp," Jesse said. "Please sit."

Vandercamp had other ideas. "Who was that man in here when I came in?"

Jesse wasn't frequently torn. He knew how he felt about things and how he should act in most situations. This wasn't most situations. He disdained organizations like the Saviors of Society and bullies like Leon Vandercamp, but the man's son had just been shot to death in Jesse's town by one of his cops. Diplomacy and charm weren't Jesse's usual default settings, but he understood that there were times to treat even the worst of people with respect and patience. This was one of those times.

"That man was Officer Davis's attorney, Monty Bernstein."

Vandercamp's fleshy face broke into a cruel smile. "Bernstein, huh? Figures." He grunted what passed for a laugh.

"How does it figure?" Jesse asked, knowing full well what Vandercamp meant.

Jesse would give the man space, but not unlimited space.

Vandercamp sat in the chair Monty had just vacated. "What was he doing here?"

"His job. But I had to inform him, as I will tell you, the investigation into your son's shooting —"

"His execution."

Jesse ignored that. "The investigation is being handled by Detective Lieutenant Mary Weld of the state police, so I couldn't be of much help to Mr. Bernstein. This morning is bound to be difficult for you. Before we head over there, can I get you some coffee, Mr. Vandercamp?"

"Keep your damn coffee. You can get me some justice for my boy."

Vandercamp was trying to provoke Jesse.

Strange behavior, Jesse thought, for a father in mourning. Stranger still, Vandercamp didn't even seem particularly grief-stricken or outraged. He was saying all the right words — execution, justice, et cetera — but the affect didn't quite match. Jesse let it go. People had a right to the way they felt and how they dealt with hard things. Even Leon Vandercamp.

Molly was at the door again. "Jesse, the mayor is here to see you."

"Send her in." Jesse knew Molly would have warned the mayor about Vandercamp.

Connie Walker dressed the part in a conservative black suit. "Chief Stone," she said, nodded to Jesse, and then headed directly to Vandercamp. Vandercamp didn't get up. "Mr. Vandercamp, I'm Constance Walker, the mayor of Paradise. I am very sorry for your loss. I can assure you —"

"I'm not interested in your assurances," he said, standing at last. He sneered down at her. "I'm not interested in his, either. I want justice for my murdered son."

Connie Walker didn't fluster easily, but as she half-turned to Jesse, he could see she needed some help.

"If you could excuse us, Mr. Vandercamp," Jesse said. "The mayor and I have to talk. I'll call ahead to the medical examiner's office to let him know we'll be heading over there in a few minutes. Officer Crane will get you what you need."

Vandercamp wasn't the kind of man to be dismissed and go without the last word. He looked away from Jesse and back to the mayor.

"Let me assure *you* of something, Mayor Walker," he said, pointing his index finger at her nose. "I'm going to get justice for my boy at all costs. We're going to have people marching in the streets of your sewer of a town every single day until that murderer gets the punishment she deserves."

When he was done, he brushed past the mayor without acknowledging Jesse.

"I dislike that man," Connie said. "I dislike him a great deal."

"I don't think he cares. He enjoys pushing people's buttons."

"I spoke to the state investigator, Jesse. She didn't come right out and say it, but —"

"I know how it looks."

"Do you think Officer Davis shot an unarmed suspect?"

He shook his head. "That's the question of the day."

"What's the answer?"

"The answer is what the evidence says it is."

"Jesse . . ."

"I know, Connie. I hired Alisha in spite of the selectmen's objections. I appreciate that you backed me up. If this goes badly, I'll resign."

"If this goes badly, Jesse, your head won't be enough. We'll both get swept out. I suppose I came here hoping you'd tell me things weren't as bleak as they seem."

Jesse couldn't help but smile.

Walker was confused. "Am I missing something?"

"If you're coming to me to cheer you up, Connie, we really are in trouble."

Mayor Walker shook her head and laughed quietly. By the time she got to the office door, she was no longer laughing. Jesse picked up the phone to call the ME. He wasn't laughing, either.

42

Vandercamp insisted on taking his own car to the morgue. Jesse had no issue with that, but when he got outside the station, he got a hint of what Paradise had coming. There were twenty vehicles — everything from pickups to 4×4s, to classic Mustangs and beat-up Buicks — lined up behind Vandercamp's five-year-old garnet Chevy Silverado. The vehicles had plates from all over the country, and many of the vehicles had flags — all snapping in the autumn wind blowing in hard off the Atlantic — attached to small plastic poles clipped to their rear door windows. The pickups had bigger flags on long poles attached to the sidewalls of their cargo boxes. Some of the flags were American flags, others were the flags of the Saviors of Society — curved swastikas et al. — but there were a few flags in particular that caught Jesse's eye. These featured bold black block lettering against a field of bright red.

ARYAN LIVES MATTER

MOURN OUR MARTYR

PUNISH HIS RACIST EXECUTIONER

Jesse knew that technology enabled you to get almost anything printed almost immediately, but he was skeptical. It had been less than twelve hours since the incident in Newton Alley. Everything, even the way the father had acted in his office, felt choreographed. It seemed that a spectacle was to be made of the younger Vandercamp's shooting. Jesse was further convinced of the father's intentions when he noticed that the last vehicle in the motorcade was a satellite news truck. Vandercamp meant to make a campaign out of his son's death.

Before the elder Vandercamp could close the passenger door of his pickup, Jesse stopped him.

"Listen, you want to use your son's death for your purposes, I can't stop you."

"Damn right you can't."

"But let's be clear. You do it within the law."

227

"Within the law!" Vandercamp sneered at Jesse. "Was your officer acting within the law when she murdered my boy?"

"Save your speeches for them," Jesse said, pointing at the cars behind the pickup. "Spread the word for them to put their headlights on and that I don't want to hear horns blowing in town, especially not near the morgue. You want to make theater out of this, fine, but other families have lost loved ones, too. Families without agendas. Understood?"

Vandercamp didn't answer Jesse but turned to his driver. "James Earl, go do as Chief Stone says."

Jesse looked past Vandercamp at the driver, hoping the man might be the soldier he'd been searching for. No luck. The driver was a younger version of Vandercamp, probably another son. He was in his early forties, not as heavy, sported a full head of blond hair, and possessed those cold gray eyes.

"I'll pull my Explorer in front of you and then we'll go," Jesse said, slamming the pickup's door shut.

The motorcade made it to the morgue without incident, though Jesse couldn't help but notice the disgusted looks on people's faces as it passed. Vandercamp and James Earl were out of the pickup by the time Jesse got to their truck.

"I take it James Earl is John's older brother," Jesse said.

"Half-brother," James Earl was quick to point out.

Jesse had no doubt which half. James Earl looked even less genuinely upset by the death than his father. It seemed to Jesse that James Earl couldn't wait to get this over with so he could find a place to get a morning drink. Jesse knew a drinker when he saw one or smelled one. James Earl wore too much cheap cologne, but it did little to cover up the stink of scotch sweat leaking out of his pores.

"Only you two," Jesse said.

The three of them walked in silence toward the building that housed the ME's office and the morgue. Being here reminded Jesse he should call Tamara. He hadn't had time to miss her since getting back into town, but he did miss her now. He stopped them just before they got to the front entrance.

"Listen to me," Jesse said. "I've been through this process too many times with too many parents identifying their children. You may think you know what this is going to be like, but it's going to be harder than that. Be prepared. After you make the ID, I'll give you all the time you want with John."

James Earl shook his head and made a face. If his father wasn't there, he'd have probably snapped his fingers and told Jesse to speed things up. *C'mon, c'mon, let's get this over with.* The elder Vandercamp didn't exactly start weeping, but he was taking loud, exaggerated breaths.

Jesse asked, "Ready?"

The father nodded. As they walked forward, the doors parted.

Jesse got what he expected from each man. James Earl took one look at his half-brother's body and was ready to move on. But Leon Vandercamp couldn't seem to stop staring at his son's body. While he didn't get weak-kneed or start wailing, he was definitely affected, probably more than he anticipated he would be.

"I'll give you some time," Jesse said. "I'll be in the ME's office when you're ready."

As he started down the hallway, James Earl caught up to him.

"Listen, Sheriff Stone —"

"Chief Stone."

James Earl rolled his eyes but made the right noises. "Sorry, Chief. Anyplace to get coffee in here . . . a vending machine or something?"

"Rough night?"

"You could say that." James Earl understood what Jesse meant and patted the right-front pocket of his jeans.

Jesse saw the familiar outline of a hip flask or small bottle.

"No vending machine, but I know they've got a coffeemaker in the break room. If you ask, I'm sure they'll brew up some for you."

"Wanna share a cup, Chief?" James Earl patted his pocket again.

"No, thanks. Don't let me catch you driving under the influence in Paradise."

James Earl winked and smiled as if they were members of the same brotherhood. "Understood."

Jesse walked away, thinking that James Earl might be a way for him to keep tabs on things for as long as this mess lasted.

43

Jesse rode back into Paradise via Swan Harbor. You didn't need to be a police chief or a seasoned homicide detective to get a sense that the bikers' confrontation at the Scupper, Felicity Wileford's assault, the cross-burning, the racist leaflets, and John Vandercamp's shooting death added up to something more than a series of one-off, coincidental happenings. Jesse couldn't be sure they were all related, but some of them had to be. He just needed to figure out which ones. If he could, maybe he'd come across some piece of evidence to help Alisha. And to his way of thinking, finding the soldier would be the key.

He drove into the area he'd driven through the last time he was in town and found several Garrison's Landscaping trucks, but not Roberto's crew. Although Jesse didn't doubt what Chief Forster had relayed to him, he wanted to talk to Roberto himself.

Maybe there was something Chief Forster had missed. Then, just as he was ready to give up and move on, Jesse spotted the men in Roberto's crew doing leaf removal on the lot of a barn-red saltbox colonial near the beachfront. He noticed Jim Garrison's extended-bed Escalade parked behind the trucks. There was one last thing he noticed as he approached the crew: Roberto was nowhere in sight.

Garrison, red-faced and already spoiling for a fight, marched up to Jesse before he could get near any of the men working the property. Though a few inches shorter than Jesse and probably a few years his senior, Garrison would have been a pretty formidable opponent, had Jesse actually taken the man up on his challenging behavior. And he had to give Garrison credit. He was still willing to do the work himself instead of just sitting on his ass at home.

"You got trouble with your hearing, Stone?"

"What?"

Garrison's lip twitched. "So you're a comedian, too, huh?"

"Not much of one," Jesse said. "Where's Roberto?"

"None of your fucking business."

"It is if I want it to be."

Garrison pulled his cell phone out of his back pocket. "I'm getting Forster down here. Maybe he can draw you a picture, since you don't seem to understand words so well."

Jesse shrugged. "Why the drama, Garrison?"

"Because I don't like you."

"You don't know me."

Garrison sneered. "I know you well enough to know I don't like you."

"I can't argue with that. Where's Roberto?"

Garrison turned away from Jesse and punched up a number on his cell.

"Yeah, Forster, that pain in the ass, Stone . . . Yeah, him, from Paradise. He's harassing my men again. Get over here before I have to take care of this my . . . No, you listen to me, Forster . . . What do you mean you can't come now? What do we pay you for? You're what . . . Who? Okay, I guess I'm going to have to live with it, but . . ." Garrison stopped talking and stared at the phone. "That son of a —"

Jesse supposed Chief Forster had hung up on Garrison. He also had a pretty good idea that Forster was sending one of his cops over to deliver a message to Jesse. It was pretty easy to figure out what the message would be: Go home.

"You always treat the police chief like a paid employee?" Jesse asked Garrison before Garrison could say anything.

"What?" Garrison got red-faced again. "He is a paid employee. Cops in this town understand their place."

Jesse didn't touch that. Instead, he reached into his pocket and pulled out the SS flier and handed it to Garrison.

"You know anything about this?"

Garrison laughed as he tore it into pieces and let the wind blow it away. He pointed at his crew.

"You deaf *and* blind, Stone? You know where those men come from. You think I would trust them with my money, with my equipment, with my customers, if I believed that stuff?"

"I don't know. That's why I asked."

Jesse could see Garrison getting ready to throw a punch when the Swan Harbor PD cruiser screeched to a stop a few feet away from them. And when Jesse saw the police officer getting out of the Impala, he smiled. The same could not be said of the cop.

"Officer Daniels," Jesse said. "I wanted to talk to you anyway."

"Chief Stone. Mr. Garrison." Daniels nodded and came over to where the two men were standing.

"Drake, will you tell Stone to get the fuck back to his town and leave my men the hell alone?"

Daniels turned to Jesse. "Chief Stone, my boss asked me to ask you to please stop bothering Mr. Garrison and that he told you everything. He said you'd understand that."

"Okay. But let's have a talk, Officer Daniels," Jesse said, turning his back on Garrison and walking toward the Explorer.

As he walked, he noticed one of the men from Garrison's work crew staring at him. Jesse recognized him from the last time but didn't know his name. He looked as if he had something to say. With Garrison and Daniels standing only several feet away, there was no chance for him to approach Jesse. Jesse didn't want to get the man in trouble with Garrison, so he kept on walking. As he walked, Jesse dropped one of his cards onto the pavement. The man gave Jesse a quick nod and went back to raking leaves onto the big blue tarp.

44

Jesse waited by his Explorer for Officer Daniels to finish speaking with Garrison and to come over and talk to him, but Daniels never came. Instead he got into his cruiser and drove off. Jesse was about to follow him when the phone buzzed in his pocket. It was Chief Forster.

"Jesse, I thought we had this all straightened out."

"We did, but I still have open cases and I still need to find the soldier."

"I would think that you'd have enough stuff to keep you busy after the . . . shooting in Paradise last night. How's that going?"

"I'm officially not part of the investigation, so I don't know."

"Doesn't look good, though," Forster said.

"No, it doesn't. Reminds me, don't you have better things to do than to run interference for a landscaper and one of your cops?"

"You manage your department however you want to. I'll do the same."

"Fair enough. Any word on the Wileford homicide?"

"It's not a homicide."

"You mean not yet."

"Stop worrying about what I mean or don't mean," Forster said. "Worry about what's going on in Paradise."

"Thanks for the advice."

"Jesse, I'm not kidding about this. Don't come into town and flex your muscles again. I won't stand for it."

Forster hung up. Jesse didn't know what to make of it. Cops were, by nature, territorial. But it was hard to know if that's what was going on with the chief of the Swan Harbor PD. Was Forster simply a wimp who was scared that the local businesspeople would kick him to the curb if he didn't do their bidding? Or was it something else, something darker than that? Jesse wasn't going to find out by leaning against the fender of his SUV, so he headed back into Paradise.

Daisy's was crowded at lunch. Jesse was happy for her and for Cole, who would be raking in the tip money, but wished that her patrons weren't mostly media types. He guessed the news-media invasion was inevitable. Even he could see that this story would play in every market. Everything about it, from Alisha's skin color to John Vandercamp's family lineage, made it a grand slam. And with Leon Vandercamp seemingly determined to exploit the death of his son, it was bound to get worse. Jesse could hear the sizzle words in his head: white supremacist, unarmed, African American, police shooting.

As Jesse was ordering his sandwich, he realized that his presence hadn't gone unnoticed. The noise of the conversations, the clatter of silverware and plates, hushed suddenly. Those things were replaced by loud whispers and the squeaking of people sliding out of vinyl booths, the rattle and scraping of chairs on the tile flooring. When Jesse turned away from Daisy, he saw four people coming at him.

The two women and two men approached him. Jesse recognized Rianne Phillips, the investigative reporter from a Boston TV affiliate. Handsome, with perfectly cut shoulder-length hair, she was impeccably dressed and made up. But Jesse knew not to dismiss her. She had always been tough but fair. He didn't recognize the other woman. She was definitely a print journalist, dressed for comfort, not for the camera. He also recognized Esai Vasquez, another reporter for a Boston TV outlet. Tom Pemberton was from the Salem daily paper.

"Chief Stone, can you confirm that the victim" — Esai looked down at his notes — "Mr. Vandercamp, was unarmed?"

Jesse held his palms up.

"Let me make this clear to all of you," he said. "I can confirm or deny nothing. I am not party to the investigation. The investigation into the incident is being handled by state police personnel. All I can say is that the Paradise Police Department is cooperating with the investigation and that we will abide by their findings. Now, if you don't mind, I'm trying to get some lunch."

Jesse knew it wouldn't end there. All he'd done was temporarily close one area for the media to pursue.

"What about the Saviors of Society fliers that have been handed out in Paradise?" asked the woman print journalist. "Do you think there is any connection between the shooting of the unarmed son of the head of that organization by an African American policewoman?"

Jesse answered with a question of his own: "Who are you?"

"Casandra Mills from *The Globe.*"

"We don't know each other, Casandra, but if you ever want me to answer one of your questions, don't put the answer you want in the question."

"Okay," she said. "Do you think there is any connection between those fliers and the incident last night?"

"Until the investigation is completed, it would be wrong for me to speculate."

Then Rianne Phillips asked the really hard question. "Did your department report a recent cross-burning incident as vandalism instead of a hate crime? If so, can you explain why?"

"No comment, Rianne."

But Jesse made a mental note to have a talk with Rianne when no one else was around. He knew the Patels hadn't leaked the information, and since his cops were under strict instructions about talking to the press during the investigation, he doubted one of them was the source. That left the person who'd burned the cross into the lawn, and if John Vandercamp was that person, he couldn't have been the source. The question the reporter asked only cemented Jesse's belief that there was more going on in his town than what you could see in the light.

45

As Jesse paid for his sandwich, Daisy nodded toward the back of the house. He understood. When he left the restaurant, he went through the alley and around to the back door. Daisy was waiting for him there.

"What's up, Daisy?"

"The kid is great and I don't want to lose him."

"But . . ."

She pointed over her shoulder with her thumb. "But I really can't have him living back here if we're going to be this busy. This ain't normal busy. This is crazy busy, and I hate to say it, Jesse, but as long as this thing is a story, I —"

"I got it, Daisy. Can you get through one more night?"

She gave him a half-smile and winked. "For you, handsome, sure thing."

"Thanks. Anything I can do for you?"

"Talk up my many virtues to Mayor Hottie."

Smiling, he turned and walked away. Finding Cole Slayton a place to sack out wasn't exactly at the top of his priority list, but he remembered that old Chinese proverb about how when you rescue someone, that person becomes your responsibility. He hadn't rescued Cole per se. Still, he felt responsible for him and felt a responsibility to Daisy. She'd given Cole a job on Jesse's say-so, and now, with her being so busy, she needed the kid.

Back at the station, Jesse seemed to be looking at his half-eaten BLT. He was still hungry, just not for food. He was daydreaming, lost in the memory of James Earl Vandercamp patting his pocket and seeing the outline of the hip flask. That morphed into a vision of a tall glass of Johnnie Walker Black with a splash of soda and a squeeze of lime. He could almost see the bubbles rushing to the surface, smell the tang of the lime in the air, hear the tinkling of the ice cubes against the glass, taste the magic on his finger after he stirred. He remembered how it felt going down, the liquid cold from the ice but spreading warmth at the back of his throat, then in his belly and then . . . *Is this how it's always going to be?* he wondered. *Am I always going to want to drink so bad?*

He remembered all of those sessions with Dix. The ones when he had talked about all the lies and rationalizations he'd come up with over the years. *It's stress. It's boredom. It's depression. It's work. It's the pain in my shoulder. It's the job. It's Jenn. It's to relax. It's to get ready.* They didn't feel like lies when he spoke them. They all seemed real and true. But what it really felt like was love.

Jesse dialed Bill's number. It went to voicemail. He didn't leave a message. He figured he wouldn't have to. Bill would know Jesse wasn't calling to discuss how badly the Patriots were going to beat the Jets on Sunday. The bottom line was, he needed to get to a meeting, sooner rather than later. He went to the online meeting list, but before he could scroll through it, Molly stuck her head into the office after knocking. There were times he'd been happier to see her face, though he couldn't recall when. Then he noticed her expression.

"What's wrong?"

"Some people are here to see you."

"What people?"

"Mayor Walker and . . . Sam Mahorn."

244

"Reverend Sam Mahorn?"

"Yep, Jesse, him."

"Send them in."

Jesse had a sense that once it got out that Alisha was African American and that the dead man was the son of the founder of the Saviors of Society, battle lines would be drawn and Paradise might become a political war zone. Now there was no doubt of it. Though not quite as much a polarizing figure as Leon Vandercamp, Reverend Sam, as the media and his followers called him, wasn't beloved by all, especially not by police. He began his career as a preacher in a storefront church in 1980 in Newark, New Jersey, but came into national prominence when he led demonstrations through the streets of that city in the aftermath of a notorious incident involving two police officers and a sixteen-year-old black girl.

The girl, Serena Jamerson, had been missing from her Ironbound neighborhood apartment for several days. Her mother reported this to the police. After her mother complained bitterly in the press that the police didn't seem to take her concerns seriously enough, rumors surfaced that people had seen Serena getting into a patrol car on the night she disappeared. When Serena turned up two weeks later at a cousin's apartment in Brooklyn, it was Reverend Sam and Serena's mom who went to bring her home. The sensational tale she told the press went viral. She said that two white policemen had picked her up off the street, got her drunk, drugged her, and had taken her to a motel in New York City somewhere. She was too out of it to remember precisely where. She couldn't remember what they had done to her, but she woke up days later in a back alley somewhere, alone and sore all over. The details of how she'd gotten from the alley to her cousin's were again sketchy at best.

By the time the smoke had cleared and it came out that the story was almost a complete fabrication, the world had changed. The careers of the two police officers in question were ruined and Serena's family was forced to move somewhere out west. Reverend Sam Mahorn was famous. He had made the jump from small-time preacher to national civil rights leader. And for the past thirty years, every time there was a high-profile incident involving African Americans and the police, Reverend Sam was there. Jesse couldn't help but wonder what angle Mahorn would play in this case. He'd find out soon enough.

46

Reverend Sam had aged well. He was a tall, slender man with a regal bearing. He wasn't particularly good-looking, but he had a lined face with a lot of character and an ingratiating smile. His head was shaved and his gray mustache perfectly trimmed. He carried himself like important men do, with a sense of style bordering on arrogance but that didn't cross the line. As a former L.A. cop, Jesse was used to this pose. He even understood that for prominent public figures, the image they projected was crucial to how they were perceived. A superstar actor once confessed to Jesse that the public believes you are only what *you* believe you are.

Reverend Sam held his right hand out to Jesse, smiling that famous smile of his. Mayor Walker, on the other hand, looked like she was about ready to be sick. Jesse realized she was probably more nervous about what her police chief would do than what the reverend would do. Jesse shook Mahorn's hand — the man had a firm grip but not a challenging one — and gestured to the chairs in front of his desk.

"It's a pleasure to meet you, Chief Stone," said Mahorn without a hint of guile. "Mayor Walker has been telling me that you fought hard to get Officer Davis on your department."

"Without the mayor's support, all the fighting I did wouldn't have mattered."

Reverend Sam bowed his head to the mayor. "I'm sure that's the case, Chief Stone, but would you mind telling me why having Officer Davis as a member of your department was worth the fight?"

"First, please call me Jesse."

Mahorn's smile turned into a sneer and he laughed a derisive laugh.

Mayor Walker got that sick look on her face again, and she stared at Jesse with no small measure of dread.

But Jesse asked, "What's that about?"

"Forgive me, Chief — Jesse — but you'll understand that I am not usually greeted with courtesy and respect by law enforcement types. Certainly, I've never been asked to address any so familiarly."

"I'm not a type, Reverend Mahorn, any

248

more than you are. Until you give me reason to treat you otherwise, you'll be treated with courtesy and respect."

"Fair enough." Reverend Sam raised his hands. "But can you answer my question about why you fought so hard for Alisha Davis?"

Jesse looked at Connie Walker, who gave Jesse a subtle nod to answer.

"I thought she was the best candidate."

Reverend Sam shook his head. "C'mon, now, Jesse, let's not play footsie with each other here. I'd like to hear the real reasons, not the pap you tell the media."

"Why do my reasons matter?" Jesse asked. "Why are you here, Reverend? Don't you always come down on the opposite side of the police?"

Mahorn puffed out his chest. "I'd like to think I come down on the side of right."

"Tell that to the two Newark cops whose careers you helped ruin."

Connie Walker got that look again as Reverend Sam shot out of his chair. "I should have known better than to think you would be reasonable."

Jesse waved his hands. "Please, Reverend, sit back down and I'll tell you why I fought so hard for Officer Davis. But if you want to march out of here, I won't stop you."

Mahorn sat.

"Paradise is changing," Jesse said. "People are moving up here and commuting to Boston. We're a more diverse place than when I took this job. I didn't think the easy way out, hiring another retired, white, big-city cop who came with twenty years of baggage, was the smart move. I wanted a young cop, another female cop, I could train. That Alisha was African American was an added benefit. A police force should reflect the community it serves or will be serving. She had the pedigree as a cop's daughter, scored the highest on the test, and was the most impressive in her interviews. And until last night, she hadn't done anything to make me seriously question my decision."

Reverend Sam clapped his hands together. "See, there it is! You've already convicted her without a trial. In your eyes, she's guilty. She's black and she shot a white man and that's that."

"No, Reverend, I don't know whether she shot an unarmed man. She says she didn't and she's never lied to me. I'll wait until the state investigation is done before I make up my mind, because I believe in right and wrong more than skin color. And I believe in evidence."

"Lip service."

Before Jesse could say anything, Connie Walker was out of her seat. "Reverend, Jesse and I have had our differences, but I won't sit here and let you question his integrity. He isn't always right, but he believes what he says. You can accuse him of a lot of things, but not meaning what he says isn't one of them."

"I'll keep that in mind," Reverend Sam said, standing.

Jesse stood, too. "Reverend, I understand the desire to support Officer Davis, but this has the potential to get ugly."

"I'm well aware of who the dead man is, Jesse. But I cannot let that deter us from the larger issue at stake here."

"You mean the truth?"

Mahorn opened his mouth to react, then rethought what he was going to say. "You're a clever man, Jesse. I won't underestimate you again."

"Do you really want to help Officer Davis?" Jesse asked as he sat back down.

"That's why I'm here."

"Then forget about marching and pray somebody finds that gun."

The next thing Jesse heard was his office door closing.

47

Jesse walked down the steps to the basement of the Episcopal church in Cambridge. He figured this was the last meeting at the church he'd be able to get to for the foreseeable future. The demonstrations hadn't yet started in Paradise, but he knew they were coming and that in the days to come he and his cops would be pushed to their limit. And once the autopsy results and preliminary forensics reports came out, things would blow up. So when Bill called him back, apologizing for not being able to take Jesse's call, he urged Jesse to get to a meeting, any meeting. But Jesse, like a lot of drunks, was a creature of routine, and after only a few meetings, he didn't feel comfortable enough to wander into an unfamiliar meeting closer to Paradise.

When he came through the doors he saw Bill was sitting in the next-to-last row, his jacket thrown over the seat next to him. Bill picked up his jacket when he saw Jesse. Anya was there, too, but not in her usual seat. She had moved up closer to the front of the room and was sitting next to a man Jesse had seen Anya talking to at the end of the last meeting. He felt a twinge. Not jealousy, but it felt like a loss to him. He'd had big losses in his life and he always abided, stoically. Taking it like he thought a man should take things. That was before he had stopped drinking. He didn't know how to feel about things without drinking. *No wonder people fall off the wagon,* he thought.

Bill noticed Jesse staring over at Anya.

"This isn't meant as a place for friendship, Jesse. Me and you, that's different. Maybe we'll be friends or maybe not. Anya, she'll have to find her own way."

"Uh-huh."

"Sorry again for not calling you back. All I had to do was read the paper to see why you'd want to drink. Rough day?"

"Going to get rougher," Jesse said.

"I won't ask you about it, but if talking about it will help you with your thirst, I'm good."

"Reverend Sam Mahorn turned up in Paradise today," Jesse said, not quite believing he was telling this to Bill.

"Oh, man. Between him and the dead

253

man's father . . . I wouldn't wanna trade places with you."

Jesse agreed. He'd been in some unenviable spots before, but not like this one. It was just as bad for his cops. Worse, maybe. His mind drifted, thinking about what he would say to them in the morning.

"Jesse, we're starting. It's serenity prayer time," Bill said, nudging Jesse's leg gently with his knee and snapping him back into the moment.

When the meeting was over, Bill offered to buy Jesse a cup of coffee. Jesse thanked him but decided he wanted to skip it and take a walk.

"Good luck, Jesse. Remember, you need me, call."

Around the corner from the church, Jesse heard something, a muffled scream. He took off running. Jesse spotted an open rear car door. The car was bouncing. He heard the muffled scream again. Jesse ran to the open car door. There was a man on top of a woman. Her hands were flailing, her feet kicking.

"Get off me! Get off me!"

Jesse grabbed the man's hair and yanked back hard. The man let out a yelp like a wounded dog as he was pulled out of the car and off the woman. Jesse slammed the man's face onto the sidewalk, stunning him.

"Jesse," the woman said.

When Jesse turned, he saw the woman sitting up in the car was Anya. Her lip was split, her front teeth red with blood; her jacket was opened and her sweater was torn. The man on the sidewalk was the guy she'd been sitting with at the meeting. She jumped out of the car as Jesse reached for his phone. She clutched his hand in hers. "No cops, Jesse."

Jesse looked at her, down at the man, then back at her. "Are you sure?"

"Please, Jesse. No cops."

"Okay." Jesse pulled the man to his feet by an arm bent behind him. It was painful. Jesse meant it to be. Jesse threw him against the car, then turned to Anya. "Walk away. I'll be with you in a minute."

"But Jesse —"

"If you don't want cops, walk away."

When Anya was far enough away, he took the man's wallet and removed his driver's license.

"Edward Perry," Jesse said, pushing on the man's bent arm until it was about to break. "I'll be sending your license to a friend, Eddie. You think you're a lucky man, but you'd be wrong." He spun Perry around and shoved the muzzle of his nine-millimeter into his ribs, hard. "You know who Vinnie Morris is, Eddie?"

Edward Perry's eyes got wide. That was answer enough.

"Good, because that's who I'm mailing your license to with a little note."

"I swear, she was coming on to me. I —"

Jesse introduced his right knee to Edward Perry's groin. Perry doubled over, and when he did, Jesse used his knee again. Perry's nose broke with a sickening sound. His face was a mess of blood, mucus, and tears. Jesse let him fall to the ground.

"Wrong answer. Get yourself to a hospital and then always keep an eye in your rear-view mirror. You'll never know if the guy driving that car behind you or sitting in the seat next to you in the theater works for Vinnie. Understand? Nod your head, Eddie."

Edward Perry nodded and Jesse walked away.

"He won't bother you anymore," Jesse said, holding his arm around Anya's shoulders. She was trembling, tears running down her cheeks. "C'mon, I'm driving you home."

She didn't argue with him.

48

Jesse didn't guess Anya for a Brookline type, but he didn't figure her for a run-down factory building in Newmarket Square, either. While it wasn't a squat, Jesse didn't think it was likely zoned for apartments, at least not the building she had him stop in front of.

"You sure this is your address?"

She didn't answer the question. "You're police, huh?"

He hadn't given it much thought, but he realized his PPD hat and jacket were on the backseat and the switched-off police scanner mounted below the dash kind of gave him away.

"Does that matter? You were pretty clear on no cops back there."

"Hank and — I don't like cops too much."

"Any particular reason?"

She didn't answer.

"What I did tonight, I did because you needed help," he said.

"Thank you, Jesse. I guess I shoulda said that before."

"It's okay. I'm just glad I stopped him."

She was crying again. She balled her hands into fists and punched her thighs. "I'm so stupid sometimes."

"We're all stupid sometimes. You can't blame yourself for what that guy did. He won't do it again."

She leaned over and kissed Jesse on the cheek. "Thanks, Jesse."

She was out of his Explorer and disappeared in the shadows of a loading bay. Jesse watched and listened. He heard a metal door scrape and creak open, then slam shut. He waited there a few minutes to see if he could spot a light popping on in the building but couldn't find one. As he drove away, he saw a reflection off something in an alleyway behind the factory building. He pulled over and spotted a lineup of motorcycles. They were all Harleys, their gas tanks painted a lacquered black, with a small, silver skull and crossbones painted on the right side of the tank. He thought back to the one time Anya's boyfriend, Hank, had come with her to the meeting. A biker, yeah, Jesse could see that. Now the factory building made sense. He thought of Sharon, a waitress he'd met years ago who had gotten in too deep with a biker gang. He'd helped her out, but he wasn't sure he had done her much of a favor. He had more hope for Anya. She was trying to change.

When Jesse was driving through Paradise after getting back from Boston, he was uneasy. It was quiet, almost too quiet for his liking. He knew there were forces at play here that might change his town forever and would almost certainly blow people's lives apart. Alisha's life for sure. Even if Vandercamp's phantom gun magically appeared or if Monty came up with some brilliant defense and got her off, she was in for years of torment. Killing, justified or not, isn't as easy as it seems. Unless you're a psychopath, you pay a price.

He was about to turn and head toward the Swap when the Bluetooth ring came across the speakers.

"Jesse Stone," he answered.

"It's me, Jesse, Gabe. Hope I didn't wake you."

"No, that's fine. What's up?"

"There's a guy here waiting for you."

"Who?"

"I don't think he speaks English. He just handed me your card."

"I'll be right there."

Jesse recognized the man from earlier in the day. He was the landscaper who worked for Garrison, the man with whom he had made eye contact. He seemed very nervous, but also relieved. Jesse shook his hand and invited him into the office. He said his name was Pablo.

Jesse turned to Gabe before heading to the office. "Pablo's visit is off the record unless I say otherwise." Then he turned to face Pablo and repeated the same thing in Spanish.

Pablo gave Jesse a tentative smile and followed him into the office.

"I speak English, a little," Pablo said, when he was seated across from Jesse's desk.

"Good. So, Pablo, why are you here?"

"Roberto, he goes away the night when you and the Swan police talk to him."

"Goes? Where did he go?"

Pablo shrugged. "Many of us share a house. Garrison, he comes each morning to get us. The morning . . ." Pablo turned his palms up, struggling for the words.

"The morning after I spoke to him, Roberto was gone?"

Pablo smiled. "*Sí.* Yes. He doesn't come. I go to his room, and his things . . . some are there, some are not."

"Maybe he went back home or went away like Miguel."

Pablo frowned, his shoulders sagging. "No, Roberto is legal. He watches out for us. He would not just leave us. Something is not right, I think."

"Do you think Mr. Garrison —"

Pablo stood up like he was shot out of the chair and waved his hands. "I say nothing about the *jefe*. I am just scared for Roberto."

"Okay, Pablo. Give me the address and I'll look into it. I give you my word."

49

The reports were in and Jesse read through them. The autopsy results weren't going to do Monty Bernstein or his client much good. As far as the autopsy went, there were no surprises. As Dr. Minter had surmised upon his initial view of John W. Vandercamp's body, any one of the three shots from Alisha's off-duty piece could have been the fatal shot.

The one peculiar and interesting piece of evidence Jesse found was in the forensics analysis, not the autopsy report. Vandercamp had gunshot residue on his right hand and clothing. Gunshot residue didn't just magically appear. You needed to either fire a weapon yourself or be in very close proximity to a weapon being fired. And Alisha had been way too far away for the residue to have come from her weapon. *There had to be a gun.* But there wasn't a gun.

"Molly," Jesse said, walking out into the main room of the station house. "Get Detective Lieutenant Weld on the phone for me."

She cleared her throat, loudly.

"Please, Molly."

But Jesse wasn't smiling.

"What is it, Jesse?"

"There was GSR on Vandercamp's right hand and clothing."

Twenty seconds later, as Molly picked up the phone, Mary Weld came into the station. She had a computer case slung over her left shoulder.

"Jesse was just calling you."

Weld lifted the left corner of her mouth, which Molly took for a smile.

"He in there?" Weld pointed at the office door.

Molly got up. "He is."

Weld waved Molly back down into her seat. "I can manage."

She knocked and waited for Jesse to acknowledge her.

When Weld entered, they shook hands. She sat herself down without the usual formalities.

"Officer Crane tells me you wanted to speak to me."

"I did."

"Let me guess," Weld said. "The GSR."

"Uh-huh. There had to be a gun."

Weld didn't answer immediately. Instead, she removed a notebook computer from her carrier, put it on Jesse's desk, and booted it up. "Oh, there was a gun, all right, Chief Stone. Just not when Officer Davis said the gun was there."

"Am I missing something?"

"Give me one second."

Weld tapped the keyboard, turned the computer so the screen faced Jesse, and pushed it toward him. She stood up, came around the desk to stand behind him, and pressed the enter key. A somewhat grainy black-and-white still image came up on the screen. The image was of a man standing behind a counter, a cash register to his left. On the wall at his back was an array of handguns and rifles of various types, calibers, and purposes.

"This is CCTV from the Magic Valley Handgun and Rifle Range. It's about five miles due west of here." Weld hit the enter key again. "You'll notice the time stamp in the upper-right-hand corner. And . . . here he comes, John W. Vandercamp, a member of the NRA, the National Association for Gun Rights, and just about every other gun organization you could name and some you can't. He was also licensed to carry in New York state."

The video showed Vandercamp approaching the counter, producing items from his wallet, and having a friendly exchange with the man behind the counter. The counterman handed ear protection and goggles to Vandercamp and pointed him in the direction of the indoor range. The image switched to the range, where another employee places three gun cases, three boxes of ammo, and nine paper targets down on the stall platform. Vandercamp appears in the frame and has a brief discussion with the employee.

Weld stopped the video. "I don't think we need to watch him, do we, Chief Stone?" It wasn't really a question. "He rented a Browning 1911, a Colt Python with a six-inch barrel, and a Luger. Note the time stamp. This session ended approximately ninety minutes before the video footage of Officer Davis, gun drawn, chasing Vandercamp, unarmed, directly past this station."

"Apparently unarmed," Jesse said. "Just because Vandercamp didn't have a weapon in his hand at the time doesn't mean he was unarmed."

"That's almost verbatim of what Mr. Bernstein and his client claim. She says that just before they come into frame on the station's camera she thought she saw Vandercamp reaching into his jacket for a weapon."

"Do you have any reason to doubt her?" Jesse asked.

"You mean besides the fact that we can't find this weapon, she was legally drunk, and she was the responding officer to the cross-burning for which Mr. Vandercamp was a person of interest? I'd say we have plenty of reason to doubt her."

Jesse's cell buzzed in his pocket. "Excuse me." He looked at the screen, saw it was Connor Cavanaugh from the hotel, and refused the call.

"Look, Chief, I'm not trying to bury your cop, but it just doesn't look good and I didn't want you to get your hopes up about the GSR."

"Thanks for the courtesy. I understand you've got your job to do. Off the record, cop to cop, is there anything at all that you've found that hints at exonerating her?"

"Cop to cop . . . Two out of the eleven witnesses who heard the shooting claim they counted nine shots, not eight, and one witness who lives on the town side of Newton Alley says she heard people talking and footsteps in the alley after the shooting. But some people heard five shots, some fifteen.

And the witness who says she heard footsteps and a conversation . . . lives on the second floor with only a sealed bathroom window onto the scene. It'll all be in the report."

"How long before you issue the report?"

"Still waiting on some of the forensics," she said, "but pretty soon."

There was nothing more for either one of them to say. It was pretty obvious what Weld's conclusions would be. And Jesse had to admit, given the evidence, he would probably draw the same conclusions: Alisha had killed an unarmed man.

50

Jesse picked his old glove off his desk and pounded the ball into the mitt. As he did, he considered what he was being asked to believe. What a jury was likely going to be asked to believe. The difference was that he wouldn't buy it, but that a jury almost surely would.

Jesse wasn't a big fan of coincidence but accepted that things did sometimes just happen. He supposed it was possible that the suspect in the cross-burning just happened to be standing twenty feet in front of Alisha at the precise moment she left the Gull. It was possible that serendipity had played a part in the suspect running directly past the police station surveillance cameras at a time when Alisha had drawn her weapon. Was it serendipity, too, that had caused John Vandercamp to flee down the only dead-end street in that end of Paradise? Was it simply by chance that he had been to a shooting range only hours before his death? Although it was a stretch to believe the innocent confluence of any two of these things, believing all of them was ridiculous. Problem was, there wasn't anything he could do about it . . . not officially, anyway.

"Molly, get in here," he said, shouting so that she could hear him through the door.

When Molly opened the door, Jesse was facing out the window behind his desk. The glove was still on his left hand and the ball was cupped in his right.

"Sit down, Crane."

"What is it, Jesse?"

"What if I told you that John Vandercamp was at a shooting range about an hour and a half before Alisha killed him?"

"I'd say that was pretty convenient if Alisha is telling the truth and Vandercamp fired first."

"I agree," he said, still facing the window. "Where are the only official CCTV cameras in this part of town?"

"Jesse, you know the answer to that."

"Humor me, Crane."

"The only cameras are surrounding the station house."

"If you were running from someone in this part of town, where would you run?"

"That's easy. I'd run into the marina. It's

pretty dead this time of year. It's dark and there are plenty of places to hide. Plenty of boats to hide on, too. You could jump into the water, use the planking for cover, and swim away. Never mind that you can access parking lots from the Lobster Claw and the Gull, and from there you can get back into town."

"So you wouldn't run in a straight line right past the station house cameras and into a dead-end street?"

"I grew up here. I'm a cop here. Vandercamp probably didn't know better."

Jesse turned to face Molly, placing the ball back in the glove and the glove on the desk. "Who in this department would you trust with your life?"

"Everyone," she said without hesitation. "I have to or I couldn't come to work."

"Good answer. Who would you trust with your kids' lives?"

She didn't answer right away. "You and Suit . . . Peter. Gabe, too. What are you getting at, Jesse?"

"Not Peter," Jesse said. "He's too by-the-book. I need to talk to the rest of you."

"I'm here. Talk to me now."

Jesse shook his head. "It needs to be all of you at once."

"I'll see what I can do," she said.

The front desk phone rang.

"You better get that, Molly."

Less than a minute later, she was back.

"It was the mayor, Jesse. There's trouble."

The calm before the storm was now officially over. When Jesse got to town hall, the battle lines had been drawn and it was pretty clear that actual battle was about to break out. The two groups of protesters had surged toward each other and several were nose-to-nose. It wouldn't take much — the first punch, a shove, one thrown bottle, a shift in the wind — to set off a full-scale donnybrook. And there, at a safe distance, cameras rolling, the media.

It was no wonder to Jesse. One look at the signs that Leon Vandercamp's people were carrying and the flags they were flying left little doubt that a fight is just exactly what they wanted. Nobody loved the United States more than Jesse, but there were times he wished the framers had done a little more tweaking of the first two amendments. As he had told Molly, there were pretty ugly aspects of freedom of speech. Mix those ugly aspects with guns and you could have a real problem on your hands.

"Molly," Jesse called in. "Get three cars off patrol and down to town hall. Call in the auxiliaries and call the staties."

When the cops and the auxiliary officers showed up, Jesse had them get between the groups and urged them at least twenty feet apart.

"Suit, line the cruisers end to end to keep them apart. Don't let the guys get in anyone's face. Nobody with a badge does anything to provoke the protesters. Let the groups shout at each other all they want, but one person from either side throws something or charges the other way, arrest them."

"Where are you going, Jesse?"

"To have a talk."

51

Jesse walked over to where Leon Vandercamp was standing. He was holding a color
portrait of his dead son but looking about
as pleased as he could. James Earl was
standing next to his father, holding a bullhorn carelessly at his side and drinking a
cup of coffee. Jesse could smell the bourbon
in the steam coming off the coffee. James
Earl gave Jesse the look that was kind of
like a secret handshake. They weren't Ma-
sons or Elks, but they were drunks. Jesse
nodded, giving the look back. He didn't
know why, but he felt kind of sorry for
James Earl, and it wasn't just about the
drinking.

"Mr. Vandercamp," Jesse said to the father.
"I was wondering if I could have a word
with you in the mayor's office."

Leon Vandercamp wasn't at all as happy
to see Jesse as his son was. He didn't answer
right away, and it seemed to Jesse he was

making a calculation.

"You have my word that my officers will do nothing to your people as long as they remain on this side of the building."

"Your word. Ha! You hired that bitch that executed my boy."

There were about twenty things Jesse would have liked to have said to that. He also would have liked to have punched him in the face. He said none of them and kept his hands at his sides. What he did say was "Mr. Vandercamp, please come inside to the mayor's office. I'm sure James Earl can handle things out here."

Jesse could tell James Earl liked that. James Earl didn't seem like a man who'd ever had much praise heaped on him or been given much responsibility.

"Clearly, Chief Stone, you aren't a very good judge of character. But I guess even James Earl can manage for a few minutes."

"Up the steps, through the door, down the hall," Jesse said. "I'll be with you in a minute."

When the father left, James Earl turned to Jesse. "Real loving man, my father. I'm the wrong son. I've always been the wrong son. You have kids, Chief?"

Jesse ignored that. "Like I told him, just

keep your people on this side and we'll be good."

James Earl lifted the bullhorn. Jesse took that opportunity to approach Reverend Sam.

"I saw you talking to the enemy," Mahorn said before Jesse could even open his mouth.

"Well, Reverend Sam, you're going to get the opportunity to express your opinion to the enemy if you'll come with me."

"Come where?"

"Into the mayor's office."

It was just the four of them in Mayor Walker's office: Vandercamp, Mahorn, Jesse, and the mayor. They had at least one thing in common. None of them was happy to be there.

"Gentlemen," Connie Walker said, "please sit."

She sat, but none of the men did. No one was going to risk showing weakness.

"Let's get this over with. The less time I have to spend in a room with him," Vandercamp said, pointing at Mahorn, "the better."

"Don't think I enjoy breathing the same air as you, you hateful racist son of a bitch."

"Temper, temper, Reverend Sam," Vandercamp said. "Your people have such trouble controlling their emotions. Got my boy killed."

Connie Walker got that sick look on her face again. She looked over to Jesse to do something, but Jesse was his usual cool, unreadable self.

"My people!" Mahorn said.

Vandercamp's unblinking cruel eyes were focused on Reverend Sam, his mouth shaped into what passed for a smile. He brushed his fingers across the skin of his cheek, rubbed his fingers together as if they were dirty, and wiped them off on the thigh of his pants. "Your people. You know what I mean."

Mahorn laughed at Vandercamp. "You think you're gonna incite me, you half-wit cracker fool."

Vandercamp was no longer smiling. He turned to walk out of the office, but Jesse stepped in front of him.

"You're not going anywhere, not yet. Neither one of you is."

"Get out of my way, Chief Stone," Vandercamp said.

"Or what?" Jesse didn't move.

Vandercamp didn't like that but said nothing.

"Listen to me, both of you," Jesse said. "I don't care about your agendas, either one of you. The people out there can do what you just did in here. But someone, anyone, throws a punch, commits an act of violence or vandalism and I'm going to hold you as responsible as the person who did it. And if you think I'm kidding, try me. This is a small town, so people are going to cross paths. You both go back out there and say what you have to say to save face, but make it clear."

"We don't believe in violence," Reverend Sam said, moving toward the door.

Vandercamp said, "We won't distract from my son's execution by doing anything but demanding justice and rightful retribution."

Jesse opened the door, let them out, and then shut the door behind them.

"Do you think that will do any good, Jesse?" Connie asked.

"In the long run, probably not. But if it buys us some time until the preliminary investigation is done . . ."

"For now, I guess it's one day at a time."

One day at a time. That was a phrase Jesse had been hearing a lot lately. But with the way things were in town, he probably wasn't going to hear it that night.

52

When Monty Bernstein walked into his office, Jesse was happy for the distraction. That was right up until Monty said, "You look like you could use a drink."

"No drinking, not anymore."

"You serious?"

Unconvinced, Monty walked around to Jesse's side of the desk and tugged on the handle of Jesse's bottle drawer. Jesse didn't stop him.

"Holy shit! You *are* serious."

"What are you doing here, Monty? You know your being here won't play well."

"Right now, Jesse, the only way they could play worse was if there was HD video and full sound of Alisha shooting Vandercamp. I can hear the prosecutor's opening remarks, because they would be mine." The lawyer stood in front of Jesse as if in front of the jury. He held up his right thumb. "One, Officer Davis was inexperienced and was hired against the objections of many of Paradise's elected officials." Index finger. "Two, she lost her cool several weeks before the shooting during a confrontation with bikers when she was called the n-word. She was so irrational during that incident that when fellow officers showed up at the scene, she was insubordinate." Middle finger. "Only days before the tragic shooting of John Vandercamp, there was a vicious assault on an African American woman in a neighboring town. This now deceased woman was involved in an interracial relationship, as is Officer Davis. This, combined with a cross-burning on the lawn of an interracial couple in Paradise, heightened Officer Davis's already hypersensitivity to racial issues." Ring finger. "And when the victims of the cross-burning asked that it be reported as simple vandalism instead of a hate crime in order to shield their young children from publicity, Officer Davis was furious and protested to her chief." Pinkie. "So that when the one person of interest in the cross-burning, John Vandercamp, appeared in front of Officer Davis, who, the evidence will show, was legally intoxicated at the time . . . I think you get the picture."

"You left out the racist leaflets," Jesse said.

"Those cut both ways. As a defense lawyer, I could use them to tie the kid to the father and make him look less sympathetic. A smart prosecutor would avoid them until he or she is forced to deal with them."

"Good point." Jesse looked at the clock. "Buy you breakfast or an early lunch?"

"Not today. Me being in here with you is one thing." Monty headed for the office door. "The two of us being seen together out there, that's something else. Good luck with the drinking. I mean —"

"I know what you mean, Monty."

53

Daisy's was even busier than it had been the day before. Jesse made sure to give his best fish-eyed stare to anyone who remotely resembled a member of the media. A few of them seemed on the verge of approaching him and then thought better of it. Cole gave Jesse a wave and a smile, which he took to be continuing progress. Chinese proverbs aside, Jesse still couldn't figure out why it mattered.

Daisy wasn't as enthusiastic about Jesse's presence. To say she didn't hide her feelings was an understatement. Before Jesse could order, she said, "You didn't find a place for him to stay, did you? Look, Jesse, I know this is a mess with Alisha and all, but I got a business to run."

"I'll take care of it right now," he said. "Can I borrow him for five minutes?"

"If you're taking care of it, sure thing. What do you want to eat?"

"Let's wait on that. If this doesn't work, you might poison my food."

"Don't give me any ideas, Jesse."

Jesse motioned for Cole to follow him into the alley. Cole looked at Daisy and she waved for him to go.

"What?" Cole asked. "I've got to get back in there."

"You can't sleep here anymore. It's interfering with Daisy's operations."

Cole sneered at Jesse. "So this is where you tell me to get out of town?"

"This is where I tell you you can come stay with me . . . temporarily."

"No way."

"Way I see it, you don't have much choice."

"There's always a choice."

"That's true," Jesse said. "You can blow whatever money you saved so far in two nights at the hotel or one night at a B-and-B, but they won't have room now, with the controversy in town. Or you can split and screw the person who gave you a job and who needs you. Or you can swallow your pride and take my spare bedroom until things settle out. I'll charge you, if that makes you feel better."

"Let me think about it."

"You don't have time to think about it."

Cole was shaking his head, though what he said was "Okay. Okay. I'm doing this for Daisy. I don't abandon people."

"I didn't think you were doing it for me."

"I'll write the address down and I'll call ahead so you can get in. It's about a ten-minute walk from here. You want to go back to work, go ahead."

Cole Slayton held his ground, a puzzled look on his face. "You don't know me and you don't owe me anything. Why would you trust me in your house?"

"Because I know you're not stupid. But even if you were dumb enough to steal from me, there aren't many things that mean that much to me."

He wasn't satisfied with that answer. "But why are you doing this for me?"

"Because, just like you," Jesse said, "I don't abandon people."

Cole sneered at Jesse again, this time with genuine anger in his face. But he didn't give it voice. "I've got to get back."

The kid turned and left Jesse standing in the alley. He was no less confused about Cole Slayton now than he had been the day he met him in the cell at the station.

At the station, Molly told him that Suit and Gabe had agreed to meet.

283

"Did they ask any questions?"

"Only where. They trust you, Jesse. I trust you."

"Tamara and I used to eat at that chain place on the highway."

Molly smiled. "The place with the two-fers and the all-you-can-eat soup and salad?"

"Uh-huh."

"We used to take the girls there when they were little. It's not cool enough for them anymore."

"Tell them to meet there around eight."

"Okay."

Back in his office, Jesse made two more calls. To do what he had in mind, he would need more help than Molly, Suit, and Gabe. Even if they all agreed to be a part of it, he wasn't sure they would be enough. But he didn't see that he had much choice.

54

The soldier had been careful to stay out of the area since the night of the shooting. It was just as well, because he still couldn't wrap his head around what he had been told to do and what he had done. That was the thing about being a good soldier: You follow your orders, even the stupid ones or the ones you know you'll have to answer for on Judgment Day. It's the price you pay afterward, once things settle in, that cost you. It's the time you spend asking yourself the questions about what can't be undone, the hauntings when you close your eyes or when you open them and there is only darkness. He had seen a lot of darkness in his time and now he used it as cover to approach the place the Colonel was staying at.

There weren't any cops around. He'd checked the perimeter, but he wasn't so much worried about the law as he was about one of the Colonel's people. A lot of them, like a lot of the people he'd served with, were good people and true believers, but true belief didn't make you smart or capable. And the last thing he needed was for one of these people to give him away. As far as he knew, only the Colonel was aware of his presence and what he'd done. The rest of them believed exactly what they were led to believe, that John W. had been shot down in cold blood. For a lot of reasons, he wanted it to stay that way, especially that last part. If he had his way, he'd take what he'd done to the grave with him. And on the night of the shooting, he was tempted to get to the grave sooner rather than later. There were times he had felt that way in Iraq and Afghanistan, too, but it had never been as powerful a calling as it was on that night. The wound of it was still fresh enough that he could swear parts of him were missing.

As he'd been instructed to do, he went around to the back of the house. But before he approached, he scanned the area one final time. He stepped out of the woods and walked the fifty paces up to the rear deck. The back door was open. He stepped in and eased the door closed. Stepped into the first bedroom on his right.

Leon Vandercamp stood up out of his

chair, came to the soldier, and threw his arms around him. He held the embrace for a good long time.

"Well done, son. Well done."

But the soldier was preoccupied by the man splayed out on the bed, snoring.

"Don't worry about him," said the Colonel. "James Earl is passed out as always. He is a never-ending source of disappointment to me. But he is my flesh and blood."

"No offense, sir, but John W. was your flesh and blood, too."

"What is the value of a crusade if you're not willing to make great sacrifices to achieve the righteous ends? You, of all men, should understand that. How many mothers' sons did you witness being slaughtered by those heathen mongrels? If I had sacrificed James Earl, who would have cared? I'm not sure even his mother would have blinked. He was always a disappointment to her as well."

"How is John W.'s mother taking it?"

"About how you would expect. She'll be arriving here tomorrow."

"Does she know that —"

"What she knows or doesn't know isn't your concern, son. The cause, *our* cause, is what matters here. Just know that I am pleased with how you handled yourself. I could not be prouder of how you have conducted yourself under terrible duress." Leon Vandercamp placed his hand on the soldier's shoulder but stared down at James Earl. "Why does God burden us so?"

"I don't know, sir."

Vandercamp's face hardened and he took his hand off the soldier. "I wasn't really asking you for the answer. You're good and you're loyal, but metaphysics has never been your strong suit."

"No, sir."

"I'm sorry, son. That was uncalled for."

The soldier moved on. "Why am I here, sir?"

"Did you take care of that other business?"

"The landscaper? Yes, sir."

"Will they find his body?"

The soldier shook his head.

"Good. There may be one or two others who will have to go."

"One or two?" the soldier asked.

Vandercamp lowered his voice to a whisper. "Keep an eye on the people who own this house. You know where their business is located?"

"I do."

"That's right. Of course you do," Vandercamp said.

"Have they given you any trouble, sir?"

"Loose ends. They're loose ends."

"Sir, I know it's not my place to question your orders, but —"

Vandercamp slapped the soldier across the face so hard James Earl stirred from the sound of it.

"You'll do as I tell you. The one time you disobeyed me nearly destroyed us, but you did what you did and now you have certain skills. Now you'll use them when I tell you to."

"Yes, sir."

"Have you built the explosive device?"

"Sir, I have not."

"What are you waiting for? I sincerely hope you're not going to disobey me?"

"No, sir," the soldier lied. He had seen the carnage that IEDs and suicide bombs could do to the human body and had hoped the Colonel would reconsider. Apparently, his hopes had been in vain.

"Okay, then, you have your orders. If they have any contact with the law, I want to know about it immediately. And, son . . ."

"Yes, sir."

"Build it."

The soldier saluted, turned on his heel, and left.

James Earl, still groggy said, "Was that —"

"Go back to sleep, James Earl. He's none of your concern and I'm really not in the mood for you, not tonight."

55

The restaurant was pretty slow, but Jesse asked the manager if he could use the party room.

"Sure," she said. "We've got nothing booked for tonight. We haven't seen you or your girlfriend around lately."

Jesse didn't bother to explain that Tamara hadn't been his girlfriend, nor that she had moved down to Austin to work for the Travis County Medical Examiner. Sometimes explanations led to more questions, and Jesse wasn't up for awkward conversation.

"Having your usual while you wait?" the manager asked as Jesse headed to the back of the restaurant. "Black Label rocks, right?"

"No, thanks. Just a club soda and lime for me."

They drifted into the room one at a time after Jesse: Molly first, Gabe, then Suit. The four of them sat pretty quietly until Healy and then Dylan Taylor showed up. Jesse told them to order drinks if they wanted to and that he had ordered appetizers. But once the appetizers and drinks were delivered and the small talk gotten out of the way, Jesse asked the server not to come back in until he went to get her.

"This about Alisha, Jesse?" Suit asked. Somebody had to.

"Uh-huh." He didn't think his answer came as a surprise to anyone.

"What about her?" Gabe Weathers wanted to know. "I don't think she would do what they're saying she did."

"I don't know," Suit said. "I don't want to believe it, either, but I was there and there was no gun. I also took witness statements."

"You're just pissed at her for the way she acted when we showed up at the Scupper and she pushed back," Gabe said.

"Bull, Gabe. I'm telling you that unless his gun grew wings and flew away, John Vandercamp didn't have a gun."

"Enough," Jesse said. "Before I say another word, I need something from the three of you," Jesse said, pointing at his three cops. "You'll be risking the most out of any of us."

Molly spoke first. "What do you need from us?"

"Either walk out of here right now or promise to keep quiet about this unless you are asked about it under oath. Even if you decide not to help, make that promise now or leave."

Gabe, Suit, and Molly stared at one another, then nodded. None of them got up.

Suit spoke for all of them. "You have our word."

Jesse laid out the case against Alisha the way Monty Bernstein had laid it out for Jesse. Their expressions grew less hopeful as he spoke.

"That's about it," he said when he was finished.

For a moment, no one spoke.

Dylan Taylor, who was basically a stranger to everyone there but Jesse, spoke. "Don't you think it's pretty convenient that John Vandercamp just happened to go to a shooting range only a few hours before he was killed?"

Captain Healy, who was now retired for about a year, stood up and came around by Jesse.

"Convenience doesn't mean it's not true," he said, pointing at the others, who remained seated. "I worked more homicides than all of you combined. I worked more of them than Jesse. But there are way too many coincidences in this case for me to accept. It's a perfect storm."

Gabe said, "I don't like it, but Suit's right, there's no gun. And one thing you've said to me from the minute you hired me was that we followed the evidence on the PPD, not hunches."

"None was found," Jesse said. "That's different than there was no gun."

Molly was skeptical. "But how is it different? Two plus two or six minus two, you get the same result."

Dylan spoke again. "And what, this guy who just happened to go shooting also just happened to magically appear out of nowhere right in front of Alisha as she came out of the Gull? C'mon. It's a setup."

"It sounds like a setup, but the staties aren't in the business of proving it's a setup," Jesse said. "They are following the evidence, and the evidence makes Alisha look guilty as hell."

Healy agreed. "Mary Weld's an excellent detective, but she's not looking for exculpatory evidence. Her case is pretty damned good, and when the rest of the forensics come back, I think it will be rock-solid."

"Then what are we here for?" Suit asked.

"Mary Weld's job may not be to look for

exculpatory evidence or to prove it was a setup, but it can be our job," Jesse said. "I'm not going to lie to you. Even if we somehow find the gun or mitigating evidence, Alisha is probably done as a cop. So this isn't about saving her job. It's about keeping her out of prison. I know Healy and Dylan are in. But the three of us aren't enough. If you need a minute, we can step —"

"I'm in," Molly said.

Gabe was next. "Me also."

Everyone turned to Suit.

"You don't see me going anywhere, do you? But what are we supposed to do to help?"

"Mostly surveillance," Jesse said.

Molly raised her eyebrow. "Mostly?"

"The other stuff will be handled by Healy, Dylan, and me. And no texting or e-mails. Calls only, and no messages with details."

Gabe asked, "When do we start?"

Jesse smiled. "We just did."

56

Jesse got to his condo before Cole, and seeing all the boxes, ninety percent of them still untouched since he moved in, made him realize just how little time he'd spent there alone and awake. In fact, he had spent very little time alone since rehab. He had never feared being alone. In spite of Jenn, Diana, and all the other women who had been in his life, Jesse liked to think he was at his best on his own. It was that self-contained thing Molly always talked about. But in rehab he had been warned over and over again about the dangers of time alone and had been counseled to find ways to fill up the empty hours he used to spend fantasizing about drinking, anticipating the rituals of drinking, and drinking itself.

His condo was still a mess. The floors and his furniture were piled high with boxes. He walked through the maze of cardboard, trying to figure out what things were in which boxes. He hadn't been around to pack up his stuff and had paid someone to do it for him. The boxes were labeled, but not specifically enough for him to find exactly what he needed to make up the guest bed. He hadn't even fully done up his own bedroom. Since his return, he'd been living out of his duffel and suitcase like a traveling salesman. The one thing he had managed to hang in his living room was his framed poster of his old drinking buddy, Hall of Fame shortstop Ozzie Smith. Other than his job, there had been only two constants in Jesse's life: drinking and the silent Wizard of Oz. Now it was down to Ozzie.

Jesse checked his watch and worked out the timing. Even if he found all the stuff he needed in the next five minutes, it was still way too late to get to a meeting. Boston was out of the question, and the close-by meetings were almost done at this point. He guessed he could call Bill, then realized Bill was probably at the meeting at the church. It wasn't so much that he felt like drinking, but he could feel himself missing the rituals that surrounded it. He remembered, with a smile, how at the end of his day he used to start thinking about getting back to the house. How during his traditional drive through town, he would rehearse the rituals in his head. Somehow, the anticipation of the drink made the drink taste that much better. As he stood there, he could almost taste the Black Label on his tongue, feel it going down, but his reverie was disturbed by the sound of his front door lock turning.

As Cole Slayton came through the door, several emotions crossed his face before he lapsed into his usual disdainful expression. But unlike when they'd first met, Cole couldn't keep that look for long. Although it had been only several days since he'd met Jesse, there had been a softening in him. That first day, the disdain was palpable and it seemed to come easily and naturally. Now Cole seemed to have to work at it, almost as if keeping with some vow he had taken or promise he had made to himself. What Jesse couldn't figure out was whether Cole's attitude was a general dislike of authority or if it was specific to him. Maybe it was both.

Jesse had met a lot of people over the course of his life who carried rage around inside them like the molten core at the center of the earth. And not all of them were people he'd met as a cop. He'd come across many of them during his time in the minors. Some matured and got past it. Some used it to fuel their competitiveness. Those men, the ones fueled by their rage, the ones who could never let it go, were the men afraid of who they might be if they didn't have the rage anymore. He understood them better now than he had ever understood them before. Jesse wasn't sure who he would be if he stayed sober.

"I didn't think you'd be here before me," Cole said.

"Neither did I, but I didn't have time to make your bed."

"Just give me the sheets and stuff. I'll do it."

Jesse laughed, "I was trying to find that stuff when you came in."

"This place is a mess."

"I haven't gotten around to unpacking."

"Yeah, I guess it's been a little crazy in town." Cole noticed the Ozzie poster. "What's with the poster?"

"Do you know who that is?"

Cole's face hardened again. "I know who Ozzie Smith is. But why do you have a poster of him on your living room wall? I mean, there's nothing hung up except that. You got your favorite rock-star poster in your bedroom?"

"Funny."

"No, really, what's with the poster?"

"He was the best at what he did," Jesse said.

"I don't get it. You think he has a Jesse Stone poster up on his wall?"

"He's a reminder to me."

"Of what?"

"Of a lot of things."

"Like . . ."

"To be who I am."

"You ever give a straight answer?"

"I was a very good shortstop, but I could never play it the way Ozzie did. I had a great arm and good hands, but he was like an acrobat or a ballet dancer. I used to dream about playing against him, but I never got the chance."

Cole said, "That would frustrate me, having him up there like that, reminding me."

"My relationship with that poster is complicated."

"Whatever." Cole waved his hand dismissively. "You gonna give me the house rules now?"

"You consider yourself a grown man?"

"Yeah."

"Then I don't have to give you rules. C'mon, let's find you some bedding."

57

When they finally had Cole's bed made up, the place looked like even more of a mess. Jesse asked if Cole wanted something to eat.

"I've got stuff to make omelets," he said, "but that's about it."

"I've eaten a lot of eggs since I started at Daisy's, but if that's all you got, sure."

Jesse stepped into the kitchen and waved for Cole to follow him in.

"How is it working there?"

"Daisy's good to work for. She doesn't expect anything of me she won't do herself. Let's face it, she didn't have to let me stay at the restaurant. She didn't have to hire me at all."

"You guys get along?"

"Yeah," Cole said without hesitation. "She is one of the only people I ever met who doesn't bullshit me."

Jesse laughed. "It's not in her. Gets her in trouble sometimes."

"People are screwed up like that. They'd rather get lied to."

"You always want to hear the truth?"

"No, I'm just tired of liars."

"Everybody's a liar, one way or the other."

Cole smirked. "Even the Paradise chief of police?"

"Uh-huh. Even him," Jesse said. "What do you like in your omelet? I've got pancetta, Jack, cheddar cheese —"

"Pancetta?"

"It's Italian bacon. It's not smoked like American bacon."

"Pretty fancy stuff for a cop."

"A woman I knew liked it in her omelets. I learned to like it."

"What happened to her?" Cole asked. "She dump you?"

"She was murdered."

Cole looked gut-punched and, for the first time since they'd met, Jesse caught a glimpse of the wounded little boy beneath the veneer of rage and disdain.

"I'm really sorry. I didn't mean to —"

"That's okay, Cole. I didn't want to lie to you."

"Still —"

"Forget it," Jesse said, putting the omelet pan on the stove and throwing in some butter and olive oil. "I also have chorizo, onions, and peppers."

"Onions, Jack cheese, and chorizo."

Jesse diced some onion and threw it in the pan, and when the onions became translucent, he broke up the bright red sausage into crumbles and watched them brown.

"How long ago did it happen?" Cole asked.

"Not too long. We were engaged. Some days it feels like yesterday. Others, a million years ago."

Cole apologized again.

"No," Jesse said, pulling his cell phone out of his pocket, "it's really okay. This is Diana."

He handed the phone to Cole.

He stared at the photo for several seconds. "She is — was beautiful."

"She was all of that. Smarter and braver than I'll ever be."

Jesse broke three eggs into a mixing bowl, added a touch of cream, whipped them up, added salt and pepper. He poured the eggs over the onions and sausage. He flipped the omelet over, laid two pieces of Jack cheese down the center, and folded the omelet into a half-moon, sliding it onto a plate.

"All I've got to drink is water or soda water."

"Water's fine. Thanks. Aren't you going to eat?"

"No, I'm good. Let me ask you something. You getting any of the Saviors of Society eating at Daisy's?"

His mouth full, Cole nodded. When he swallowed, he said, "A few, yeah."

"How did Daisy react?"

"She told me their money was as good as anyone else's and that as much as she hated what they stood for, she wasn't a hypocrite. She said that if she refused to serve them, it would give power to people who didn't want to serve people like her."

"How were they, the people you waited on?"

Cole shrugged. "They just seemed like people eating lunch or breakfast. They didn't try to recruit me or anything."

"That's the problem with evil," Jesse said.

"What is?"

"The people who practice it look like everybody else."

Cole laughed. "My mom always said the devil wouldn't have horns, but that he'd look like the mailman."

"Smart woman."

Cole smiled, but then his old self returned. "Thanks for the food," he said, picking up his plate and bringing it to the sink. "I'm going to bed."

58

Jesse could see some resemblance between Clarissa Vandercamp and her late son. John W., like James Earl, had Leon's eyes but otherwise didn't share much in the way of looks with his father or brother. Clarissa Vandercamp was a sturdily built woman, blond, with high cheekbones and sad eyes. Jesse guessed the sad eyes were inevitable. He wondered if the sadness was in her even before her son's death. She was younger than he expected. She was certainly too young to be James Earl's mother, as they seemed to be about the same age.

Jesse came out from behind his desk to greet her. Molly stood behind the woman, off to one side.

"Can we get you anything?" Jesse asked.

Clarissa Vandercamp stared directly into Jesse's eyes. "Justice for my boy," she said, a quiver in her voice.

Leon Vandercamp's pleas and protestations always sounded like sound bites or propaganda to Jesse, as if microphones were recording his every word or a large audience was listening. With Clarissa Vandercamp, it was personal. Jesse led her to the seat facing his desk.

"Would you like some water or coffee?" he asked.

"No, thank you," she said, her voice steady. She turned toward Molly. "Does she have to stay?"

"It's policy," Jesse said. "What can I do for you?"

"I think I already made that clear."

"Mrs. Vandercamp, I'm sorry, but I have nothing to do with the investigation into your son's death. I thought your husband would have told you."

Her skin flushed and her mouth went from sad to angry. She tried to wipe the look away before Jesse could see it but was unsuccessful.

"I haven't seen Leon," she said. "I've been on the road for hours and came here first thing."

"I'm sorry. Are you sure you don't want coffee?"

Clarissa Vandercamp looked at Molly. "Black with two sugars, please."

Jesse nodded for Molly to go ahead.

"The investigation is being headed by the state police," Jesse said as he wrote. "This is the number of Detective Lieutenant Mary Weld. She's the person you need to speak to about your son's death."

"Thank you. I'd like to see my boy now."

"Are you here alone, Mrs. Vandercamp?"

"I don't see what that's got to do with anything or that it's your business."

Jesse said, "No matter how prepared you think you are for this, there's no way to be ready. And your son's been the subject of an autopsy. That makes it worse for some people. It might be easier if you weren't alone."

Her face, which only seconds before had been red with anger, blanched. Jesse noticed.

"Maybe your husband can meet you there, or James Earl."

The mention of James Earl's name changed Clarissa Vandercamp's expression yet again.

"James Earl's a good-for-nothing and he's not mine."

Molly came back into the office. "Here you go," she said, handing Clarissa Vandercamp the coffee.

"Thank you."

"You can go, Molly," Jesse said.

Molly gave Jesse a stern look. "Are you sure?"

"Go ahead, but stay close."

Jesse waited for Clarissa Vandercamp to take a few sips of coffee before he spoke again.

"I didn't think James Earl could be your son, but —"

"Both James Earl and Lee are Gloria's boys. Gloria was Leon's first wife."

"Divorced?"

"Dead."

Curious as he was, he didn't think it was appropriate to interrogate a grieving mother. But he was interested in the mention of a third son.

Jesse said, "You mentioned another son, Lee?"

She made that face again. "James Earl's the oldest, but he's always been a screwup. Lee Harvey, now, he was Leon's pride and joy until he went and joined up."

" 'Joined up'?"

"Enlisted in the Army right after the 9/11 conspiracy. Gotta give the Israelis and the Saudis their due. Had almost everybody fooled, but Leon saw right through that, the way they got together and got us to fight their wars for them."

Jesse kept calm, ignoring the conspiracy

theory. "Lee enlisted?"

"Leon and I were just newly married back then, and Johnny . . ." She stopped, bowed her head, and swallowed hard. "John was so young. Lee had just turned eighteen and there was nothing Leon could do to stop him — not legally, anyhow. Doesn't mean he didn't try. He told Lee that it was all a big lie and that he wouldn't really be fighting for us. Told Lee that the Army was a sewer, full of nig— blacks and all types of inferior peoples. But Lee wouldn't listen to reason. They didn't talk for years after that."

Jesse wanted to push her but decided to let it go for now. "Are you sure you don't want someone to go with you. Molly can —"

She stood. "No. I'm okay, but I would appreciate you calling ahead."

"I'll do it right after you leave."

Molly stepped back into Jesse's office after he was done speaking to the ME.

Molly asked, "How was she after I left?"

"She's a believer and a grieving mother. Molly, do me a favor."

"Sure, Jesse."

"Try and get hold of the U.S. Army service records for Lee Harvey Vandercamp."

"Lee Harvey as in Lee Harvey Oswald?"

"Makes sense. James Earl, John Wilkes, Lee Harvey."

Without another word, Molly turned and left.

59

Jesse had time to start digging. Since he was convinced that all of the incidents in recent weeks were connected, he decided to go back to the beginning, to the incident at the bar between Alisha and the bikers.

The Scupper was located in the heart of the Swap and, for many years, was as close to a dive bar as you were going to find in Paradise. Over the years, a thousand names were carved into its booths and walls, and it still smelled like cigarette smoke twenty years after smoking had been banned. It had once been the favorite haunt of the fishermen who lived in the Swap and who had once been a huge part of Paradise's economy. It was also traditionally the place where the fathers of Paradise brought their sons for their first legal drinks. Lately, it had become a place where the few hipsters in town crossed paths with the Boston transplants. The O'Brien family had owned it for all the years Jesse had been chief, and it was Joey, the oldest of the O'Brien children, who had been tending bar and called the PPD the day the bikers came into town.

There was no one seated at the bar or in the booths when Jesse got there. Joey O'Brien was behind the bar cutting fruit, a towel slung over one shoulder.

He nodded. "Jesse."

"Joey."

"Johnnie Black? You want it straight up or with club soda? As you can see, I got plenty of limes."

"How about some club soda and two of those lime wedges?"

O'Brien half smiled at Jesse and winked knowingly. "One day at a time, huh, Jesse?"

"That obvious?"

"Only to a fellow traveler," Joey said.

"How long?"

"Going on two years now."

Jesse gave the barman a skeptical look. "C'mon, Joey, we had a couple of snorts together a few months ago."

Joey gave Jesse a full smile and pulled a half-empty bottle of expensive bourbon off the shelf behind the bar. He grabbed two rocks glasses and poured doubles in both.

"Go ahead, Jesse, pick it up, take a slug." Joey didn't wait for Jesse, grabbed the glass and took the double in a single gulp. When he was done, he took Jesse's glass and drank it down, too. Then he laughed. "It's tea. You brew it just right with the right blend of leaves and it looks like good bourbon. As a bar owner, it doesn't help the image not to drink with the customers."

He fixed Jesse's soda and lime. "If you're not here to drink, what can I do for you?"

"A few weeks back, when those bikers were in town, you called the PPD."

"Sorry, Jesse, I meant to ask, how's Alisha doing?"

"Not so good. I can't talk about it."

"I understand, but man, those bikers were pushing her hard," Joey said. "I don't think I could've controlled myself the way she did. Then one of them called her a — the n-word. I guess that set her off a little. I would've smacked the guy after that."

"You don't have surveillance cameras in here, do you?"

Joey shook his head. "Only on the back door and the alley."

"You wouldn't have the footage from that day?"

"Give me a day or two and I can check."

"Can you describe any of the bikers?"

Joey shrugged. "They looked like bikers. I don't know. The men were bald — most of them, anyway. They wore black leather jackets and black boots. You know."

"How many?"

"Ten. Maybe fifteen. I wasn't counting. Sorry."

"No problem. You didn't know something would happen."

Jesse sipped his club soda, giving Joey O'Brien time to think. As a detective, Jesse had learned that there was a time for rapid-fire questions and a time to ease off the pedal. Silence and time could be more effective than pressure or threats. It worked.

"You know the funny thing, Jesse?"

"What?"

"Thinking about it, they acted kinda strange. When they first came in, they behaved themselves. Just went over there in those back booths," Joey said, pointing to his left, "and ordered a few pitchers. Then it was almost like showtime."

" 'Showtime'?"

"I don't know. I know this sounds stupid, but it seemed staged. All of a sudden one of them stands up and starts spewing crap about mixed races and religion. It was like he was trying to provoke a fight. That's when I called. I don't know. Maybe I'm just remembering it wrong or my mind's put it together that way." He shrugged again. "But when Alisha showed up, their focus turned just to her. Almost like they expected her to come. I'm not sure that helps any."

"Me, either, but thanks." Jesse finished his soda, stood, and waved to Joey.

"I'll check on that footage for you. And, Jesse . . ."

"Uh-huh."

"Good for you, man. Life's better without alcohol in it."

"Better not let your customers hear you."

"Most of them can handle it. We can't."

Jesse left the Scupper, walking out of the dark bar into the sunlight. He wasn't sure what Joey had to say about the bikers was any help beyond reinforcing his belief that everything that had gone on recently was of a piece. He also wasn't sure about that other thing Joey had said. As far as Jesse was concerned, the jury was still out on whether his life was any better without alcohol in it.

60

It had been a long time since Jesse had seen or spoken to anyone in Anthony deAngelo's family. For the first few years after he was killed, there had been a lot of contact between the PPD, Paradise town officials, and the family, but everyone had since moved on. It was the nature of things. Word was Anthony's folks had retired to the Carolinas somewhere. His wife had remarried and moved down to Chelsea.

Every time one of his cops would tell a story involving Anthony, or sometimes on the date marking the anniversary of his murder, Jesse would consider calling deAngelo's parents or his wife. He could never think of what to say or how to make it not be awkward. It was strange how he had managed to be a comfort to so many homicide victims' families but couldn't find the words for Anthony's family. Maybe that was why it had taken him this long to check on

Drake Daniels's story about having grown up with Anthony and about how Anthony had shared the details of Tammy Portugal's murder.

Once again, Jesse had thought about calling but decided dropping by the address in Chelsea on his way to the AA meeting at the Episcopal church was the right thing to do. Sophia lived near Mary O'Malley Park in a red-brick house in the Admirals Hill section of Chelsea. Jesse parked his Explorer on the street and in the fading daylight rang the doorbell.

"Coming," said a woman on the other side of the door.

When the door pulled back, both Sophia and Jesse stood in silence.

"Chief Stone?" She tilted her head, trying to make sense of the man at her door. "Jesse, what are — I'm sorry, come in. Come in."

"Hello, Sophia."

He offered his hand as she moved to embrace him, and then, seeing each had misread the other, switched. They stopped and laughed. They hugged. Jesse followed Sophia into the kitchen.

"Sit. Sit. Can I get you something to drink?" she asked. "I'm getting dinner ready for the kids."

"No, thank you."

They exchanged the expected small talk. Sophia explained about how she had met Ronnie on a dating site and that they had hit it off immediately. That Ronnie had a good job at an investment banking firm and that they had two kids, both boys, the oldest named Anthony. *Ronnie insisted.* Jesse kept it simple, talking mostly about Molly, Suit, and Peter. He kept the conversation far away from his personal life.

"So, Jesse, not that I'm not glad to see you, but why are you here after all this time?"

"Do you remember if Anthony ever mentioned a friend named Drake —"

"Drake Daniels," she said, making a face not unlike Clarissa Vandercamp had made at the mention of James Earl. "I remember Drake."

"I take it you didn't like him much."

"How about not at all. Anthony and him grew up together. You know how that is, growing up with somebody. You don't see their faults because, well, you're friends and you don't see them or you look past them."

"Uh-huh."

"Well, that was Anthony. He couldn't see what a jerk Drake was."

"How so?"

"What's this about, Jesse?"

Jesse explained about how Felicity Wileford was found in the school parking lot with the word *slut* written across her belly in red lipstick. He told her about how Drake Daniels spotted the similarities between the Wileford case and Tammy Portugal's murder.

"Daniels said Anthony had shared the details of the murder scene."

Sophia bowed her head, turning away from Jesse. "You have no idea how badly that murder scene affected Anthony. He had bad dreams about that poor woman's body left out there in the middle of the parking lot."

"So Anthony would have shared the details with Drake?"

She nodded.

"Sophia, if you don't mind me asking, why did you think Drake was a jerk?"

"He . . . he didn't like people."

"People?"

"Black people, especially, but other people, too."

"What other people?"

"Pretty much everybody who wasn't white or Christian."

Jesse bought what she was saying, but he felt there was something else.

"There's more to it than that. Isn't there, Sophia?"

"One time, Anthony went out to get some beer for us and Drake . . . he cornered me in the kitchen and . . . He tried forcing me to do something. I was going to tell Anthony. I was, but I was afraid he would do something stupid and get in trouble. I miss him sometimes, Jesse, but sometimes I forget what he sounded like or felt like."

"Are you happy now?"

"Very."

"Anthony would be good with that," Jesse said. "That's what counts."

Jesse had gotten what he came for, but it didn't necessarily clear anything up. Daniels had told the truth. Anthony deAngelo had shared the details of the Portugal murder. And if Sophia was to be believed, Daniels was also a racist and a molester. Did that mean he had anything to do with what had been done to Felicity Wileford? Maybe not. But maybe it did.

61

Bill was there. Anya was not, nor was Edward Perry anywhere to be seen. Jesse shook Bill's hand and patted him on the shoulder.

"Has Anya been here?"

"I haven't seen her," Bill said. "Why?"

"The older guy she was sitting with last time."

"What about him?"

"Good thing I turned your offer of coffee down. When I was walking back to my Explorer, I found him on top of her, tearing her clothes off."

"Holy shit! What did you do?"

"I broke his nose and took his driver's license."

Bill laughed and shook his head. "I get breaking his nose. He's lucky you didn't do worse, but why'd you take his —"

"I told him I was sending his license to Vinnie Morris."

Bill's eyes got wide at the mention of Morris's name. That was a common reaction among Bostonians. Jesse had known Morris for many years now, knew his reputation, but he sometimes forgot that Morris's reputation was well deserved.

"You know Morris?" Bill asked, a hesitant look on his face.

"I do."

"You friends?"

"Not exactly. You ever have dealings with him when you played for the other team?"

Bill rolled up his left sleeve and showed Jesse a bulge on top of his forearm. "Broke it in two places so close together the bone wouldn't knit right."

"What happened?"

"Deal went bad. I had a guy lined up to take some merchandise from one of Gino Fish's boys at a fair price, but the guy got cold feet before the exchange was made. I had to scramble to find a new buyer and the new buyer knew he had me. He paid a dime on the dollar instead of a quarter. Morris took it out on me as an example."

"Sorry."

"Don't be. It helped wake me up. Besides, I was the lucky one," Bill said. "The original buyer ate through a feeding tube until the day he died."

"Hard to stay clean when you play in the mud."

Bill laughed again. "Same could be said of a lot of the cops I've known."

Jesse nodded. Although he was usually on the right side of things, Jesse knew he had made a lot of compromises he never imagined himself making when he graduated from the academy. In the end, it was doing right that mattered, no matter what it took to do it.

"I've been watching the news, Jesse. You got real trouble in Paradise."

"Un-huh."

"You think you're gonna be able to keep a lid on things?"

"I don't know. A lot is riding on the findings of the investigation and what the prosecutors choose to do with them."

Before Bill could say another word, Jesse's cell buzzed in his pocket. He breathed a sigh of relief when he saw it was from Connor Cavanaugh. This made two calls he owed Connor, but with all that was going on, and given that the meeting was about to start, Jesse let it go to voicemail.

After the meeting, Jesse bought Bill coffee and then they went their separate ways. Jesse's separate way took him back to the run-down factory building in Newmarket Square. He wasn't completely sure why he was there except that he was concerned for Anya. He didn't want one jerk to ruin AA for her and drive her back to drinking. Jesse understood the price people paid for being violated. Even if he had stopped Perry from doing his worst, Jesse knew Anya had blamed herself. He sat there in his Explorer for about a half-hour, watching, waiting. Nothing happened. No one went in or out of the door Anya had used when he dropped her off. He drove around to the alley. The motorcycles were gone. And seeing that, Jesse was gone, too.

62

It was a bad day to begin with. Lundquist had called to tell him that Felicity Wileford's parents had arrived in Swan Harbor and, after their prayers and good-byes, had removed their daughter from life support.

"She didn't last ten minutes without the machines," Lundquist said. "It's my case now, officially, but you've got your own headaches. I just thought you'd want to know."

"I don't know if this is any help, but last night I had a conversation with Anthony deAngelo's wife."

"Refresh my memory."

"He was one of my officers who was killed in the line of —"

"Right. The cop who was killed at the mall. The one at the Tammy Portugal crime scene who was pals with the Swan Harbor cop. What about it?"

"She says that the Swan Harbor cop,

Daniels, *was* an old friend of deAngelo's, but that he was also pretty much a racist ass."

"Jesse, you know we don't like to say it out loud, but a lot of —"

"Yeah, we had 'em in L.A., too, and even here when I first got the job. But here's the kicker. She says Daniels once cornered her and tried to force himself on her."

There were a few seconds of silence, but Jesse could almost hear what Lundquist was thinking. He could hear it because he had had the same thought.

"You thinking that maybe Daniels was involved in the Wileford attack?" Lundquist asked.

"Remember when I first talked to Daniels I mentioned those volunteer firemen who started fires so they could rescue people and be the hero?"

"I remember."

"What if Daniels wasn't trying to be the hero but trying to save his own neck?"

"Come again."

"Let's say he's one of the guys who attacked Wileford. Things went too far or not far enough. Who knows what was in their minds? Either way, they've pretty much beaten her to death. He remembers the Tammy Portugal case and rigs things up to mimic what happened to her. But he gets nervous, thinking maybe no one will make the connection, so he makes a mistake. He points it out and draws attention to himself instead of away from himself."

"That's a lot of what-ifs and maybes, Jesse."

"But worth looking into."

"Absolutely."

"I'm persona non grata in Swan Harbor these days, but the first places I'd be looking at would be the stores in and around town that sell the brand of lipstick they used to write *slut* on her abdomen."

"Maybe I already figured that out for myself."

"Sorry."

"You still think this is all connected?"

"More and more."

"Me, too."

"You going to put someone on Daniels?" Jesse asked.

"When we get off the phone."

"Keep me posted."

Lundquist hung up before answering.

Then things got worse. The phone rang. Molly came running into Jesse's office.

"Jesse, that was Connie Walker's assistant on the phone."

"Uh-huh."

"She says you should turn on the TV."

"What channel?" he asked, clicking on the old set.

"Any."

And there she was, Detective Lieutenant Mary Weld in front of town hall, standing behind a lectern crowded with microphones. Cameras clicked away. There was a low murmur in the background. At Weld's back was Ron Kennealy, the DA. Mayor Walker was off to her left. Weld signaled that she was about to begin, and the murmur quieted.

"I'm Detective Lieutenant Mary Weld of the Massachusetts State Police. I was charged with leading the investigation into the fatal shooting of John Wilkes Vandercamp by Paradise Police Department officer Alisha Davis. We have completed that investigation and have shared our findings with both District Attorney Kennealy and with Mayor Walker, both of whom will make brief statements and take questions from you following my statement.

"My team has found no evidence to support the claims by Officer Davis, who was legally intoxicated at the time, that she was fired upon by Mr. Vandercamp. Furthermore, we retrieved no weapon on or near

329

Mr. Vandercamp's body. And while there is strong evidence to support the fact that Mr. Vandercamp tried to evade Officer Davis, we can find no justification for the level of force used in this matter. As to the charges Officer Davis will face, those will be determined by Mr. Kennealy. On a personal note, I want you to be aware that I take no pleasure in these findings, but that it is crucial for all law enforcement agencies that the people we serve have confidence in us and our decision-making processes. To that end, we must hold the people charged with upholding the law to the highest standards. Now I'll turn the microphones over to District Attorney Kennealy."

Jesse turned off the set. Molly was about to ask why, but one look at Jesse's face changed her mind.

63

An hour later, Jesse was standing in front of Connie Walker's desk and he was no less angry than he had been while watching Weld's statement on TV.

"I know you're upset, Jesse, but there wasn't anything I could do to stop it."

"In football you get a two-minute warning. Your assistant gave me five seconds."

"I didn't have much more time myself. Kennealy marched in here, told me the investigation was over, gave me a summary of the findings, and announced there was going to be a press conference. He thought I should prepare something to say. So, you see, I was caught by surprise as well."

"How about the fact that I should have been there?"

"Bad optics."

Jesse wasn't having it. "Bullshit. You didn't want me standing there looking unhappy or trying to defend Alisha."

"Can you blame me? It was better this way. You aren't associated with or tainted by what Alisha did —"

"Is alleged to have done."

"C'mon, Jesse, really? Aren't you always the man touting that your cops follow the evidence and not their hunches? Look at the evidence."

He wasn't going to argue. Jesse knew that everything Weld had pointed to Alisha shooting an unarmed man, but he could not get the series of coincidences out of his head.

The mayor wasn't finished. "And even if you believe that Vandercamp had a gun that grew legs and ran away, there's no getting around the fact that Alisha was drunk. I mean, for goodness' sakes, Jesse, John Vandercamp wasn't even actually a suspect. He was someone you wanted to question. Use your smarts. Let it go. You and I will both survive the hit if you ease off. You hired her and I backed you. Everyone makes mistakes. Voters can be very forgiving."

"Is everything calculus for you, Connie?"

"For better or worse, I'm a professional politician, Jesse. That's how it works. You know the saying about how no one wants to see the sausage being made . . . Well, imagine if the sausage was being made by someone who didn't know how to make sausage. Politics is sometimes an ugly process, but I'm good at it and I know what I'm doing."

Jesse hated politics. Most cops did. Still, Connie Walker had a point. Politics was bad business, but police work could be sausage making at its ugliest.

When Jesse tracked Mary Weld down, she was eating a grilled cheese sandwich at Daisy's. He didn't bother asking the statie if she minded him sitting across from her. Neither Daisy nor Cole approached the table. You didn't have to know Jesse Stone at all to read the keep-your-distance look on his face.

"You hung Alisha out to dry," Jesse said.

"Not my call," Weld said, putting her sandwich down.

"It's SOP to announce you've finished your investigation and that you're turning over the findings to the DA. I get that. But since when do you hold a press conference to announce your findings?"

"Since I got told to."

"By?"

She shook her head.

Jesse said, "That's how it is?"

"That's how it is. I take orders just like

333

everybody else."

"How is she supposed to get a fair trial now?"

Weld looked around, and when she was sure no one could hear her except Jesse, she leaned forward. "There won't be a trial."

"What do you mean?"

"Look, Chief Stone, I didn't like what I did today any more than you, but think about it. Your town is full of people looking for someone on the other side to light the match and start the fire. What my releasing the findings did was to pour water on everybody's matches. By the time they dry, the warring factions will have moved on."

"At the price of doing the right thing."

She laughed without joy. "The right thing. What's that?"

"You denied my cop of any chance to clear her name."

Weld had had enough. "Your cop was drunk and emptied her clip down a darkened alley into an unarmed man, so don't give me any right-thing or justice crap, Chief. The DA will go to a grand jury, get an indictment on the most serious charges, and then, with a nod and wink from all sides, plead her down and give her most of her life back. John Vandercamp won't have that chance."

Weld stood up and threw a ten on the table.

"What about your sandwich?" Jesse asked.

"Lost my appetite."

She left.

Jesse didn't have much of an appetite, either. It seemed to him that almost everyone was willing to do whatever it took to make this all go away. He understood how Mayor Walker and Detective Lieutenant Weld saw it. Their way was certainly the easier way, but it wasn't the right way, and no one could convince him that it was.

64

That late afternoon, following her shift, Molly Crane drove into Swan Harbor and parked across the street from the offices of Garrison's Landscaping. Jim Garrison's Escalade EXT was right out front. Dylan Taylor was also in Swan Harbor, waiting for Drake Daniels to come off his shift. Jesse trusted Lundquist would keep his word to put someone on Officer Daniels. What Jesse couldn't be sure of was Lundquist's willingness to share information. It was easy enough for Healy to find his assignment for the evening, because as soon as the sun went down, James Earl Vandercamp headed to the nearest bar. Suit followed Leon Vandercamp.

Jesse pulled his Explorer into the parking lot of the Magic Valley Handgun and Rifle Range. There were two alleged coincidences that really stuck in Jesse's craw: that John Vandercamp just happened to be shooting handguns in the hours prior to his death and that he then fatefully appeared twenty feet in front of Alisha Davis when she stepped out of the Gray Gull. It struck Jesse that these things were too damned convenient to be believed. With Vandercamp's clothing and skin covered in gunshot residue and in the absence of a weapon on the scene, it would be impossible to find evidence to support Alisha's claim that she had been fired upon first. Jesse thought it even more unlikely that serendipity was responsible for John Vandercamp's appearance at the Gull. As he opened the Explorer's door, he thought, *First things first.*

But before Jesse got out of his SUV, his phone vibrated in his pocket. He pulled out the phone and got back inside the Ford. It was Connor Cavanaugh again, and this time Jesse answered.

"Connor, I'm sorry I haven't returned your calls."

"No problem, Jesse. I know this has been a crazy week for you."

"*Crazy*'s one word for it."

That was followed by a long silence. Jesse put an end to it.

"So, Connor, what's up? You called me, remember?"

"That Cole guy, the one who stayed here

for a few days."

"What about him?"

"You know I had to pack up his things in a hurry, right?"

"I do. What's this about?"

"Well, Jesse, I don't know if this means anything, but when I was packing up the kid's stuff I found something that was a little . . . I don't know, strange. Weird, maybe. I'm not sure."

"You've got my attention. What did you find?"

"A picture."

"A picture?"

"A photo."

"Of?"

"You, I think, and a woman. She was very pretty — beautiful, really. She had dark hair and a real dark tan and a great smile. You were much younger, with sunglasses on, and you were wearing an LAPD uniform. She was sitting on your lap with her arms around your neck."

Jesse said, "Did it say anything on the back? Was it dated?"

"I don't think so. I don't like snooping at personal stuff, and if I didn't think I recognized you in the picture, I wouldn't've even looked as closely as I did."

"I understand."

"What do you think it means, Jesse?"

"I'm not sure. Thanks for the heads-up."

"Like I said, no problem. I just thought you should know."

Connor's call had brought it all back to him in a rush. Jesse didn't like focusing on his life in L.A. The way things ended for him out there with Jenn's cheating, his dive down the bottle, and his getting fired, it was all pretty ugly stuff. One thing was clear, the woman in the photo wasn't Jenn. He'd dated a lot of women before hooking up with Jenn, but there weren't any very serious relationships before her, not in L.A. He tried matching Connor's description of the woman with a name. Problem was, it fit a few women from those days. That wasn't the real issue. The issue was why Cole Slayton should have a photo of Jesse with any woman. Whatever the reason, it would have to wait. Jesse walked across the parking lot and through the range's front door.

The somewhat acrid smell of gunpowder was noticeable as Jesse stepped inside. He recognized the man at the front counter from the video Weld had shown him.

"Can I help you, Officer?" the counterman asked.

"That obvious?"

"You work a place like this, you get to

recognize professionals from the buffs and the freaks." Then, realizing what he'd said, the counterman looked around to make sure no one other than Jesse had heard him.

Jesse flashed his chief's shield. "I'm Jesse Stone, Paradise police chief."

The smile slid right off the counterman's face. "Tough news today about your cop. You're not here to shoot, are you?"

Jesse shook his head. "I'd like to look at all the footage from the day John Vandercamp shot here."

Jesse could see the counterman's wheels turning. "Look, Chief, it's not my place. Maybe I better call the owner and see what he says."

"You could do that and I could bring a warrant. But that would piss me off and I would have to ask the state police to sit outside in the parking lot night and day for the next few weeks, maybe searching some of the patrons' vehicles for weapons that —"

"Right this way, Chief."

65

Jesse wasn't exactly sure what he was looking for, but that was sometimes what police work was all about. It was especially true of reviewing surveillance tape. Luckily for Jesse, he didn't need to run through endless footage, because he already knew the time John Vandercamp had arrived and the time he'd left.

"It's cued up, Chief," said the counterman. "I've got to get back out front."

Although he was fifty feet removed from the indoor range and two sets of concrete walls separated the office from the range, Jesse could still hear the dull echoes of shots. When he listened carefully, he could distinguish between the eager amateurs who were there for their first times or there on a dare. They were the ones wasting their ammo with long bursts or the ones who kept pulling the triggers on their rented pistols. The experienced shooters took their time between shots. They fired two-round bursts. They weren't interested in shredding their targets into confetti. Jesse stopped listening and turned back to the monitor.

The screen was divided in four for the four cameras that covered the front entrance, the counter, the shop, and the indoor range. Jesse hadn't asked how to isolate footage from the individual cameras, because he wanted to see as much as he could see as fast as he could see it. He had no doubt that the counterman was back up front calling the gun range owner, who would be displeased. The relationship between law enforcement agencies, who often supported more restrictive gun laws, and the people who profited from the sale and use of firearms was an uneasy and frequently unfriendly one.

Jesse watched John Vandercamp shoot. It was obvious he knew how to handle the weapons he had rented. Though he didn't know Vandercamp at all, it seemed to Jesse that something had been bothering him. The video wasn't crystal clear, but it looked to Jesse as if Vandercamp's arms were shaking and that he was working very hard to steady himself. At least three times during his session, Vandercamp stopped, bent over, and took deep breaths. *Nerves?* What, Jesse wondered, was he nervous about? And when he brought his paper targets forward, Vandercamp seemed disappointed in the results. Jesse could see the hits on the targets were all over the place, very erratic. Odd for someone so familiar with handguns and for such an experienced shooter. But there wasn't anything Jesse could put his finger on, nothing he could use to help Alisha's cause. And then . . .

Just as John Vandercamp was finishing up, another young man came onto the range. He took the lane directly to Vandercamp's left. The two men nodded to each other, and there was something in their nods that indicated more than a casual greeting between strangers. They knew each other. Jesse was sure of it. And there was something else. The shooter to Vandercamp's left looked familiar. It was Gary Cummings Jr., the owner's son from the convenience store/gas station, who had sold the kerosene for the cross-burning to Vandercamp. Jesse pumped his fist without being conscious of it. This was a break, finally. He didn't know what it would ultimately mean or how significant it would be, but it meant one thing for certain: The younger Cummings was somehow connected to Vandercamp. Weld would have had no way of knowing the significance when she reviewed the footage. But this wasn't enough to bring to her or the DA. It proved nothing by itself. Since everybody involved seemed willing to believe in preposterous coincidences, they would count this as just one more. Jesse froze the video right where it was, with both Vandercamp and Cummings in the frame.

He wanted the counterman to see where he'd stopped it, because Jesse meant to start a fire of his own, one that didn't require kerosene.

"You done?" the counterman asked when Jesse emerged from the office. "My boss is pretty pissed off at me for letting you back there."

"You'll live."

"Easy for you to say. It's not you who just got yelled at on the phone."

Jesse ignored that. "Gary Cummings Junior come to shoot here much?"

A flash of panic crossed the counterman's face before he recovered. "Who?"

Jesse laughed at him. "I hope you're better with that," Jesse said, pointing to the SIG Sauer holstered to the counterman's hip, "than you are at lying."

"Lying?"

"You know Cummings. It was all over your face when I mentioned his name."

344

"Look, Chief, I don't know who you're talking about."

Jesse leaned over the counter and put his face very close to the counterman's.

"Listen to me. I worked LAPD Robbery Homicide for ten years. I've been lied to by stone-cold killers, so don't try to play me. I'm going to ask you again: Does Gary Cummings Junior shoot here much?"

"Twice a week," the counterman answered as the front door opened.

"That's better. Now get me the records."

"Don't you do a damned thing if you want to keep your job."

Jesse turned around to see a fit man in his mid-fifties, bald and sporting a gray goatee. He had a football player's neck and was decked out in khaki camo. He aimed his fierce brown eyes at Jesse's.

"You want anything, you come back here with a warrant. Otherwise, get the fuck out."

Jesse asked, "Who are you?"

"Ian Kern. I own this place. And don't go start making threats," he said. "I'm no dumbass like him." Kern pointed to the counterman. "All my paperwork is in order. I'm in compliance with every freakin' law, rule, and regulation you bastards can throw my way."

" 'You bastards,' " Jesse repeated. "I've

been called worse."

Kern smiled with all the dead-eyed warmth of a feeding shark.

Jesse came right up close to him and whispered in his ear, "You tell Cummings I know the truth and that when he looks over his shoulder, that'll be me."

Before Kern could answer, Jesse walked out of the range and headed straight to his Explorer.

66

Jesse didn't waste any time making his threat a reality. He drove straight from the Magic Valley Handgun and Rifle Range to the Cummingses' place of business just outside of Paradise. He'd lit the spark, and now it was time to fan the flames. And it was apparent from the second Jesse walked in that Kern or his counterman had called ahead and delivered the message. What made it even better was that Gary Jr. — who struck Jesse as more than a little arrogant and full of himself — was on duty and that his daddy was nowhere in sight. Junior's face flushed and his body language said he was girding for a fight.

Jesse walked straight up to him, smiling the whole time.

"Who called you, Kern himself, or did he make the guy who works the counter do it?"

That confused Junior. He had expected Jesse to come at him, but angrily, not smiling and not sideways. But Jesse wanted to keep Junior off balance. So far, so good.

"Relax, kid," Jesse said, knowing the "kid" would get under Junior's skin. "Far as I can tell, you haven't broken any laws . . . yet."

"What's that supposed to mean?" Junior asked, puffing out his chest.

"You speak English, right, kid? It wasn't a hard sentence to understand."

"Get out of here. Go bother someone who cares."

Jesse laughed at him. "You always talk this way to the police? Your father had more respect."

"My father hates cops as much as I do. He just thinks acting polite means something."

"But you don't, do you, kid?"

"Fuckin' A. And stop calling me 'kid.' I'm not a kid."

"Really? You tie your own shoelaces and cut your own meat?"

"Go fuck yourself. You guys are a waste of time and taxes. You let people alone to take care of justice, there'd be no crime in this country. We'd know who to watch and keep in their place. We wouldn't let them run things the way they do."

"Who would you watch, kid? Which people?"

Gary Jr. smiled a knowing smile at Jesse. "You know who. We'd make sure they stayed where they belonged. They like the jungle, so let them live there and leave us alone."

Jesse switched gears. "So, how long did you know John Vandercamp?"

"Who?"

"You're going to play it that way? Okay, kid. Let's you and me make a bet."

"What are you talking about?" Junior said, as off balance as Jesse had hoped.

"They told me you shoot twice a week at Magic Valley. My guess is you shoot on the same days all the time, but this past week, I bet not. It was no coincidence that you shot on the same day as John Vandercamp or that you took the stand right next to his in an otherwise empty range." Jesse held his right hand out to Junior. "A bet?"

Jesse was half hoping the kid would swat his hand away so that he could get just physical enough with Junior to throw a real scare into him. But Junior left Jesse's hand hanging and told him to get out.

"That's impolite," Jesse said, taking back his hand. "If I don't get out, what are you going to do about it? You going to come around the counter and do something about it or are you going to call your daddy to come rescue you?"

Junior's face turned bright red and the veins in his neck were really popping out. Jesse almost had him provoked enough to take a swing at him, but the door to the convenience store opened and a young woman stepped in and broke the tension. She handed Gary Cummings Jr. a twenty-dollar bill.

"Twenty dollars on . . ." she said, turning back to look outside. "My car's on pump four." She had a Boston accent thick enough to cut with a knife. "Where you keep ya tallboys at?"

"Beer's over there," Junior said, and she walked to the beer case.

"C'mon, call your daddy. I'm going to speak to him soon, anyway. Tonight works as well for me as tomorrow."

But Junior had regained his footing. "Look, you want to stand there all night, stand there. I don't care. You want to talk to my father . . ." Junior looked at the digital clock. "He'll be here in seven hours."

When the woman brought the six-pack of bottles to the counter, Junior was smart enough to ask for proof.

"Yaw kiddin' me, right?" she said.

Junior pointed at Jesse. "Police."

She shook her head, showed him her license, paid for the beers, and went to pump her gas.

Jesse just smiled at Junior. "Tell your daddy I'll be in tomorrow to speak with him."

"I'll think about it."

"Don't think on it too long, kid. Not your strong suit, thinking. And I'm curious to know how it was that you knew John Vander-camp but your daddy still alerted the police to his buying the kerosene here and told us he didn't recognize him."

Jesse didn't wait for an answer. He turned around and left.

The soldier was sitting in his camo Jeep. He had parked it so that it was covered in shadows cast by the walls surrounding the trash compactor at the side of the store. It was where he had parked the night he had sent his half-brother to buy the kerosene. He had already taken note of Jesse Stone's arrival and now checked his watch as the Paradise police chief drove away. He'd been inside for a while and had come out empty-handed. That could only be trouble.

67

By the time Jesse got back to his condo after making his ritual goodnight drive through Paradise, Cole Slayton was fast asleep in the spare bedroom. Jesse hadn't really had much opportunity to think through what Connor had said about Cole having that old photograph. He wasn't sure why Cole would have it or how he came to possess it, but there was an easy way to find out. Still, it could wait until morning.

It was too early in the game to call Molly, Suit, Healy, or Dylan Taylor to discuss the connection between John Vandercamp and Gary Cummings Jr. They were all still probably on stakeout. Jesse was most hopeful for results from Healy. James Earl was definitely the weak link, and Healy was an old pro at extracting information. Plus, as Jesse knew from experience, Healy could hold his liquor and keep his wits about him. In spite of his hopes and the first bit of good news in terms of aiding Alisha's cause, Jesse's mind kept drifting back to thoughts of the photo of him in his LAPD uniform and the beautiful woman on his lap.

He looked around the room and saw that Cole had neatened up, put some of the contents of the boxes in logical places: towels in the linen closet, cleaning products under the sink, et cetera. But Jesse was looking for the box that contained his old photographs. He knew he had probably posed for many photos of himself in uniform with women he had dated in L.A. It was funny how there was something about the uniform itself that attracted women — not all of them, though. Jesse wasn't egotistical, but he knew he wasn't half bad to look at, especially back then, his body still in baseball shape. He found the box he was looking for, the one with his old photo albums and the envelopes processed photos used to come in.

As he had done on his previous visit, the soldier scouted the area before approaching the Cummingses' property. Good thing, too, because he spotted the big man sitting in his Dodge pickup on the side of the road, about a hundred yards from the front of the house. He always had mixed feelings about his father, the Colonel. Even before they had had their falling out over 9/11 and his enlisting, it was never easy to know how to feel about his father. Regardless, Lee Harvey couldn't deny that the man had been right to be wary of the Cummingses. The Colonel had an uncanny ability to see trouble coming around the corner when most people couldn't even see the corner. He supposed that was how his father had survived all this time with so many enemies at his heels.

He had texted the Colonel to meet him in the woods behind the house. He watched the Colonel come out the rear door and walk into the woods. The soldier watched and waited before approaching to make sure his father's midnight stroll hadn't attracted the attention of anyone in the house or other curious onlookers. No one followed. No lights went on in the house that hadn't been on before. There were no signs that anyone had noticed, so he circled around to where the Colonel stood.

"You were right, sir," the soldier said. "Stone has stumbled onto something. He showed up at the gas station and spent several minutes inside with the son. He also has a tail on you. One of his deputies is parked about a football field down the road from this development."

"Stone is a problem," said Leon Vander-camp. "He was at the shooting range earlier and knows that there was a connection between John W. and Cummings's son. Cummings Senior came to me and reported that Stone pushed his boy pretty hard, but that the kid did not break."

"Yet," said the soldier. "The kid is weak and has a big mouth."

"Agreed."

"Would you like me to make a move on Stone, sir?"

"Possibly, but not just yet. There are intermediate steps to be taken first. If you catch my meaning."

"I do, sir."

"The father and the son will be at work together in several hours. I will see to things. As to the other matter we discussed. Have you taken care of it?"

"I have. It's is built and operational."

Leon Vandercamp stepped forward, reached out his hand, and stroked Lee Harvey's face. "With John W. lost and James Earl lost to himself, you're all I've got left, son. You're a good boy. I am sorry for what happened between us."

"Yes, sir" was what Lee Harvey said before about-facing and disappearing into the woods.

Jesse sat on the couch in such a way that Ozzie Smith might look over his shoulder at the old photos. Most of the shots on the top of the box were of Jenn and him. It was odd how he felt about her these days. There was a time when he couldn't think of her or hear her name without his insides knotting up. Even after the love had gone away, she'd kept a strange and powerful hold on him. Now he smiled at the good memories and waved off the bad ones. She was happily married, and the dysfunctional energy that once bound them together was gone.

In the next layer of photos were the shots with the women he had dated between the time he had arrived in L.A. and when he had met Jenn. His memory was accurate. There were many, many shots of him in uniform with various women. As he looked at the photos, he smiled. It surprised him that he could remember all of their names, how and where they had met, and where they had gone on their first dates. First dates were almost never to the movies, because the only movies Jesse loved were Westerns, and even back then there were hardly any being made.

There were a few photos with women sitting in his lap, but only one that fit the description Connor Cavanaugh had given. He was right. Celine was a beautiful woman. She was a trauma room nurse at UCLA Medical Center who lived in Woodland Hills. Cops and nurses, like that ever happened. Jesse put the other photos back in the box. He took the one of Celine and him in his back pocket.

68

Jesse's cell phone vibrated off his nightstand and thumped to the hardwood floor. It was the thump that woke him up.

"What is it?" Jesse said, his voice still thick with sleep.

"Jesse, it's Brian."

"Brian?"

"Lundquist. You better get over here."

"Where's here?"

"The Cummingses' gas station."

"Why, they file a complaint against me for bothering the kid?"

"Just get over here."

There was a click on the other end of the line.

Jesse got out of bed, went to the bathroom, and threw some cold water onto his face. Fifteen minutes later, he was showered and dressed. He knocked on the spare bedroom door on his way out, but Cole was already gone to work. Whatever they had to discuss could keep. Whatever Lundquist had to discuss, apparently, could not.

Everything about the Cummingses' place cried murder: the state prowl cars, the unmarked cars parked every which way, the stunned and curious looks on the faces of bystanders, and the crime scene tape. But nothing more so than the ME's car and the meat wagon. Jesse had seen too much of both lately to suit him.

He pulled his Explorer up next to Lundquist's car, got out, and ducked under the tape. Once he stepped through the convenience store's door, Jesse knew his sense of things was right. Whether real or imagined, Jesse tasted the metallic mist of blood still suspended in the air. But he needn't have relied on his sense of smell or taste, because there was blood and brain spatter all over the wall behind the counter. A big man like Suit, Lundquist was hunched over the counter, speaking to someone blocked from Jesse's view. Dr. Minter, no doubt. One of Lundquist's men walked up to Lundquist, tapped him on the shoulder, and pointed at Jesse. Lundquist waved Jesse to come on.

"Take a look," Lundquist said.

Jesse leaned over the counter and saw the ME squatting next to Gary Cummings Jr.

He had collapsed in a lifeless bundle of flesh and bone, his right leg caught beneath him, his left leg splayed out at an unnatural angle. He was missing his right eye and a big chunk of the back of his skull. He didn't seem nearly as arrogant or full of himself in death. Nothing so humbling, Jesse thought, as a bullet through the brain. Bullets cared little for bravado or pretense.

"The father's in the back," Lundquist said. "One through the back of the head. Most of his face is gone."

"Hollow-points."

"Looks that way."

Jesse noticed that the kid's sidearm was still holstered. "The father's sidearm still in its holster, too?"

Lundquist nodded.

"Well, you should have it all on video. They've got a —"

Lundquist wasn't nodding any longer. "No video. I checked. Been turned off."

"What? Doesn't make any sense. Why would they turn the video off?"

Lundquist shrugged.

Jesse was thinking to himself aloud. "Not unless they were asked to turn it off."

"What did you say?" Lundquist was curious.

"Look, both of these guys were experienced with handguns and the kid was the type who would have been looking for any excuse to pull his weapon and fire. But both of them are here, bullets through their heads, and the surveillance system turned off. What does that say to you, Brian?"

"A lot of things, possibly."

"One of them being what?"

"They knew the assailant."

"I vote for that one."

Lundquist wasn't buying, not yet. "Big leap for someone who's been on scene for all of three minutes and hasn't even had a good look. What makes you so confident?"

Jesse tilted his head, motioning toward the front door. "We need to talk."

"Okay, let's step outside and take a walk."

They went around to the side of the store.

"All right, what's up, Jesse?"

"John W. Vandercamp and Gary Cummings Junior knew each other. On the day Vandercamp was killed and was shooting at the Magic Valley Handgun and Rifle Range, Cummings was shooting in the lane right next to him, even though the rest of the range was empty."

"You know this how?"

"For now, just take my word for it."

"For now. But this proves what?"

"By itself, nothing. Still, don't you find it

odd that the Cummings kid knew John Vandercamp but the father showed me video of John Vandercamp buying the kerosene used to burn the cross on the Patels' lawn? If they knew him, why show me the tape at all? And if they were going to show me the tape, why not just identify him?"

"We're never going to know the answer to that now," Lundquist said.

"That's my point. I was in here this morning around midnight and confronted the Cummings kid about Vandercamp. I almost had him talking, but a woman came in to buy some gas and beer. By the time she left, the kid had regained his senses."

"So even if Vandercamp and Cummings knew each other, what does it prove?"

"That homicide scene in there, does it look like a robbery to you?"

Lundquist said, "Money is missing from the register."

"That's not what I asked you, Brian." Jesse didn't wait for an answer. "Looks more like an execution staged to look like a robbery."

"What if it does?"

"All I know is something doesn't add up. They show me video of a kid buying kerosene. They claim they don't know him, but they in fact do. When I'm here, the father pointed out that all of their people were licensed to carry firearms because they were never going to be robbed again without a fight. Yet eight hours after I connect Cummings Junior to Vandercamp, both Cummingses are murdered during a robbery without drawing their weapons and the video system just happened to be shut off. C'mon, Lundquist."

"Let's say I accept your version of things. What does it add up to?"

"I don't know yet, but it proves there's more going on here than a series of unlikely coincidences."

"I can't deny that."

"Any witnesses?"

"Guy who called it in says he thinks he saw a green Jeep passing him in the opposite direction when he was turning into the gas station, but it was still pretty dark out and he can't be sure if the Jeep was coming from the station."

That's when it hit Jesse. He thanked Lundquist and left without another word.

69

Molly was resting her head in her hands, and when she looked up to see who was coming through the station door, Jesse saw that she was bleary-eyed and yawning.

"Anything happen last night?" he asked.

"Nothing. Garrison stayed in his office until about nine, then went home. I sat on his house until midnight. He didn't go anywhere. Bedroom light went on at eleven and I saw the TV flickering. When the flickering stopped and the light went off, I stuck around another half-hour to make sure it wasn't a ruse."

"Good."

"What's the old expression about the cobbler's kids going shoeless? Garrison's lawn was dead and the hedges overgrown."

"And the contractor's house is always the one in the worst shape. How about the military records on Lee Harvey Vandercamp?"

That perked Molly right up. "Funny you should mention that. I'm getting the run-around."

"I thought you had good sources, Crane."

"I usually do."

"What do you think it means?"

She raised her eyebrows. "I can't be sure, but my guess is Lee Harvey probably did either classified stuff or the dirty jobs we never get told about."

"I'll make a call," Jesse said.

"Anything on your front?"

"A lot."

Jesse told Molly about the gun range, his visit with Gary Cummings Jr., and the murder scene he'd just been at.

"Holy sh—oot! You know Suit trailed Leon Vandercamp to a gated community in Swan Harbor. Want to take a wild guess at who lives there?"

"Who?"

Molly smiled and said, "The Cummingses. Suit couldn't trail Vandercamp past the gate but checked this morning before he came on."

"When I was at the murder scene, I realized two things that I should have realized before."

"What's that, Jesse?"

"How did John Vandercamp get from the

gun range to the Gull? And, if we're working on the assumption that his appearance
in front of the Gull wasn't happenstance,
how did he know Alisha was there?"

"You're right. Someone had to be watching her."

"Check all the local cabs and car services.
My guess is there won't be any record of
him being driven from the range to town.
Have we had any reports of abandoned cars
in the restaurant or business lots in town?"

"Not for months."

"Then unless John W. Vandercamp flew,
someone drove him. Get as much surveillance camera footage from local businesses
as you can."

"Okay, Jesse, but what am I looking for?"

He thought about it for a second. "Start
with a green Jeep, and if you come up
empty, we'll see."

In his office, Jesse sat with the phone
pressed between his ear and his shoulder,
his right index finger hovering above the
numbered keypad. Jesse usually wasn't a
man to care about what the person on the
other end of the phone would think of him,
but this wasn't usually . . . not even close.
He punched in the number and waited.

"Federal Bureau of Investigation, Special

Agent Rosen speaking, how may I help you?"

"Abe, it's Jesse Stone."

The silence that followed was as uncomfortable as silences could get. Abe had been a colleague of Diana's and had been in love with her for years, though nothing had come of it. Like Diana's family and just about everyone else, Abe held Jesse responsible for Diana's murder and for letting her killer escape. Of course, what Abe could never know, what all of them could never know, was that her killer hadn't escaped at all and had died a very long and torturously painful death.

"What?" Abe said at last. "This have anything to do with what's going on in Paradise?"

"Uh-huh."

"It must be important for you to call me for a favor."

"You know it is."

"What is it?"

"We're getting the runaround with the military. We're trying to get ahold of Lee Harvey Vandercamp's service records."

"Nice family, the Vandercamps."

"If you like cockroaches."

"Cockroaches are what they are," Rosen said. "The Vandercamps choose to be what they are."

"Good point."

"I'll get those records for you."

"Thanks, Abe. I know you're not inclined to help me."

"She loved you, Jesse. That gets you some credit with me."

"Thank you."

"You ever think about her?"

"Every day when I get up in the morning and every night before I close my eyes."

"Me, too," Rosen said, then hung up the phone.

70

Jesse drove his Explorer across the bridge to Stiles Island and Dylan Taylor's cottage. He sometimes forgot how beautiful Paradise and the surrounding area could be. When he first arrived in town and for many years after, he was struck by the differences between the stark desert allure of his Tucson youth, the seductive, hypnotic blue of the Pacific, and the rocky, white chop charm of the Massachusetts coast. It was easy to think about beauty when remembering Diana.

Jesse had been careful to avoid Alisha since the evening of the shooting, but after getting off the phone with Abe Rosen, he arranged a meeting. Dylan Taylor's cottage on Stiles, away from the press corps' prying eyes, seemed the logical choice. Monty Bernstein's Porsche, Dylan's Range Rover, and Alisha's Miata were parked on the gravel driveway. Jesse parked around back.

"Nice place," Jesse said when Dylan

greeted him at the door.

"Like the Range Rover, it comes with the job. Come on in."

Monty Bernstein waved at Jesse, but Alisha didn't seem to know what to do or how to react. Jesse took care of that himself. He walked over to her and shook her hand, making sure to hold on to it and to squeeze it so that she knew he was with her. It was better than him trying to express it with words. She understood.

"Thanks, Jesse," she said, staring up at him. "Dylan told me what you're doing for me."

"I'm just trying to do what's right. If what you say is true, you don't deserve to get railroaded."

"You believe me?" she said.

"I believe the evidence, and I don't think Weld had all of it when she made her findings public."

They all gave Jesse perplexed looks. He told them about the connection between Vandercamp and Cummings and the murders earlier that morning. Monty Bernstein got a glint in his eye.

"Finally, something." the lawyer said, raising his hands to the ceiling.

"But what does it mean, Jesse?" Alisha asked.

"I don't know yet, but I can accept only so many coincidences. I was there last night, pushing the Cummings kid hard, and now they're dead. Another coincidence. Sorry, not buying. They shut off their security cameras and their weapons were still holstered. They knew the person who executed them. I'd bet on it."

"But it doesn't help my client," Monty said.

"No, but it's creating room for doubt, and that's something I hear you're pretty skilled with, Counselor."

Monty smiled his expensive white smile.

"Even Weld will have to wonder about the Cummings murders," Jesse said. "It won't take much more for one of us to find something out and get her to reopen the investigation."

"But, Jesse," Dylan said, "you wanted to talk to Alisha. Was it about this?"

"No. I wanted to go over the statement she made to Weld about what happened that night."

Alisha frowned at hearing that. "I've been over this a thousand times with them. Please don't make me —"

He raised his palms to her. "I understand. What I'm interested in isn't what you said to Weld. I'm interested in what you didn't tell her."

Alisha jumped to her feet, anger replacing her hurt. "Are you accusing me of something, Jesse?"

"Uh-huh."

"Of what?"

"Of being human and following your training."

"I'm confused, Jesse."

"It's simple," he said. "I trained you and you're the daughter of a cop. You've been told to never add anything to an answer, to never embellish or fill in details that weren't asked for. I know. I told you that myself. And as a human, there are things you might have wanted to say during your statement that made you feel foolish or were embarrassing, so you didn't say them. I've been at this a long time, Alisha, and I know there's always something else or something more. You're not in court now and you're with friends. Is there anything you didn't tell Weld? It doesn't matter how insignificant it seems or how silly."

She bowed her head and in a whisper said, "The cat."

"Cat. What cat?" Monty asked. "You never mentioned a cat."

"Like Jesse said, I felt stupid."

Jesse pushed her. "Tell us about the cat."

"Right at the end of the chase, when Vandercamp was approaching Newton Alley, I got the sense that there was someone else there besides the suspect and me, in the shadows, mirroring my movements. I heard a plastic garbage can fall and swung my gun around, but a gray tabby cat came out of the dark."

"Exactly where was this?" Jesse asked.

"You know where the back of the last building on Newton Alley bumps out on Bridge Street, where the people put out their trash in the triangle between the back of the building and the street?"

"And this sense you were being mirrored, was it just a feeling or was it something you heard?"

Alisha looked embarrassed and bowed her head again. "I thought I was imagining it because I was a little drunk, I guess."

"Let's never mention that last part ever again," Monty said.

Jesse stood up. "That's good, Alisha. It gives us more to work with."

Monty walked him to the door.

"Do you really think this means something, Jesse? Or is it grabbing-at-straws time?"

Jesse shrugged. "We'll see, Monty. As of right now, you're still her best hope."

The lawyer grabbed Jesse's biceps. "Then you better find something solid and soon."

71

Jesse parked his Explorer on Bridge Street across from where Alisha said she heard the garbage can fall and where the cat came out of the shadows. He'd been down this street hundreds of times, but now he pushed his familiarity with it out of his mind. Holding a copy of Alisha's statement in his hand, he walked slowly back to the Gray Gull and retraced the steps she had taken that night while pursuing John Vandercamp. Although he was doing this in full daylight, Jesse was constantly checking to see if there were places along the way where someone could have kept out of sight while mirroring Alisha and Vandercamp's movements.

It didn't take long for him to become discouraged. While there were a few places at every juncture along the route where someone might have been able to stay completely out of sight in the dark of night, Jesse didn't see any way a third person could have mirrored the chase without Alisha spotting him or her. Even on a moonless night or if Alisha had been more intoxicated than she was, another person could not have remained completely out of Alisha's line of sight. And she likely would have heard him as well. But as Jesse came back to his Explorer and the place where the back wall of the last building on Newton Alley jutted out onto Bridge Street, he had another thought. *What if that third person already knew where the chase would come to an end?*

If Alisha's instincts were right and there had been someone else there the night of the shooting and that person knew John Vandercamp was headed for Newton Alley, he wouldn't have had to follow every inch of the chase. He might have been there the entire time, waiting for Vandercamp and Alisha to come his way. But that led to a question Jesse had no answer for — not yet, anyway: *Why?* Even if Jesse was correct and this was all part of some larger scheme, he still couldn't grasp what that third person might be doing there.

Jesse stood in the little triangle where the plastic garbage can had fallen and from where the gray cat had emerged. Even on a night with a full moon, it would have been easy for someone to hide himself in the shadows by simply pressing himself against the wall. While that was true, it didn't help answer the question. *Why?* Jesse stepped away from the wall and looked around. He knew there was something he wasn't seeing. Then he remembered what his drill sergeant had hammered into his unit in Marines boot camp. *The enemy don't always fight you at eye level. Looking up and down and side to side may save your life.* He'd had them sing it out as they ran. *Up and down and side to side may in battle save my worthless hide. Up and down and side to side may in battle save my . . .*

Jesse stood at every point in the triangle formed by the back of the building and the street. He looked from side to side. Nothing. He stood across the street where Alisha would have been and where his Explorer was now parked. He looked from side to side. Nothing. He followed the same pattern, scanning the pavement as he moved. Nothing. When he did it a third time, keeping his eyes focused above him, Jesse saw something at last: possibilities. He left his SUV where it was, walked to the corner, and turned down Newton Alley.

As he made his way down the alley, he waved through the art gallery windows at the proprietors. Art had never been his thing and there was a certain sameness to the paintings and sculptures displayed in the windows and on the walls of the galleries on Newton Alley. Lots of seascapes and paintings of whaling ships, bronzes of native Indians and pilgrims, photos of beached driftwood, of lonely gulls soaring over grassy dunes. Some of the stuff was more daring, but in a town like Paradise you had to give the tourists what they expected.

Jesse stopped outside the Pembroke Gallery, the last gallery on the alley. It was to the right of the Pembroke where John Vandercamp's body had fallen. Gayle Pembroke was nowhere in sight, but the lights were on. Jesse tried the door and it gave way. A bell jingled as he stepped inside. Gayle Pembroke, a retired high school art teacher well into her seventies, was a native daughter of Paradise and living her dream.

"Jesse!" Her face lit up as she came out of the gallery office. "Good to see you."

"Nice to see you, Gayle."

"Ugly business lately." She stepped past Jesse, went right to the front window, and pointed. "You know he died right over there."

"Uh-huh."

"Of course you do," she said. "How silly

of me. I'm sorry. What can I do for you?"

"You own this building and the one next door?"

"I do. When Sam died, I sold our house, took the insurance money, and bought both places. Good thing I bought when I did, too. With all the Bostonians and New Yorkers moving in, I'd be hard pressed to pay half what they're worth now. Sorry for rambling on."

"Do you think I could have a look around next door?"

She turned her head and squinted at him. "That's an odd request."

He didn't want to explain, nor did he want to raise awareness by getting a warrant. "Maybe so, Gayle, but what do you think?"

Gayle Pembroke retreated into her office, returning a few seconds later with a set of keys.

Jesse took the keys and thanked her. "Shouldn't take long. And, Gayle, you've got a tenant in there, right?"

"Maryglenn. She rents the top-floor loft." Gayle had a big smile on her face and walked over to a haunting painting of one of the old Victorians on the Bluffs. "Maryglenn's a painter. This is her work."

"Beautiful."

"It's sold," Gayle said. "I have some of

her other work here. Would you like to take a look?"

"Not right now, Gayle. I'll be back down in a few minutes."

72

The blood had been scrubbed off the pavement where John Vandercamp died, and with the blood the patina had been removed as well. In an odd way, the clean spot called almost as much attention to itself as the blood had. Jesse hoped foot traffic and weather would take care of that before it became a shrine to Leon Vandercamp's followers. Jesse had no desire for swastika-shaped wreaths to be laid on the spot.

The weathered red door to the building next to the gallery complained when Jesse pushed it in. The building had once served as a carriage house, but the carriage doors had been removed and bricked over so long ago that it was impossible to distinguish the old brick from the new. Old or new, the bricks now bore scars from Alisha's bullets that had missed John Vandercamp. A dangling pull cord hit Jesse in the forehead as he stepped inside. He tugged on the cord and an old fluorescent light fixture flickered to life. To his left was warehouse space where Gayle and the other gallery owners stored some of their stock, unused fixtures, business records, and boxes. Much of the artwork was wrapped in plastic or draped with fabric sheets all covered in a light downy layer of dust.

In front of him was a too-steep wooden staircase, the steps warped and worn shiny. They groaned under his weight as he climbed to the artist's loft above the warehouse. The ladder to the roof was right in front of him, but he hesitated. He stared at the black metal door of the loft. He could hear music, strings and a harpsichord, leaking out from the gap between the threshold and the bottom of the door. He decided that whatever there might be to see on the roof could wait, but that he should talk to Maryglenn while he was sure she was in. Jesse knocked on the door hard enough to be heard above the music.

He was surprised when the door pulled back. Given the haunting painting in the gallery and the classical music, Jesse pictured the artist as a contemporary of Gayle Pembroke. Maryglenn was a nice-looking woman in her early forties. Her brown hair was threaded with gray and cut at an angle matching her jawline. Her face was round and pleasant. Her black T-shirt and ripped black jeans were speckled with a rainbow of paint. She didn't look happy to see Jesse.

"Haven't I talked to enough of you people already?" she said, a lot of Nashville in her accent.

That caught Jesse as off guard as her appearance had, then he remembered he was wearing his PPD hat and jacket.

"I'm Jesse Stone, the Paradise police chief."

"I'm sorry," she said, realizing how her greeting must have sounded. "That was rude of me. Come in."

Jesse stepped into the loft and could immediately see the appeal of the place for an artist. Two sets of large angled windows on the Bridge Street side of the loft filled that area of the space with tons of natural light, and it was there that Maryglenn had seemed to set up shop. There were several easels, and shelves with arrays of paint tubes, cans, and brushes. Various-size canvases — some blank, some not — were stacked and piled in a few places on either side of the easels. The wooden flooring was, like the artist's clothing, covered in drips and speckles of different colored paints.

"Pardon me, but is Maryglenn your whole name?"

"There's a last name, too, but I don't use it. How can I help, Chief?"

"Please call me Jesse. I take it you were at home on the night of the shooting."

"I was. Look, Chief — Jesse — I've gone over this twenty times."

"How about once more? It could be very important."

Maryglenn offered Jesse tea, which he refused, but he did sit with her at the card table in the small kitchen area of the loft. After some preliminaries to help put the artist at ease, Jesse began.

"How many shots did you hear?"

"I was dozing off," she said, "so I'm not sure. I heard one loud explosion that woke me up and then I heard a lot of shots. I don't know, eight or nine, maybe ten altogether."

"Did any of the shots sound closer to you than the others?"

Her eyes got a faraway look in them, the way people's eyes do when they're trying to picture or remember something from the past. "The first shot, the one that woke me up, sounded louder, I guess, so that might mean it was closer. But I don't know anything about guns or acoustics."

"Was there a lapse in time between the first shot, the louder one, and the ones that followed?"

"I don't know . . . maybe. I was asleep."

"Did you hear anything unusual other than the gunfire? Anything at all? Was there noise on the roof or —"

"Don't tell Gayle, but we have squirrels and rats, even raccoons and opossum sometimes climb up on the roof." She pointed at the ceiling. "Gulls perch up on there, too."

That got Jesse's attention. "So you heard something on the roof?"

"Maybe. Things scurry around up there all the time. I mean, if I heard anything, it wasn't that different than stuff I'd heard before."

"And the only window on Newton Alley is your bathroom window."

She nodded. "Yeah, it's next to the shower, but it's small and cloudy so it lets light in. You can't really see much through it."

"Can I take a look?"

Maryglenn got up and showed him the window. She was right. Even if she had been at the window, staring down at Newton Alley while the shooting was going on, she wouldn't have been able to see much. In the dark, she wouldn't have been able to make out shapes. Jesse shook her hand, thanked her, and told her he was going up onto the roof.

"Jesse," she said. "I'm sorry about being rude before."

"No worries. By the way, I thought your painting of the house on the Bluffs was haunting."

She smiled up at him, letting go of his hand. "Thank you."

As he climbed the ladder to the roof, Jesse could not get Maryglenn's smile out of his head. When it came to women, Jesse didn't have a type per se, but Bohemian wasn't usually a sensibility that got his attention. Maryglenn had changed that.

Up on the roof, Jesse walked to the back ledge and looked down where the rear wall of the building ran perpendicular to the rear wall of a building on Connecticut Street and intersected the sidewalk on Bridge Street to form that triangle where the trash cans were kept. He knelt down, checked the tarred wall of the ledge, and found the type of damage — two angular scars dug so deep into tar they had chipped the brick beneath — he had hoped to find. He stood and walked in a straight line to the ledge on the Newton Alley side of the building. Even as he walked, he saw the same type of pits dug into the tar. Jesse stood at the ledge and, looking down, saw that he was standing almost directly above the spot where John Vandercamp had been killed, the freshly cleaned area on the pavement below marking the spot.

As he climbed back down the ladder and then the stairs to the street, Jesse thought he might now be able to explain how Alisha's claim of being fired upon first could be true although no weapon was found on or near Vandercamp's body. But explaining it wouldn't be good enough. He would have to prove it, and that wasn't going to be easy.

73

Molly was looking pleased with herself when Jesse got back to the station.

"What is it, Crane?"

"Check out the video footage I sent as attachments."

"What am I going to find?"

"I think I found how John Vandercamp got to the Gull."

"Green Jeep?"

Molly smiled. "Close, but no cigar."

"The person who made the nine-one-one call at the Cummings murder scene said he saw a green Jeep passing him in the opposite direction when he was heading in to get gas."

"It's not green," Molly said, "at least not all green. In the color footage it looks like it's painted in a hunter's camo print."

"It's progress. You get a tag number?"

"Not really. The footage, even the color footage, isn't clear enough, but you can see a driver and a passenger at one point, and then at another point only a driver. The time stamps match, Jesse. The Jeep has a passenger just before the incident with Alisha begins, and then there's only a driver after that."

"Anything else?"

"I don't know what strings you pulled, but we got the records on Lee Harvey Vandercamp. I printed it out. It's all on your desk."

"You look at it?"

Molly nodded.

"Let me guess," Jesse said. "He was a Ranger with extensive special-ops experience."

Molly's face went blank again. "I'm not even going to ask this time."

Jesse smiled. "I think Alisha's version of events that night could be true."

"That she was fired on first? How, Jesse? I want to believe her, too, but there was no gun."

"There was no gun found. That doesn't mean there was no gun."

"It's not like you to parse language like that."

"I'm telling you what I think, but I need more proof before I can go to anyone with it. For now, this is between the two of us.

We don't want to give false hope to Alisha."

"My lips are sealed, but why not tell Monty?"

Jesse shook his head. "If I'm right, we can bypass Monty and go straight to Weld and the DA."

"How about Alisha's job?"

"Let's save her from prison first. I'm heading into my office. Did Healy call?"

"He did. He wants you to call him back."

Molly was right. The Jeep was painted in a camo pattern and was outfitted for severe off-road use. Its suspension had been lifted to accommodate bigger tires and to allow for more ground clearance. It had a rack of roof lights and a heavy-duty front bumper with a towing winch, and its exhaust had been modified so that it could drive through several feet of water without stalling out. But Jesse was frustrated because Molly had also been right about the plates being unreadable. He couldn't even tell what state the plates were from. On the other hand, the locations of the Jeep and the time stamps put it near the Gull and then, only ten minutes after the shooting, heading out of Paradise.

Jesse had gotten a little better at using a computer and tried to zoom in on the faces of the driver and passenger, but it was no use. They were shadows and blurs. When he enlarged their images, they became even more indistinct. When he zoomed in on their faces, they became dark blotches. He wondered if the state tech people might be able to do more with the footage. But for the moment, Jesse didn't want to alert anyone about what he thought he'd found. His sense was that his presence at the Cummingses' store had already resulted in a double homicide. If the Cummingses had been involved in the cross-burning and the rest of it, they deserved to be punished. But they didn't deserve to be executed. No, until what he had was more than conjecture, he didn't want to involve another outside agency. He shouldn't have even shared as much as he had with Molly.

He looked through Lee Harvey Vandercamp's service records. As he anticipated, Lee Harvey had received just the type of training that would allow him to operate in all types of conditions as a member of a small specialized unit. But Jesse was looking for a very particular type of training, the kind that involved missions in a rugged, mountainous country like Afghanistan. Specifically, the type of training that involved climbing and rappelling. *Bingo!* Lee

Harvey had excelled in the mountain phase of his Ranger training at Camp Merrill in northern Georgia. And his abilities at rappelling from a helicopter were noted by his instructors.

For most of his time in the military, Lee Harvey had served with distinction, but things had ended badly. He'd been brought up on charges for threatening a superior officer and for disobeying a direct order. There hadn't been a court-martial, though he was dishonorably discharged. From what Jesse could glean from the records, a member of Lee Harvey's unit had been wounded and captured by al-Qaeda. Ordered to withdraw, Lee Harvey refused to stand down and had some choice words for his commanding officer. He went after the captured soldier. The reason there hadn't been a court-martial became clearer as Jesse read on. Lee Harvey had found the body of the captured soldier in a mountain pass and had carried it back to a place where an Army Blackhawk could safely pick them up. A court-martial would have made for bad press during a very unpopular war.

Jesse put the file down. It didn't make any sense to him that a man who would risk his life and career for a fallen comrade like that would deliver his half-brother to be sacrificed. But if Jesse was right about the shooting on Newton Alley, that was precisely what Lee Harvey Vandercamp had done.

74

Healy was happy to hear back from Jesse but didn't have any breakthroughs to report about his time spent drinking with James Earl Vandercamp.

"Mostly, he feels sorry for himself. He's a typical drunk —" Healy caught himself. "Sorry, Jesse, you know what I mean. Nothing's his fault. He's got a thousand woulda-dones and shoulda-dones, but nothing went his way. It was all someone else's doing."

"I know. I've been going to AA meetings lately and you hear that a lot. Almost everyone gets up there and says that they used to blame everyone and everything but themselves and the alcohol for what went wrong in their lives."

"But all is not lost," Healy said. "I got the sense that there's a lot of pent-up anger in him, and that with the right push he'd have a lot to say."

"So."

"The thing is, I was a stranger to him and I'm an old fart in his eyes. My guess, you'd have more success with him. He even mentioned you after he'd had a few. Said you seemed like a good guy for a cop."

"High praise."

"Don't laugh. He asked me about you, whether you were hard on the people you arrested or whether you were fair."

"You think he had anything specific in mind?"

"Nah. I don't think he's got a friend in the world, old James Earl. He wouldn't talk about his dad or about the Saviors. I tried bringing them up, pretending I didn't know who he was. He clammed right up."

"Thanks. Try him again tonight," Jesse said. "Maybe with him being more familiar with you, he'll open up."

"It's worth a shot. You getting anywhere?"

"Maybe, but nothing solid."

Healy was curious. "Want to talk it over?"

"Not yet." Molly knocked and came in. "Hold on a second," Jesse told Healy, putting his hand over the mouthpiece. "What is it, Molly?"

"Joey O'Brien from the Scupper's on the phone for you," she said. "Says he remembers something."

"Tell him I'll head over there in five minutes."

Molly gave Jesse a thumbs-up and left.

"Healy, you there?"

"Yeah, Jesse."

"We'll talk tomorrow."

Jesse walked into the Scupper, hoping that what Joey had to say would be something tangible. So far, what Jesse had added up to a lot of smoke. He could see tendrils, but if he tried to grab on to them, they'd blow away. He had a theory, but theories didn't hold up in court.

There were a few people at the bar. They nodded hellos as Jesse walked by. His conversation with Healy had gotten him started thinking about booze, and now the smell of scotch was strong in the air. He didn't want a drink but found he was fantasizing about his old nighttime ritual with Johnnie Walker and Ozzie Smith. Jesse was no fool. He knew it wouldn't be long before the ritual fantasy would transform itself into thirst. So he was glad when Joey noticed him and waved him to the end of the bar.

"Molly says you remember something from the day those bikers were in here."

"Yeah. I was watching this thing on cable

last night about the Holocaust, and when they showed film of that Himmler guy, I remembered."

"Remembered what?"

"It was his hat," Joey said.

"I'm not following. What about his hat?"

"There was this silver skull-and-crossbones thing on his hat, but not like a pirate skull and crossbones. On this thing, the skull was really big and seemed to be facing slightly to the right. The bikers who were here that day, they had the same thing painted on the tanks of their bikes."

"You sure?"

"Hundred percent."

"Thanks, Joey."

"Does that help?"

"Maybe more than you know."

While it wasn't exactly what he'd hoped for, it was another tendril, this one more than smoke. With a little luck and someone's help, he'd be able to grab on to this one and use it. Sitting in the Explorer, Jesse used his phone to research the skull and crossbones. It was called the *Totenkopf,* the death's head, and was the insignia of the Nazi SS. That figured. Jesse wanted to kick himself for not recognizing it on the motorcycles parked outside the warehouse the night he'd dropped Anya off after the attempted rape. He called Molly and told her he was going into Boston and that he didn't know how late it would be when he got back.

75

Bill was there in his usual seat, but Anya was nowhere in sight. This was the first time Jesse had come to a meeting without the meeting being the point. Anya — or, more accurately, Hank, her boyfriend — was the point. Jesse sat through the entire meeting, but even Bill could tell Jesse's mind was elsewhere.

"What's up, Jesse?" he asked during a coffee break.

"Sorry, Bill, I can't really talk about it."

"Police business?"

"Something like that."

The minute the meeting ended, Jesse was out the door and headed to the factory building in Newmarket Square.

The motorcycles were parked where they had been when Jesse dropped Anya off before. This time he got out of his SUV and was careful to take a closer look at the silver skull and crossbones painted on the gas tanks. There was no mistaking it: the *Toten-kopf.* Jesse got out his cell phone and took a few shots of the gas tanks. He texted them to Joey O'Brien. Before he went into the factory building, Jesse needed to be certain the image on these gas tanks matched the one Joey had seen outside the Scupper on the day things almost got out of hand with Alisha.

Joey got back to him almost immediately with a thumbs-up emoji and the words:

Xactly the same

Before he stepped into a potentially dangerous situation with only his nine-millimeter and no backup, Jesse texted a photo of the building, the photos he'd just sent to O'Brien, and his location to Molly. Beneath the photos he wrote:

If u don't hr from me in 1 hr, call BPD

Jesse put his phone away and made his way to the door through which Anya had disappeared. He had a tough choice to make. Although he wasn't thrilled about it, he was going to need these people to help, and walking into someone's home or clubhouse with a drawn weapon wasn't usually the way to encourage people's cooperation. On the other hand, he was walking into a potentially hostile situation and he couldn't be sure that Hank and/or Anya were going to be present. Even if they were, there was no guarantee they would stand up for him. But he made the choice to keep his weapon holstered.

The door was closed but unlocked, and Jesse was able to pull it back with only mild protest. It led into a long, dimly lit hallway. It smelled faintly of gasoline, exhaust fumes, and motor oil. He took his cell back out of his pocket and, using it as a flashlight, carefully made his way down the hall. There were offices on either side of the hallway, most of them empty. One of the offices at the end of the hallway was clearly in daily use. It contained a desk, chairs, a phone, a computer, and posters on the walls. Most of the posters were of customized motorcycles or suggestively clad and positioned women. Many featured both. Along with those posters there was an enlarged, framed photo of the *Totenkopf.* Jesse stepped into the office and looked at the paperwork on the desk. No racist manifestos, but supplier invoices for motorcycle parts.

He left the office and walked a few feet to

the end of the hallway. Here there was a locked steel door, the top half of which was glass framed in metal, the kind of glass with thin strands of metal wire running through it. Although it was fairly dark on the other side of the glass, Jesse could make out that it was a mechanic shop. Work benches, tool cabinets, and metalworking machines were visible along the walls. There were motorcycles in various states of construction in jigs and on lifts. Jesse tried the door one last time to no good end. Then he found an old-fashioned black button doorbell mounted on the side wall. He pressed his finger down on it and held it there. He thought he could just make out the sound of its buzzing somewhere beyond the shop door.

It took about thirty seconds, but eventually a door opened at the back wall of the shop, a shaft of light illuminating the shop floor. With the light Jesse could see that the place was actually pretty comprehensively equipped. There were tire racks against one wall. Engines on shelves along with belts, chains, filters, frames, and all manner of motorcycle parts. Then a big man appeared in silhouette in the doorway at the other end of the shop, his frame blotting out some of the light. He lumbered across the shop floor toward where Jesse was standing.

When he got to the half-glass door, Jesse realized that *big* didn't do the man justice. He was huge, probably six-foot-six, and thick as an oak tree. He had a mountain-man beard that ended at mid-chest. His nose had been rearranged a few times, and he had a mouth full of missing teeth.

"Who the fuck are you and what the fuck do you want?"

Jesse couldn't see the gun but could tell by the way the waistline of the big man's jeans were stretched that he was carrying. He decided to play it friendly instead of tough, remembering that he needed them and they didn't need him at all.

"I'm Jesse," he said, loud enough to be heard through the glass. "I need to speak to Hank and Anya."

"Who?"

Jesse was willing to take the friendly approach only so far. "Cut the crap. Anya and I are friends and I've met Hank. Anyway, I'm not leaving. And don't go for your piece. That would be a mistake."

The big man thought about it, then, as he turned, said, "Wait there."

Two minutes later, Hank and Anya appeared at the door, the big man at their backs.

"What the fuck do you want?" Hank

screamed it with all the venom he could muster.

Jesse understood that Hank had to play the tough guy. There are fewer places in the world in which macho behavior is more highly valued than within motorcycle gangs. Not even a sports locker room compared. And Jesse was willing to play his part if it got him what he wanted.

"I'm sorry, Hank," he said. "But I really need to talk with you guys. Please."

Hank looked over his shoulder. "It's okay, Nitro. I can handle this guy."

"You sure? Smells like the law to me," Nitro said.

"I'm sure."

When Nitro was halfway across the shop floor, Hank opened the door. He and Anya stepped out instead of letting Jesse in, but neither of them was happy to see Jesse. Jesse understood and suggested they talk outside.

76

It was pretty chilly outside. Neither Hank nor Anya was clothed for it. Hank was dressed only in a Harley T-shirt, worn shiny jeans, and square-toed boots. His neck tattoos were now clearly visible: a *Totenkopf* on one side, a swastika on the other. Anya had on a Harley sweatshirt and athletic shorts.

"Okay," Hank said. "What?"

"Anya told you I was a cop?"

He nodded.

"I'm the police chief in Paradise." Jesse said it and was careful to see if that registered with Hank. It did. His eyes widened and there was a quick flash of fear across his face.

"So what? Look, I know you saved my old lady from some bad shit, but what do you want?"

Jesse sensed that Hank had already figured out what he was doing there. "C'mon,

Hank, you know why I'm here. A few weeks ago some bikers rode into my town and picked a fight with one of my officers, an African American officer."

"So? What's that got to do with me or my people?"

Jesse pointed at Hank's neck tat. "The *Totenkopf* was painted on those bikers' gas tanks just like it's painted on the gas tanks of your bikes, like the tattoo on your neck, and like the poster in the office. I'm not a big believer in coincidences. You didn't show up in my town by accident. You didn't pick that fight by accident. I want to know who put you up to it and why."

Hank shook his head. "No way. I don't talk to cops."

"I'm not interested in you or your gang. You believe what you believe. I think it's wrong, as wrong as you can be, but you've got a right to it. Nobody's got a right to do what happened in my town. Nobody."

"You wanna talk about what's right, huh? Your cop killed an unarmed man."

"What if I told you John Vandercamp wasn't unarmed and that his family set him up as a sacrificial lamb? Nothing like a martyr to push a movement forward."

"Lies. That's all you traitors to your race know how to tell. Lies and more lies."

"You believe what you want, but I know your people showing up in my town and picking a fight with my officer didn't happen by chance. You swear to me I'm wrong, I'll turn around and walk away."

Hank didn't say anything, but Jesse could see he was thinking about it. Hank's continued silence confirmed it, but he needed more than confirmation. He needed to know who had set the wheels in motion for what had been going on in Paradise and Swan Harbor. Without a name, without some idea of what the end game was, this would be a wasted trip.

"Any violence from here on out is on you," Jesse said, turning to go. "Then I will be interested in you and I can promise you you won't like it if I start paying attention. I know some people down here who can make life very hard for you."

"You aren't wrong," Anya said, stopping Jesse in his tracks. "You aren't wrong. It was a setup."

Hank was fuming. "Shut up!"

"No, Hank. Jesse saved me from being raped. If I can help him, I'm gonna help him. If you're afraid of those morons inside, go on back in. They don't scare me half as much as they scare you."

"A soldier," Hank said. "He didn't bother

giving us a name. Paid us five grand to go into your town and stir the pot. He told us where to go and when to go. Said the nig— your black cop would show. All we had to do was to get under her skin." Hank sneered when he said "skin." "The soldier didn't want us to get physical unless we had to and said that if we had to, he'd supply us with a lawyer."

Jesse reached into his jacket pocket and pulled out a copy of a photo from Lee Harvey Vandercamp's service file. "This him, the soldier who came to you?"

"Yeah," Hank said. "That's him. His eyes are crazier now and he's older than in that shot."

Jesse was curious. "Why'd he pick your gang?"

"We done some work for the SS before. And no, I ain't gonna talk about it. We finished?"

"We are. How's the not drinking coming?" Jesse asked Hank as he started away.

"I'm strong. I don't need those stupid meetings. I'm doing fine on my own."

"That's what I used to think, too. Don't fool yourself."

Hank gave Jesse the finger and tugged Anya's arm to come with him. She yanked her arm out of his grasp and told him she'd be there in a minute. He didn't like it, but Hank went back inside.

"I wanted to thank you again, Jesse. I haven't slept so good since that night, thinking about what he woulda done to me."

Jesse shook his head. "No need to thank me. But you shouldn't stop coming to the meetings because Hank thinks he can handle it on his own. I used to believe I could do it that way, but . . ."

"I'll think about it. I promise. But that's not what I wanted to say to you."

"I'm listening."

"You don't believe in coincidences, but without them we wouldn't be standing here."

"Fair enough. Listen, I can see you love Hank, but you're better than this. You're a smart woman. I can see that. You have to know this, the stuff they believe in is just wrong. If you need help to get out, all you've got to do is ask."

"This isn't like the other night, Jesse. You can't save someone who doesn't want saving. But thanks. Maybe I'll see you at a meeting."

She turned and went into the building. Jesse stood there for a moment, fighting the urge to go in there after her. The thing is, she was right and he knew it. If she wanted out, she would have to do it on her own. There was something else he realized: He probably wasn't ever going to see her at another meeting.

77

Jesse texted Molly that he was fine and that she could stand down. Almost as soon as he had finished texting, the phone vibrated in his palm.

"Jesse, what was that about?" Molly asked, her voice strained with worry. "What were you doing?"

"Filling in another piece of the puzzle."

"You're getting cryptic on me again."

"The incident with Alisha and the bikers was no accident. Like I thought, it was a setup."

"But who set it —"

"Soldier boy, Lee Harvey Vandercamp. No doubt on behalf of his father."

"So are we going to go wide with his photo and flush him out?" Molly asked.

"I don't think so. A guy like him, he'll go to ground. For now, the best thing for us is to let him be overconfident and think we don't know who he is or what he's been up to. What's up with Garrison?"

"Not much. Same routine as last night. Late hours at the office, then home."

Jesse looked at his watch. "Go home and get some rest. I think we're all going to have to meet again tomorrow night."

"You sure, Jesse? I can put in a few more hours."

"Go home, Crane."

She clicked off.

About twenty minutes later, Jesse's Bluetooth kicked on and cut off the music he was listening to. His dashboard screen told him it was Dylan Taylor on the line. He picked up.

"What's going on? You're on the Swan Harbor cop, right?"

"Drake Daniels," Dylan said. "Yeah."

"This about him?"

"Maybe more than just him. What was the name of the guy with the landscaping service?"

"Garrison."

"Well, two minutes ago Daniels pulled his cruiser into the driveway of a house with an Escalade EXT in the driveway. The driver's-side door has a tree logo painted on it and —"

"*Garrison* written over the top of the tree."

"That's it."

"Molly was sitting on the house until a little while ago. I told her to go home. Good thing you were on Daniels."

"What do you think it means, the two of them getting together?"

Jesse considered the question for a moment. "I think they're probably nervous."

"About what?"

"About being loose ends," Jesse said. "Garrison's head landscaper, a guy named Roberto, has vanished. The Cummingses were murdered. If Garrison and Daniels are involved in this somehow, they've got to be wondering if they're going to be next."

"Or maybe that's wishful thinking."

"Only one way to find out. I think it's time I had a talk with Lundquist and Chief Forster."

"Talk? Talk about what?"

"Relax, Dylan. I don't have enough to go to Weld with, but cop to cop, I think I can raise some questions and get cooperation."

"What should I do?"

"Head home. Daniels and Garrison aren't going anywhere at this hour."

"Okay, Jesse, but I wish you'd let me know what's going on. Alisha's crawling out of her own skin. She feels so powerless in all this. I'm afraid she might do something stupid if this drags on much longer."

"Go be with Alisha. We really can't afford for her to act out."

"Give me something to tell Alisha, Jesse."

"Tell her I believe her."

"That'll mean a lot to her," Dylan said. "I think the thing that's weighed on her most was thinking you thought she killed an unarmed man. She knows what you risked for her, and the thought she's let you down has been eating at her."

"Dylan, you're ex-military, right?" Jesse said, changing subjects.

"Army. Why?"

"Can you still rappel without breaking your neck?"

"Sure, but —"

"Can you take tomorrow morning off?"

"Until noon, not a problem. But, Jesse, I don't understand."

"You will. Meet me at the station at eight and don't say anything about it to Alisha, please."

"If it helps, of course."

"It will help. Tomorrow at eight."

Jesse pressed the disconnect tab on his steering wheel before Dylan Taylor could ask another question.

By the time he got back to his condo, Cole

was once again long asleep, and Jesse was in no mood to wake the kid up and question him about the photo. He figured that would keep until the opportunity presented itself. In the meantime, he had some calls to make and a bed to crawl into.

78

Lee Harvey stood at ease, hands clasped behind him as the Colonel paced back and forth. The only other time he had witnessed his father acting this way was on the day he told the Colonel he'd enlisted. That was a day he wasn't ever likely to forget. Although there were many people involved in the movement given to histrionics, the Colonel had always been the rock who let everyone else carry the emotion. He was the puppet master. But on that day the Colonel had changed from the eye of the storm to the storm itself. He'd been pacing just as he was now and then exploded, charging at his son, raging, calling him a traitor.

"This is betrayal from which there is no return, son," the Colonel had shouted at him, face red, spit flying.

If it hadn't been for James Earl holding his father back, there would have been blood spilled. Of that Lee Harvey had no doubt. The Colonel liked to say that was the only time in James Earl's life he had been of any value.

"You're dead to me, boy. Dead!" the Colonel had screamed, clawing at the air as James Earl held on to him. "Do you hear me? Dead. Dead. Dead."

Lee Harvey had heard it then, and watching his father pacing in front of him, he heard it now.

"If what you say is true, we may have to pick the pace up on things," the Colonel said at last.

"It's true, sir. I can feel it sure as I used to know when the enemy was near my unit in the mountains. Chief Stone is putting things together, and killing the Cummingses both helped and hurt."

"You second-guessing me, son?"

"No, sir. The Cummingses had to be dealt with. They would have been easy to break and it all would have collapsed. At the same time, their murders are causing a lot of attention to be paid by the police."

"What would you suggest, Lee Harvey?"

His father had rarely called him by his given name since they had reconciled, so when he did, Lee Harvey knew it was a serious question.

"As I see it, you've got three options, sir.

417

One, you ramp up the schedule so much that outside interference can't possibly react quickly enough to prevent you from achieving your ultimate goal. Two, a delaying action to distract the enemy long enough to achieve your goal without having to accelerate the schedule too drastically." Lee Harvey hesitated long enough to get his father's attention.

"The third option, son. What's the third option?"

"Kill the head and the body dies."

"Indeed it does," the Colonel said, but he wasn't smiling. "Killing Stone might make us pay too heavy a price, though he does seem to be the only one of these cops who can see the bigger picture. It'd be nice to have someone like that on our side."

Lee Harvey's face twisted in confusion.

"Don't worry, son. I'm not thinking of approaching him, though he does seem to get along with that worthless brother of yours." The Colonel rubbed his cheeks as he thought. "If I was to choose the third option, how would you go about it?"

"I think it would be best if I kept that to myself, sir. It insulates you and the movement."

"At least I've got one son with a brain in his head. Okay, keep eyes on Stone, but don't expose yourself. Keep your distance. I'll inform you of my decision as soon as I formulate it."

"Yes, sir."

As the soldier was leaving, the Colonel called after him. "I wished you hadn't betrayed me that way, Lee Harvey. You don't know what it did to me."

"But if I hadn't enlisted and received the training and experience I did, think of how much less value I would be to you. With all due respect, sir, where would you be now without someone like me?"

"I had in mind for you to lead, son, not to scurry about in the shadows and to bloody your hands."

"I like the shadows, sir. They're where I'm comfortable and where I belong."

The Colonel watched his son leave. He knew Lee Harvey was right and that he was a very valuable asset to him in this situation. It was just as clear to him that the war had turned him into someone else, something else. In a way, all three sons were lost to him forever. But like all men of his ilk, Leon Vandercamp saw it only in terms of what the cost was to him. He didn't much dwell on the price his sons had paid.

79

Lundquist was standing on Newton Alley a foot to the right of the spot where John Vandercamp had died, exactly where Jesse had asked him to wait in the message he'd left on his phone. The statie was a few minutes early for his meeting but kept checking his watch. At precisely nine, Jesse stepped out of the door of the Pembroke Gallery and stood to Lundquist's left.

"What's this about, Jesse?"

Jesse looked at his watch and said, "You're about to find out. Pay close attention."

With that, Jesse removed a firecracker from his pocket, lit it, and tossed it a few feet in front of him. In the second or two it took for the fuse to burn down and for the firecracker to explode, two things happened: Jesse unholstered his nine-millimeter and Molly appeared at the opposite end of Newton Alley.

She lit a string of firecrackers, tossing

them. That's when the narrow, dead-end street exploded with noise. Jesse's firecracker blew. *Bang!* Molly's blew. *Bang! Bang! Bang! Bang! Bang! Bang! Bang! Bang! Bang!*

Jesse fell to the pavement, the tiny bits of clam and oyster shell locked in the asphalt glistening in the morning sun. He dropped his nine-millimeter at his side. As Lundquist wheeled to his left to see if Jesse was all right, he was shocked to see another man wearing a combat hood kneeling over Jesse. The hooded man picked up Jesse's sidearm, tucked it into his waistband, and grabbed a knotted rope that extended from the roof of the old carriage house/warehouse down to the pavement. Before Lundquist could even react, the hooded man had climbed halfway up to the roof. And before Lundquist could pull his weapon, the hooded man had disappeared over the roof ledge, the knotting rope vanishing soon after. When Lundquist turned back around, Molly was racing down the street toward him and Jesse was standing up, brushing off his clothing.

"That's how it happened," Jesse said to Lundquist. "Vandercamp had a weapon. He did fire on Alisha first." Jesse turned and looked up at the warehouse roof and pointed. "That's why no one found a gun when they checked the crime scene. And that's why the setup had Vandercamp at a range shooting before this went down. With the gun disappeared, the only explanation for GSR on the body would be that he'd been at the range. Pretty solid plan. It almost worked."

"It still might, Jesse," Lundquist said. "This was a very fancy demo, but it proves only that it could have happened this way, not that it did."

Molly, slightly out of breath, said, "C'mon, Brian. This is how it happened and in your gut you know it."

"My gut isn't proof, Molly. None of this is."

"If I had a more solid case," Jesse said, "I would have played this out in front of Weld and the DA. The thing I may need is help from you."

"You're kidding me, right, Jesse? You have to be. I've got three murders to deal with in the towns surrounding Paradise and you're asking me to help you possibly step on the toes of the DA and interfere with the investigation of —"

"Four," Jesse said.

"Four what?"

"I believe there have been four murders and they're all related." Jesse turned to

Molly. "Go to the station, cue up the video footage, and make another copy of the soldier's service jacket. We'll be there soon, but first there's something I need to show Brian."

Less than five minutes later, Jesse and Lundquist were standing on the roof of the warehouse and Jesse was pointing out the deep pits in the tar.

"See these," Jesse said. "These were here when I came up yesterday. They were caused by the prongs of a grappling hook. I checked." Jesse moved two feet to his right and pointed at two fresh marks in the tar. "These are almost a match, but these were made only a few minutes ago by my accomplice." He moved to the rear ledge and showed Lundquist the two sets of prong marks there. "I wanted to show you that not all of what we played out for you was conjecture. Those first set of marks didn't get there by magic."

"Jesse, even if my gut and instinct tells me you're right, it's not proof. None of this changes anything."

"Not yet. Let's get to the station. I think you'll be a little more convinced after that."

Lundquist was partway down the staircase when Jesse dropped off the ladder from the roof. When he hit the landing, the door to the artist's loft opened up and Maryglenn stepped out.

"Hello, Jesse." She smiled. "Were you shooting off fireworks in the street before?"

Jesse raised his arms. "Guilty as charged."

"Next time, let me know. I love fireworks."

"It's a deal," he said.

Maryglenn smiled at him again and went back into the loft.

When they got down to the street, Lundquist asked who that was on the landing.

"A woman who loves fireworks" is what Jesse said. "A local artist."

As they got into their separate cars, neither of them spotted the man with the binoculars on a rooftop two blocks away.

80

Lundquist looked at the footage of the camo-painted Jeep on Molly's computer.

"My bet, that's the Jeep your witness spotted pulling away from the Cummingses' murder scene and it was driven by this man," Jesse said, placing Lee Harvey Vandercamp's photo in front of the statie.

"Maybe . . . maybe not. My witness says the Jeep was green."

"Your witness was driving fifty in the opposite direction in the dark. C'mon, Brian, read Lee Harvey's service record. Those walls would have been nothing for him to scale and rappel from. It all fits."

"All except the part where you actually produce a weapon and have a man setting up his own brother to be killed."

"Half-brother."

"Still . . ."

Jesse changed course. "Any luck with the lipstick?"

Lundquist made a face, and not a happy one. "You're all over the map. Are we talking about Wileford, the Cummingses, John Vandercamp, what?"

"The bikers coming into Paradise, the murders, the leaflets, the cross-burning, they're all pieces of one thing. And I don't think it's over."

"This I've gotta hear."

Jesse said, "First, the lipstick."

"Someone fitting John Vandercamp's description bought it just prior to closing at the old pharmacy and lunch counter on Main Street in Swan Harbor on the night of the attack."

"There's no surveillance footage, right?"

"No, these days it's a pharmacy in name only. Most of their business is small convenience items and the ice-cream counter."

"Convenience items like lipstick or sunblock, a bottle of aspirin?"

"What's the point, Jesse?"

"The point is that someone from out of town wouldn't have known to buy that lipstick at a place with no CCTV. He's the same person who would have known about Tammy Portugal's murder and how to throw the cops off by making what happened to Felicity Wileford look like a copycat crime."

"Daniels."

Jesse nodded.

"Let's say I buy that Daniels and Vander-camp were the perps on Wileford. I can see how it went too far and then Daniels came up with a way to throw us off, but what's this got to do with some big conspiracy?"

Jesse didn't answer directly. Instead, he put a small digital voice recorder on the desk. He said, "I made this recording last night. It's not the greatest sound quality because I had to keep it out of sight, but you'll be able to make out what I need you to hear." Jesse hit the play button.

What Lundquist heard was the discussion among Hank, Anya, and Jesse.

"That was the start of it," Jesse said. "The Saviors of Society were setting Alisha up. You heard the recording. Lee Harvey Vandercamp gave them specifics. They wanted Alisha."

"Let's say I accept your premise — and I'm not saying I do — that this was all part of a setup to get a black female cop to kill a young unarmed white man. I still don't see where all the other stuff fits in. They wanted Alisha. They got Alisha. Why all the rest of it?"

"I'm not a hundred percent sure myself. All the couples involved were interracial couples. I think they wanted to create an atmosphere where Alisha would feel threatened."

"Why kill the Cummingses?"

"To quote that great philosopher Mike Tyson, 'All my opponents had a plan until I hit them in the face.' Plans are great on paper, but they depend on people, and people screw up. I think two things went very wrong: the Wileford assault and my seeing the connection between the Cummings kid and John Vandercamp."

"Again, Jesse, they got Alisha. Look, it's gotten some national press and no one comes out looking good in this thing. She'll lose her job and do time. The kid is dead, but the world goes on. If they were trying to start a revolution or a race war, they've failed."

"That's what worries me. When this began, I thought it was about Alisha. But what if it's not?"

Lundquist stood up. "If I was you, I'd worry less about theories and more about finding some evidence that will stand up in court. Because right now, all you've got is four pit marks in tar, a lot of maybes, and not much else. Even if those bikers were to testify in court, what would it prove? That someone was willing to pay a lot to harass a cop."

"Are you willing to bet I'm wrong? These people have killed three, maybe four people to get to this point. What if that's just the opening to more bloodshed?"

Lundquist let out a sigh and sat back down. "Okay, Jesse, what do you want?"

"We need to get to one of the loose ends before they do."

"Who'd you have in mind?"

"You'll see."

81

Lundquist made sure Drake Daniels saw Jim Garrison being escorted out of the interview room at the Swan Harbor PD station house. The look on Daniels's face told Lundquist Jesse was probably right and that with a little encouragement, the Swan Harbor cop would break.

It hadn't been easy for Lundquist and Jesse to convince Chief Forster to let them interrogate Garrison and Daniels at the Swan Harbor station. The truth was that Lundquist could have done the questioning at a state police facility or even in Paradise, but Jesse insisted it be done in Swan Harbor.

Jesse said, "Daniels will really feel the pressure if we do it in his own station. I want him to see the other cops stare at him, whisper, and shake their heads while he sits in the hall and waits to go in."

One condition Chief Forster insisted on

was being present for the interviews.

"If you think you're going to come in here and use me as a prop, you're wrong," Forster had told them. "This is my town, my station house, and my cop. And I'm the one who's going to catch hell for you guys hauling Garrison in here."

Jesse wasn't happy about Forster's presence. Lundquist wasn't happy about any of it. But there was no avoiding it. Once they had started down this road, there was no turning back.

"Okay, Daniels," Lundquist said, after letting the sight of Garrison sink in. "You're next."

Daniels tried to keep a bored I've-seen-it-all-before expression on his face. It didn't last.

"Hey, what's this all about?" he said, his tough-guy resolve quickly vanishing. "This is bull. I'm not talking to you. I got nothing to say." He turned and looked up at Chief Forster. "Chief, what's going on here? You're not gonna let these two railroad me."

Forster patted his cop on the shoulder. "Drake, if I were you, I'd answer Captain Lundquist and Chief Stone's questions honestly and get back to work. I'm sure you've got nothing to hide and that this is all a big mistake."

"What are you talking about, Chief? What's a big mistake?"

Forster didn't answer but made sure to stay behind Daniels.

Lundquist said, "Look, Daniels, I'm not buying what Chief Stone here is selling, and so far, at least, neither is your chief."

" 'Selling'? What are you talking about? Selling what?" Daniels was already sweating, his breathing rapid and shallow. He turned back to look at his chief for support.

"Stop looking at him," Jesse said, voice chilly and calm. "He can't save you. No one can save you, because there are two people in this room who know the truth: you and me."

"What are you talking about?" Daniels looked behind him again. "Chief Forster, I swear I don't know what —"

"Felicity Wileford," Jesse said. "You think you fooled me for one second with that lipstick routine? It must've seemed like a good idea at the time. I figure it was Garrison, the kid, and you, and things got out of hand. It happens that way sometimes, but you remembered the Tammy Portugal homicide and thought you could throw us off the scent." Jesse put his face very close to Daniels's. "The kid's dead and Garrison is a tough guy, but he'll roll over on you eventually. They always do. It's called self-preservation. People want to save their own skins. How about you?"

Daniels jumped out of his chair. "That's it! We're done in here," he said, voice cracking.

Lundquist put a big paw on his shoulder and shoved him back in his seat. "We're done when I say we're done. And I've got to tell you, the way you're acting makes Chief Stone's version of things sound better and better."

"You guys need a scapegoat and you're trying me out for the part," Daniels said, catching a second wind. "It's not going to work. If you had anything on me, you wouldn't be playing games with me. So either show me something or let me out of here to go do my job."

Forster spoke up. "I told you my man wouldn't have been involved in anything like this."

"Thanks, Chief," Daniels said. "Now can I go?"

Lundquist waved for him to calm down. "In a second. Relax. Chief Stone, Chief Forster, can you give us a minute?"

Forster agreed immediately.

Jesse shrugged. "I don't like it, but this is your case." He pointed at Daniels. "Lundquist, I'm telling you, he's dirty."

When the door closed, Lundquist sat opposite Daniels. "It's just you and me now, you idiot. Don't speak unless I tell you to. Just sit there and listen. Like I said, I'm not buying that you had anything to do with the Wileford assault . . . but there's no doubt you helped them cover it up. I don't want you, but I've got an open case and you're going to help me close it one way or the other. I don't want to hurt a cop, not even one as worthless as you. I might even see my way to guarantee you keep your benefits. Just give me Garrison and the kid and tell me what the plan was."

Daniels stood up out of his chair. "Screw you and screw them guys. The next time you want to talk to me, it'll be with a lawyer present. I got nothing to say to you."

"Fair enough," Lundquist said, grabbing a file off the table. "But before you go, I've got something you need to look at." He opened the folder and spread out crime scene photos from the Cummings homicides. "These two were loose ends, also. This is how your friends deal with loose ends like you and Garrison."

"Friends? What friends?" Daniels said, his tough-guy act even less convincing now.

"If they execute you and Garrison, at least

I'll know who did it and I can wrap up all the open cases at once." Lundquist got up. "Those are copies. You can keep them. They're like a gift from the ghost of Christmas future. Your future, which, given how you're acting, will be a short one. So, last chance. You want to talk to me now?"

Daniels swept the photos off the table and stormed out.

82

Jesse waited until he was certain Daniels had left the station before returning to the interview room.

"Hate to admit it, Jesse," Lundquist said, "but that man is guilty of something. He is spooked."

"Of course he is. Did you show him the pictures?"

Lundquist nodded. "Daniels turned white and then made a show of throwing them to the floor. He's worried."

"He should be. That was the point. What did he say when you tried to be good cop to my bad cop?"

"I could tell he was thinking about my offer, but given that Wileford is now a homicide, he pushed back. He's not a total idiot. He knows that if he admits to taking any part in the assault itself or the coverup that he's burnt. He'll lose his job and his pension. Probably also do time, regardless of my intervention. I could make all the fancy promises in the world, but he knows that there's no coming back from an admission like that."

Jesse smiled. "He may know it, but he hopes what you're saying is true. People build all sorts of fantasies out of a little hope. You've set yourself up as his life preserver. He thinks he can turn to you if things go wrong and gets it in his head that they really are coming after him. Now all we have to do is drive him into your arms."

"Do I want to know how you're going to do that?"

"Probably not."

The soldier had set up in the park across the street from the Swan Harbor police station and waited. He had already watched Jim Garrison leave. Garrison, perpetually red-faced and angry at something or someone, looked shaken and worried. As the landscaper came down the steps of the station, he'd kept checking over his shoulder, as if to make certain he wasn't being followed. Problem was, Garrison had been shadowed. When he got into his Escalade EXT and drove off, an unmarked Ford trailed half a block behind. And when Drake Daniels exited the station, he too checked over his shoulder. He looked even worse than Garrison had. Another unmarked car followed him.

Lee Harvey knew trouble when he saw it, and this was trouble. The disturbing part was that the police were being so obvious. They wanted Garrison and Daniels to know they were being tailed. And that meant one thing: They were being squeezed. The police were putting on the pressure, figuring one of them would break. The only thing working against them talking was the seriousness of the charges, but that would work for only so long.

Shortly after Daniels drove away, he watched Jesse Stone and the state police captain come down the front steps of the station. He focused on Stone. The police chief wasn't smiling. Stone didn't strike Lee Harvey as a man who smiled much, but still there was something about the cop that worried him. Stone was the key. Eliminate him and it would give them the time they needed. Lee Harvey reached into his pocket for his cell.

Before Jesse got to his Explorer, his phone vibrated in his pocket.

"What's up, Molly?"

"Mayor Walker's in your office waiting for you."

"Alone?"

"She's got lots of company."

"You want me to guess?"

"Reverend Sam, Reverend Weber, Father Stroby from Saint Rose, Rabbi Kaplan, and an imam from the Islamic Society in Roxbury."

"Sounds like a setup for a bad joke."

"No one's laughing, Jesse. You better get over here."

"Any idea of what's going on?"

"No clue, but it must be big."

"Tell them I'll be there in about a half-hour."

The Colonel was not pleased to have to answer his phone. He had the bullhorn in his hand and was ready to whip up his followers in front of Paradise town hall.

"This had better be important, son."

"Looks like Daniels and Garrison were questioned by Stone, Lundquist, and Forster."

"Did they break?"

"They walked out of the station in Swan Harbor and they were followed."

"I see."

"You've got choices to make, sir."

439

"That I do."

"There's more, sir. Stone has figured it out."

"What's that?"

"How John W.'s gun disappeared."

"I think that just made my mind up for me, son. Do we understand each other?"

"We do, sir."

"Tonight, then. Before he can cause any more trouble."

"Understood."

Lee Harvey got off the phone and began formulating the murder of Jesse Stone.

83

Molly pointed at the conference room. "They're waiting in there. I ordered in some food from Daisy's."

Daisy's. Cole. He remembered the photo of Celine sitting on his lap all those years ago. Tonight he would finally get a chance to ask Cole about why he was carrying that photo around with him. Over the last few days Jesse had been too busy to give it a lot of thought. He smiled now, recalling his time with Celine. In every way except for her dark hair and coloring, she was a prototypical California girl. When she wasn't at the hospital, she was outdoors. She loved surfing, biking, and hiking. She was a little too much into healthy eating to suit Jesse, but mostly he remembered they had fun together.

"Earth to Jesse Stone," Molly said, snapping her fingers. "Earth to Jesse Stone."

"Sorry."

"Where were you, Jesse? You had a weird cast to your eyes and a goofy smile on your face."

"Back in L.A."

"Thinking about Jenn?"

He laughed. "I wouldn't be smiling."

"Have you heard from her lately?"

"No. Knowing Jenn, I think she feels somehow responsible for what happened to Diana."

"Because of the wedding? That's silly."

"You know Jenn. Everything's about her. I better get in there."

All eyes turned away from the food to Jesse as he entered the conference room. Mayor Walker stood up and intercepted Jesse, looping her arm through his and marching him back outside into the hallway.

"Where are we with the investigation? Have you made any progress in mitigating what Officer Davis did?" the mayor asked. "Because I don't mind telling you, Jesse, we're being slaughtered in the press. And the men in that room are looking for something to hold on to."

Jesse thought about his answer before he gave it. His instinct was to not share until he had some evidence that would stand up in court, but he owed Connie for backing him when he hired Alisha.

"I think Alisha's telling the truth," he said. "She was returning fire when she killed John Vandercamp."

The mayor looked stunned and puzzled. "What? How is that —"

"I can't prove it yet, but we're close."

"Who's 'we'?"

"Lundquist and Chief Forster from Swan Harbor."

"Should I say anything to them? They're pretty desperate to hear something positive. While it's not exactly civil war in the streets, tensions are running pretty high. And like I said, we're getting killed in the press. With all of Vandercamp's and Reverend Sam's people here, it won't take much for things to explode."

"You can't say a word, not yet," Jesse said, his tone firm. "I can't prove anything, and we can't risk a leak. No one can know anything about what I've told you. No one, Connie. We can't give anyone a chance to cover their tracks."

"Okay, Jesse, your people have done a good job of keeping the peace so far and I trust you, but I'm afraid something's going to give soon."

Jesse pointed at the conference room. "What's this about, anyway?"

"They want to hold a town hall prayer-vigil thing at the old meetinghouse tomorrow night. I'll let them explain."

Jesse and the mayor walked back into the conference room. Jesse understood the impulse to show unity. The tension was palpable and a prayer vigil might be a way to vent some of the steam, but it could also be trouble.

"Gentlemen," he said, nodding. "The mayor tells me you want to hold a prayer vigil in the old meetinghouse tomorrow night."

Rabbi Kaplan, a tall and slender man with a kind face, stood and gestured toward the imam.

"Jesse, this is Imam Muhammed Talib from the Islamic Society. For many years we have served on the Council for Religious Unity, and when Father Stroby suggested we do this, I thought of the imam."

"As-salamu alaykum," Jesse said.

Imam Talib, an older, olive-skinned man, smiled. *"Wa alaykumu s-salam.* Where did you learn this, Chief Stone?"

"When I worked in Los Angeles there were two mosques in my patrol sector."

Reverend Sam had had enough of the pleasantries. He stood up and strode over to Jesse. "I'm good at reading faces, Chief

Stone. I can tell there's something about this you don't like."

"I understand the symbolism of this happening in a place connected to the Underground Railroad. I can't stop you, but not everyone will be inside the meetinghouse praying and holding hands."

"Meaning?" asked Reverend Weber.

"There's bound to be protesters outside the meetinghouse, and they're not going to be polite."

Father Stroby said, "You mean Vandercamp's people."

Jesse nodded. "They've been fairly well behaved to this point, but if you know anything about their history, it won't last. They wait for events like you're planning to show their real colors. I suggest you go on the Web and see what they do."

"We must never let the haters win," said the rabbi. "We are all agreed."

All the clergy nodded in affirmation.

The imam said, "We realize this will make it difficult for you, most especially because of the incident which seems to have sparked all this. But people of faith must never be intimidated by such people as these."

"We're sorry, Jesse," said Father Stroby, "but this is going to happen. We just wanted you and the mayor to be prepared."

Jesse and Mayor Walker shook their hands as they left.

"Well, Jesse, it looks like your people are going to be getting even more overtime."

"Connie, at this point, I think they'd trade it in to make this go away."

She patted Jesse's forearm. "If that was the way things worked, I'd resign in a second."

As he listened to the mayor's heels clack on the linoleum floor, Jesse realized that he might need to push the envelope more than he'd wanted to.

84

It had already been a long day by the time Jesse sat across the table from Detective Lieutenant Mary Weld at the Lobster Claw. Before leaving the station he'd filled Dylan Taylor, Healy, and Molly in on what he had planned. He asked Molly to fill in the other two members of the shadow investigation on how things had progressed and what needed to get done.

Weld ordered a beer. Jesse, a lime in a tall glass of club soda.

Weld twisted up her lips and shook her head at that. "I heard you were a drinker."

Jesse said, "Past tense."

"I'm not keen on seafood, Chief. So if we're not here to drink, what are we doing here?"

"I wanted to have a conversation."

She was shaking her head again. "Up to right now, I gave you a lot of credit. You haven't stuck your nose into my investigation and you haven't bellyached too loud about me going public with the results. Oh, I know you and your people have been sniffing around the edges of things, but I expected that. I would have thought less of you if you didn't want to stand up for one of your cops."

When the drinks came, Jesse asked the waitress not to return to the table until he signaled for her. Weld and Jesse clinked glasses. Jesse put his glass down. Weld sank half her beer.

"Okay, Stone, you want to talk, then talk."

"Officer Davis *was* returning fire like she claims she was. You need to hear me out on this."

Jesse told Weld about how Alisha had omitted the sense she was being followed and the cat coming out of the shadows from her statement because she was embarrassed. About how he had gone back to the scene, talked with Maryglenn, and found the grappling hook's pit marks on the roof ledges. He explained about the demonstration Molly, Dylan, and he had done for Lundquist's benefit.

Weld took it in and Jesse could see she was thinking about what she would say next. She took another sip of her beer.

"We took a statement from this Maryglenn McCombs woman," she said, "but she said she hears critters on the roof all the time. Still, I admit we should've checked out the warehouse roof. I'll get a tech up there first thing. It gives Officer Davis's lawyer something to work with, but proving something could have happened doesn't mean it did happen. I hope you've got more than this or it's going to be a one-beer conversation." Weld finished her beer.

"Fair enough," Jesse said, then waved to the waitress for another beer. "There's more."

Weld took a pull on her second beer when it arrived. "I'm listening."

"You heard about the double homicide at the gas station outside of town?"

"I did."

"What if I told you that Gary Cummings Junior was shooting at the stand right next to John Wilkes Vandercamp the day Vandercamp died?"

"Helluva coincidence."

"Uh-huh. Hell of a coincidence that John Vandercamp just happened to be shooting hours before he was killed so that he was covered in GSR and so that if he had fired at Officer Davis, there'd be no way for you to tell."

Weld held up her beer. "Three quarters of

a glass left."

"I'm sure your investigation uncovered the cross-burning we had in town."

"At your old house. That's why Officer Davis claims she wanted to interrogate John Vandercamp."

"John Vandercamp purchased the kerosene for the cross-burning at the Cummingses' station. The father notified us. Funny thing, though. The surveillance footage doesn't show Vandercamp driving up to the pump. He walked to and from the pump. Odd, huh?"

"There's a point here somewhere, right, Stone?"

"There's more than a point. There's a conspiracy. Alisha was set up. You also know about the Wileford homicide in Swan Harbor."

Weld nodded and sipped.

"Wileford was staying at a bed-and-breakfast with a white man. The Patels, the people who bought my old house, are an interracial couple. And Officer Davis is —"

"Involved with Dylan Taylor, a white man. None of this proves anything, Stone."

"If the coincidences piled up any higher, we could climb them to the top of the Hancock Building. Just keep an open mind because we're right on the verge of getting a confession on the Wileford homicide. When that breaks, it's all going to break. If it goes the way I think it's going, you and the DA might want to give yourselves some room to maneuver."

"So you're doing all this to save our careers, me and the DA, huh?"

"I'm doing what's right."

"And so who's at the center of this grand conspiracy?" Weld laughed as she spoke. "Leon Vandercamp? You're going to sit there and tell me he sacrificed his son?"

"That's exactly what I'm telling you. And he used another one of his sons to do it." Jesse slid Lee Harvey Vandercamp's military file across the table to Weld. "Keep it. Study it. Then tell me I'm crazy."

"Okay, Stone, you make a good case, but here's where it falls apart. Conspiracies are usually meant to produce some desired effect. What's this gotten Vandercamp except a dead son and a cop who'll go to jail? This hasn't caused a race war or a revolution, and a week from now no one outside of Swan Harbor or Paradise will remember it. It'll be just another cop shooting a civilian, and the details of race and the rest will be forgotten."

Then it hit Jesse like a slap from a hand he didn't see coming. He threw a twenty on the table and ran. As he did, he called back to Weld, "You're right, but you're wrong."

85

Drake Daniels kept muttering to himself not to look over his shoulder, but it was no damned good. He was just plain scared. Cops, especially ones in a town like Swan Harbor, didn't have much occasion to fear for their lives. Still, he knew neither his badge nor his gun would mean a freaking thing to the soldier. He'd seen the man's handiwork. He hadn't been able to get those crime scene photos out of his head, featuring the bloodied bodies of the Cummingses.

As he trotted up the granite steps to Jim Garrison's house, Daniels wanted to smack his head against the door instead of knocking. *Why did I get involved with these people to begin with?* That question had chased the crime scene photos around his brain like a dog chasing its own tail since he'd walked out of the Swan Harbor station house. Sure, the money was a nice inducement and the turn-on of being the bad guy when the three of them surrounded Felicity Wileford was about the biggest thrill of his life. He had never witnessed human fear like that. And of course it had all gone too far and too wrong. *Fucking Garrison!* He was such a hothead to begin with, and after the woman kneed him, he lost all control. Not even the Vandercamp kid could control him. *That stupid kid, he was almost as scared of Garrison as the woman was.* Daniels cursed himself again because the kid was dead and he was tethered to Jim Garrison.

When Garrison opened the door, he looked over Daniels's head and around him to make sure he didn't see anyone or anything suspicious.

"What the hell are you doing here?" Garrison said, his breath stinking of vodka.

"What do you think? We're in this together now. One of us talks, we're both screwed."

"Shut your pie hole, idiot! You wearing a wire?"

"What?" Daniels made a confused face. "No. why would I be —"

"Step into the hallway and strip."

"No way."

Garrison took his hand out from behind his back and shoved an old Colt .45 Peacemaker in Daniels's face. "Do it or get the fuck out of here. The only way you're getting in this house is by showing me you ain't wearing a wire."

Daniels considered his options. As much as he didn't like having a gun shoved in his face or the idea of stripping down in front of Garrison, he knew he was better off talking this out with Garrison than leaving. Together they might have a chance against the soldier if he came for them. Individually, they didn't have a prayer.

"Okay, all right, but get that thing out of my face."

Daniels stepped inside, closed the door behind him, and removed every stitch of his clothing.

"Satisfied, Garrison?"

"Satisfied? You're fatter and uglier to look at without your clothes. Get dressed before I puke. I'll be in the den."

It was all Daniels could do not to pick up his off-duty piece and blow out the back of Garrison's head. Instead, he got dressed and met Garrison in the den. Garrison was sitting in a leather recliner, a half-empty bottle of vodka at the side of the big black chair. He pointed to his dry bar.

"You want something to drink, help yourself."

"No, thanks. I think it's better if we stay sober in case he comes for us."

Garrison laughed. Even his laugh was rife with cruelty and anger. "Too late for me. So you think that son of a bitch will really come after us the way he did the Cummingses?"

"You tell me," Daniels said. "Did you tell him we were questioned?"

Garrison laughed again. "Are you stupid? Why would I tell him? But you've got to know that Stone or that Lundquist guy spread the word. One way or the other, he'll know. We gotta hope that he won't hurt us because it'll look too suspicious. Stone and Lundquist would know it was him."

Almost before that last word came out of Garrison's mouth, a bullet ripped through the den window, carved a hole in the draperies, and tore apart the glass and face of the antique grandfather clock that stood a few feet behind the recliner. Both men froze for a second and then dived onto the floor.

"So much for things looking too suspicious," Daniels said. "We're dead men."

"Calm down, you fat piece of —"

But Daniels had already made up his mind as to what he was going to do. "Shut up, Garrison. For once, shut up," Daniels said, pointing his Beretta at the place on Garrison's body where most people have a heart. "Stand up!"

"But —"

"But nothing. Up!"

Garrison stood and opened his mouth, but before the landscaper could say another word, Daniels shot him three times in the chest. Garrison was dead before he hit the floor. Daniels waited a full minute to make sure no more bullets were going to come through the den window. When he was as sure as he could be, he grabbed Garrison's Peacemaker, stood where Garrison had stood, and fired two shots at a spot a foot or two beyond where Daniels had fired from. He wiped the handle clean of his prints, placed Garrison's limp right hand around the grip, index finger on the trigger, then dropped it.

All the shots would have the neighbors calling 911. Now all Daniels had to do was stay away from the windows until his Swan Harbor colleagues showed up. The safest place for him would be in a cell in the Swan Harbor jail. Not even the soldier could get to him in there. In the meantime, as sirens wailed in the distance, Drake Daniels worked on the story he would tell the cops and wondered what kind of deal he could get from Lundquist.

86

Jesse had done a lot of hard things in his life. He played minor-league ball and was one step away from the majors. He'd been in the Marines, been an L.A. street cop and detective. He'd run a police force and been through a divorce. He'd had to kill men and watched as a man murdered his fiancée right before his eyes. Maybe the hardest thing he had ever done was to give up alcohol. That was different from not drinking. He'd done that for long stretches in the past. What he'd done by going to rehab and meetings was a commitment he meant to honor for himself and for Diana. But he was about to test himself and he wasn't at all sure he'd pass.

The Scupper was buzzing with activity, every barstool taken, the booths and tables full. The juke was blasting Aerosmith's "Dream On," and half the guys in the place were playing note-for-note air guitar along with Joe Perry. And the rush of it all came roaring in as Dix had warned it would. *It's as much about the rituals and atmosphere as the drinking itself.* Although Jesse tended to be a solitary drinker, he did enjoy the occasional bar night out. He was distant from it now, observing, watching the alcohol-induced smiles and camaraderie, the back-slapping and hugging, listening to the laughter that was a little too loud for the joke that was told. The problem was he wasn't sure how long he'd be able to hold it at arm's length.

There were two faces in the mix he was happy to see. One belonged to the person he'd come to find — James Earl Vander-camp — and the other belonged to the barman.

Joey O'Brien called out to him. "Yo, Jesse, what's up?"

Jesse leaned in close to the bar. "Listen, Joey, you know that special scotch you keep on hand —" O'Brien raised his palm to stop Jesse. "Understood." The barman winked. "Only the best for you, Chief."

"Good. I'll be with him at that table." Jesse pointed at James Earl. "Make his doubles of what he's drinking. I'm buying. Send a round over now and keep them coming. Remember, mine is from your special bottle."

Joey's face showed that he didn't much approve of Jesse's company, but bar owners can't afford to be judgmental types, not if they want to stay in business. "Whatever you say, Jesse."

Jesse could see that James Earl was already half in the bag and raring to go for the gold. James Earl's face lit up when he noticed Jesse standing by his table.

"Hey, Chief. Sit down. Sit down." James Earl shooed away his minder. "You, get lost," he said, pointing at the dull-eyed man of forty across from him. "I'm not likely to get in much trouble if I'm with the chief of police. Go on to my daddy and tell him I'm in good hands."

The man hesitated but left. Jesse had no doubt he'd call Leon Vandercamp the second he got outside, so Jesse had to work fast.

"I got a round headed our way," Jesse said as he sat down. "There are certain privileges that come with being the top cop in town, and a bottomless glass is one of them."

"I'll drink to that." James Earl sucked down the bourbon in front of him just as the round Jesse ordered arrived.

Jesse threw a twenty on the waitress's little

round tray and said, "Keep 'em coming."

He picked up his rocks glass of dark amber liquid and raised it at James Earl. They both sucked their drinks down and slammed their empty glasses on the table. Jesse couldn't quite believe how the act of drinking, regardless of the fact that there was only tea in his glass, brought the buzz back. He felt the warmth at the back of his throat, in his belly, and spreading out into his body. The mind, he thought, was incredibly powerful. They repeated this two more times before Jesse spoke. By his third double of tea, the placebo effect had, thankfully for Jesse, disappeared. The real stuff was getting to James Earl.

"How you feeling, James Earl?"

"It's all good, Jesse Stone. It's all good."

"Your daddy always have clowns like that guy trailing you around?" Jesse asked, hoping it would bring out whatever rebelliousness James Earl kept alive inside of himself.

"Fuck that guy and my daddy. Man, you have no idea what a curse it is to be born into the world I was born into."

"I think I can imagine."

Jesse thought he should wait for another round before he pushed, but James Earl had stuff he wanted to say.

"No you can't even, Jesse. I don't hate

461

Jews or blacks or Chinese people. I don't hate no Mexicans. I never really met none except the ones screaming at me and Daddy. My life is like living in a walled city where everyone in it is like a brick. Sometimes I think I'll choke on all the hate. I don't hate people. I swear I don't. I like people. I like you."

"And I like you, James Earl," Jesse said, patting him on the shoulder. "But I hate what people like your daddy stand for."

Jesse felt sorry for James Earl. Over the course of his life, Jesse had met many people who felt trapped by circumstance and family dynamics. He thought particularly of gang members in L.A. They were born into lives that often seemed predetermined: short and violent ones. Lives from which escape seemed impossible.

"C'mon, let's get outta here," Jesse said, slurring his words slightly for effect. He wanted to make sure they got out of there before Leon Vandercamp sent reinforcements to collect James Earl. "We'll go for a ride."

James Earl gave Jesse a bleary-eyed look. "You sure you should be drivin'?"

"I'm police chief!"

"That's the truth. Sure, let's go."

87

Jesse drove James Earl up to the Bluffs, to where the Salter house once stood overlooking the ocean. After a young woman had been shot to death in the old Victorian and the family's unsavory business practices had been revealed, the Salters had decided to demolish the place. When Jesse first came to Paradise, the Bluffs were crowded with Victorian manses built by the nineteenth-century movers and shakers of Paradise. Now only a few remained. But Jesse found the Bluffs to be the most peaceful and beautiful part of Paradise. And he thought it might have put James Earl in the right mind-set to unburden himself.

"Jesse, it sure is quiet and beautiful up here. A man could learn to like a place like this."

"That's why we're here. Thought you might like to have some quiet time away from it all."

"I'm not dumb, Jesse. I hope you don't think I'm dumb."

"I know you're not. That's why I wonder why you stay on with your father if you don't believe that crap he spews."

The Explorer got dead silent. James Earl slumped forward and Jesse thought he might be about to get sick. But it wasn't that at all. James Earl was crying, first quietly and then loudly. Jesse let him cry. It was time to let James Earl talk if he wanted to.

"They killed my brother."

Jesse knew better than to fill in the empty space.

"They killed him and I stood by and let them do it. I am so fucking ashamed of myself, Jesse. Every time I think I can't sink any lower . . ."

"There's always lower, James Earl. I know that from experience."

"Can a man kill himself jumping off these cliffs?"

"It's been done, but I won't let you do it. You've got a choice to make," Jesse said. "You can get John W. some justice or you can keep feeling sorry for yourself."

James Earl was crying again. Jesse knew there were only so many tears in a man, even one as drunk as James Earl.

"They thought he was disposable because he wasn't really one of us. He was Clarissa's boy."

"John Wilkes?"

"That's right. Daddy never had much regard for him, though I guess he loved him in his way."

"What about you? Does he love you?"

"In his way."

"Tell me how they did it, James Earl. Let me get some justice for your brother."

"I can't."

"Can't or won't?" Now Jesse was pressing him. When James Earl didn't answer, Jesse said, "How about I tell how it went down. Your brother Lee Harvey drove John from the shooting range to the Gray Gull and handed him a gun John W. must've thought was fully loaded. But your father couldn't risk John actually hitting Officer Davis or having a slug recovered. So the gun was loaded with blanks. After the shots were exchanged, Lee Harvey rappelled down, collected the gun, and climbed back up onto the warehouse roof. By the time Officer Davis got to John W., Lee Harvey had already rappelled down the other side of the building and was driving out of Paradise in a camo-painted Jeep."

"Holy shit! How the hell can you know

that?" James Earl stared at Jesse as if he had pulled a rabbit out of a hat where there was no hat. "You can't know that."

"But I do. C'mon, James Earl, this is your chance to break away and to put an end to the hate right here and now."

James Earl was thinking about it. Jesse gave him a last push.

"How about getting your brother a little justice."

"All right, Jesse. What do you need?"

"The missing gun would be best, but I'm sure it's been disposed of. Short of that, a sworn state—"

Now James Earl was laughing. "The gun ain't been disposed of. My daddy thinks I don't know it, but he's keeping it to put in a museum someday. You don't understand him, Jesse. He sees himself as some kinda messiah. He thinks there'll be a time when people see him like George Washington, that they'll build monuments to him for what he's done. And he thinks that gun will be part of a shrine or some such thing."

"You know where it is?"

"I do."

"Will you give me a statement now? I have a voice recorder. Tomorrow, I can have it transcribed and you can sign it."

James Earl hesitated but agreed.

■ ■ ■ ■

When James Earl had finished, Jesse could not believe how much of the plan he had been right about. There were missing pieces. For instance, James Earl didn't know what had happened to Roberto or about the motorcycle gang.

"You can't go back home now," Jesse said. "You know that, right?"

James Earl nodded.

"I'm going to make a call and arrange things."

But before Jesse could punch in the number, the phone buzzed in his hand. Lundquist's name appeared on the screen.

"You were right, Jesse," Lundquist said.

"Uh-huh. About what?"

"Daniels is waiting for his lawyer, but he's going to talk. He went to Garrison's house this evening and the soldier took a shot at them. Garrison panicked and tried to kill Daniels, but Garrison was drunk and missed. Daniels planted him with three in the chest. Where are you?"

"The Bluffs. You better get Lee Harvey's photo out there wide," Jesse said, but something was bothering him.

He liked being right about Daniels and

that the case was coming together, but there was something about the soldier screwing up that felt wrong. He was about to say something to Lundquist about that when he heard the roar of the engine and saw the lights coming at them.

Bang! The truck must've been doing fifty when it hit the passenger-side door. The door caved in with a telltale groan. James Earl's head snapped sideways with a dull crack as his neck broke. The left side of Jesse's head smacked hard into the window, briefly stunning him. As the Explorer was being pushed toward the edge of the Bluffs, a hundred thoughts went through his head. The loudest one was about stepping on the brakes and pressing the ignition switch. His only hope of survival were the airbags, and they wouldn't deploy if the Explorer went over without the engine on. Jesse felt for the brake pedal, found it, jammed down as hard as he could, and pressed the ignition. The engine turned over, caught, and . . .

88

There was nothing in his world but hurt. It pushed everything else out of him so that there wasn't room for thoughts or ideas. Every part of him was in pain. Moving his head nearly gutted him, and there was a vague feeling of nausea deep in the pit of his belly. His left arm and right leg were stiff and unmoving. It was dark when he opened his eyes, and he thanked goodness for it because even the tiny bit of ambient light split his head in two and made the nausea rise up from deep within him into his throat. He shut his eyes and let the pain and the sounds of the sea sing him back into unconsciousness. The last thing he remembered were the smells of gasoline, iron, and salt in the air.

As he drifted in and out with the waves, he thought he heard loud voices, the grinding of metal against metal, and a woman's mournful gasp. There were sparks. He could swear there were sparks and flashes of different colored lights. He felt himself rise up, and as he rose, so, too, did the pain. It was pain like he had never felt before. In his head he was tumbling, endlessly tumbling, waiting to crash to the rocky infield in Pueblo, but he never hit the dirt, never felt his shoulder crack. From somewhere on a distant planet he heard a voice calling to him, but the words were scrambled and made no sense. Then the sea sang again, and with it came the blackness.

The next time he opened his eyes, his head didn't quite explode and the pings and whooshes he heard were distinctly not of the sea. Nor were the odors that filled his nose. The salt, iron, and gas had been replaced by that odd mixture of ammonia, isopropyl alcohol, and humanity. There was a blurry shape to his left, a familiar human shape.

"Mol— Molly," he said, his voice no more than a raspy whisper.

But she didn't answer. Instead, she disappeared. Jesse heard her footfalls. "Nurse! Doctor, he's awake," she said, her voice very much louder than his whisper. "Jesse's awake. He's awake!"

"I don't mind telling you, Chief Stone,

you are a lucky SOB. I'm amazed you survived that tumble down the Bluffs. More than that, you're going to leave here in a few days with nothing more serious than a concussion, two black eyes, a badly sprained elbow and knee, and every inch of you is bruised. You won't be playing softball anytime soon, but in six weeks you should be fine. I've got a drip going with something for the pain, and when I release you I'll give you a script. For now, all you've got to do is rest."

By the end of the doctor's talk, Jesse had already begun to fade. He was confused by what the doctor had said about the tumble down the Bluffs because he was having trouble remembering. He meant to ask Molly, but he was out cold before the questions reached his lips.

In the scrambled pieces of his sleep, Jesse put some things back together, but not so that they made much sense to him. He remembered the sound of a truck engine and lights. He remembered rolling and bouncing, remembered opening his eyes and the sound of the sea. But there was something he could not get his head around, a hole in his memory that he could not fill in.

The next time he opened his eyes, there were two much larger human shapes to his left: Suit's and Lundquist's.

"Where's Molly?" Jesse asked, his voice not much stronger than it was before.

"She left here hours ago, Jesse. You trying to hurt my feelings?" Suit laughed as he said it. "A guy could get a complex."

"Sorry, Suit. It's good to see you."

"You look like crap." Lundquist leaned over Suit's shoulder. "But you did good work, Jesse."

Jesse was confused all over again. Both Lundquist and Suit could see the confusion on his face.

"Drake Daniels won't shut up. He's scared out of his wits. He's corroborated a lot of what's on the voice recorder," Suit said. "That was smart to record James Earl like that."

Lundquist was smiling. "Yeah, we recovered it and listened to it. James Earl really gave up the whole bunch of them, including his father and brother. My people and Weld's people are executing warrants as we speak."

"James Earl," Jesse said to himself, but

loud enough for the others to hear.

Lundquist shook his head. "Dead when they got to you guys. Too bad about him. There might've been hope for him as a person. Not like the rest of those crazy bastards."

Jesse didn't speak because he was letting the puzzle put itself together in his head. First he remembered the sound, and then came the image of James Earl's head snapping sideways when the truck plowed into the passenger side of the Explorer. He still couldn't remember the rest of it. He was sure there was something else, but it stayed just beyond his reach.

"Jesse, you okay?" Suit asked.

"James Earl died before we went over," Jesse said. "His neck broke when the truck hit us."

"Yeah," Suit said. "We found the truck at the bottom of the Bluffs next to your Explorer. Stolen from a yard on Trench Alley. You were lucky there, too. Truck could've landed on top of you."

Jesse felt that missing piece getting a little bit closer to his grasp. "Do you have the soldier, Lee Harvey Vandercamp, in custody?"

By the looks on Suit's and Lundquist's face, he had his answer.

"He's the dangerous one," Jesse said. "You've got to get him."

Lundquist put his hand on Jesse's shoulder. "We'll get him. In any case, we've ruined their party. Looks like Officer Davis is in the clear, at least as far as the shooting goes. You had it exactly right, Jesse."

That's when the last piece came within his reach, and Jesse grabbed it. Weld's words about a race war and revolution rang in his head.

"What time is it?" Jesse said, sitting up in bed, his head pounding.

Suit looked at his watch. "Seven-fifty-two. Why?"

"What time is the vigil at the old meetinghouse scheduled for?"

Suit looked puzzled. "Eight."

Jesse pulled the IV drip out of his arm, stood up from his bed, and went down to his knees.

"Get back in bed, Jesse," Lundquist said, pulling him to his feet.

"No." He swatted Lundquist's arms away. "We've got to get to the vigil. Now! Get me some scrubs to wear and my gun."

Lundquist didn't understand. "Why?"

"That's the target. Think of the symbolism of the old meetinghouse. Vandercamp means to declare war. Real war."

89

Suit called ahead as Jesse demanded and had the cops working security at the vigil begin clearing people out of the building by the time they arrived. The old meetinghouse was large for the era in which it was built but had no more square footage than a modern McMansion. Lundquist had already arrived by the time Suit and Jesse got there. Suit fished his pump-action shotgun out of the trunk.

"Jesse, you look like hell," Gabe Weathers said as Suit helped him out of his cruiser. "And your holster looks pretty silly over hospital scrubs."

Jesse ignored that. "Any trouble?"

"They're pretty pissed. I guess they feed off things like this." Gabe pointed at Vandercamp's people across the street from the meetinghouse, some of them draped in Nazi flags, others carrying signs with hateful slogans written on them. But it was the things they were chanting that sickened Jesse most of all, things he had hoped he would never hear again.

"Any sign of Leon or Lee Harvey Vandercamp?"

Gabe shook his head. Jesse really didn't like that, but it confirmed his worst fears, that something big, something bad, was going to happen.

"All right," Jesse said. "Try and pick up the pace and get everyone out of the area."

That's when Reverend Sam approached Jesse.

"Lord, Chief, what happened to you?"

"We can discuss it some other time. Right now I need you and the other clergy to get everyone out of the meetinghouse and out of the area."

Mahorn wasn't pleased. "Look, I know you have our best interests at heart, but we won't be bullied by the likes of haters like those people." He pointed at the small line of Vandercamp's supporters marching across the way.

"They're not the problem, Reverend."

"Then what is?"

That was when the first burst of automatic-weapons fire hit the windows on the second floor of the old meetinghouse, raining glass down on the street below and

476

forcing people who were exiting to retreat back inside for cover. Jesse grabbed Reverend Sam with his good arm, yanked him down to the sidewalk, and threw his body over Mahorn's.

"You okay?" Jesse asked.

"Fine. I'm fine. Anyone hurt?"

"Doesn't look that way."

There was another burst of gunfire, driving people back into the old meetinghouse for cover.

Then another.

"Reverend, I need you to crawl to cover, so I can deal with this. Can you do that?"

"I can."

"Go!"

Jesse rolled off Mahorn and the reverend combat-crawled into the building. Jesse crawled in the opposite direction and got behind Suit's cruiser, where Suit was kneeling and scanning for where the shots were coming from.

"Where's the shooter, Suit?"

Suit pointed to a storefront about a half-block away. There was a fourth burst of gunfire.

"Here's the crazy thing, Jesse. I don't think the shooter's trying to hit anybody."

"My bet, it's Lee Harvey. And it's not crazy," Jesse said. "I think he's trying to

477

drive everyone back into the old meeting-house. He wants as many people inside as possible. Watch the door. He'll fire whenever people try to leave."

Suit turned to look at the meetinghouse doors and, just as Jesse predicted, the minute people tried to leave, there was a spray of bullets aimed at the street twenty yards in front of the doorway. The bullets ricocheted, pinging into lampposts, lodging in trees, and smashing car windows.

"Why does he want people inside? He could cut a lot of people down in the panic."

"Maximum damage. I think there's a bomb planted in there. Demolition was one of Lee Harvey's specialties."

"Oh my God!"

"Do you think you can make it inside?"

"Sure, Jesse," Suit said, voice cracking slightly.

Jesse grabbed Suit's arm. "Look, Luther, I know you don't ever want to get shot again and you're newly married —"

"It's not that. What am I supposed to do when I get inside? I can't tell the people there's a bomb. That'll just make the panic worse."

"Remember why the place is a landmark and why they had the vigil here tonight."

That goofy smile of Suit's lit up his face.

"The Underground Railroad."

"Let's hope Lee Harvey didn't stop to read the plaque if and when he planted the bomb."

"Okay, Jesse."

"First, give me your radio and your shotgun."

Suit handed Jesse the shotgun and undid the radio from his belt and uniform shirt.

"Keep low," Jesse said. "He won't fire at you if you're going in. Get those people into the tunnel as fast as you can. Even if the building blows, I think you should be safe. And, Suit, one more thing . . . I couldn't be prouder of you. Now go save those people."

Jesse wasn't much for praying, but as Suit crawled toward the meetinghouse doors, he closed his eyes and prayed.

90

Lundquist was hunkered down behind his cruiser.

He called to Jesse, "SWAT team's on the way. Bomb disposal, too."

Jesse, the initial rush of adrenaline wearing off, was dizzy and nauseated, the pain of his bruised ribs and sprained limbs reminding him he'd come within a few inches of death less than twenty-four hours ago. He waved for Lundquist to come his way as he knelt over and sucked in large gulps of air.

"For crissakes, Jesse," Lundquist said, reaching him. "You going to be sick?"

"No. Listen. We can't wait for SWAT or the bomb squad. We've got to get people away from the outside of the meetinghouse now."

"Agreed. But what about the people inside?"

"Suit's handling it. My cops will give us

covering fire and then we're going to move along the cars parked on the opposite side of Salter Street until we pass the gunman's position. You're going to give me covering fire and I'll take him out."

"You're in no shape to walk, let alone take anyone out."

"My town. My call."

Lundquist was skeptical. "Let's see you make it there first. You know he'll be expecting something like this, right?"

"We don't have a choice."

Jesse got on the radio and ordered Molly to get the people away from the meeting-house.

"I don't care who they are or what you've got to do, but get them as far away from that place as fast as you can. That's an order, Molly. Get the auxiliaries to help."

Before she could question him, Jesse started barking orders at Peter Perkins and Gabe Weathers.

"When I give you the word," he said, "start firing at the shooter. If you take him out, fine, but I want as much lead thrown at that storefront as you and the rest can muster. Lundquist and I are going to be approaching from the opposite side of the street. Have someone keep eyes on us. Once we get close to his position, stop firing.

When you're done, clear out. Get away from the meetinghouse. All of you. That's a direct order. No heroics today." He turned to Lundquist. "Ready?"

"You know, when I got Healy's job I thought this kind of crap would be over forever, but I guess I'm as ready as I'm ever going to be."

Jesse keyed the mic. "Fire away."

Storefront glass shattered almost immediately, and the noise of all those nine-millimeters firing away was louder than Jesse thought it would be. As he and Lundquist made their way along Salter, Jesse hoped that Lee Harvey would be distracted and return fire, but Lundquist was right. Lee Harvey was expecting them to come for him, and Jesse had little doubt he would be better prepared for them than they were for him. He was definitely better armed.

When he and Lundquist were past the storefront, Jesse took a few seconds to try and regain some strength. He lay facedown on the sidewalk, exhausted and sick. The shotgun was dangling over the curb in his right hand.

"Can you see him?" he shouted to Lundquist above the gunfire.

But before Lundquist could answer, the covering fire ceased. He got close to Jesse and said in a whisper, "I can do this. Give me the —"

"No." Jesse forced himself up, leaning against the car. "Move back that way until you're directly across from him and start firing. Don't wait, just fire. Here's my nine so you won't have to stop to reload."

"But —"

"If I can't get at him with the shotgun, my nine isn't going to do me a bit of good."

Lundquist moved okay for a big man, though not as smoothly as Suit did. Lundquist did exactly what Jesse had asked him to do. He got into shooting position and began firing across the street at where Lee Harvey was holed up. Jesse could make out the soldier's silhouette as he scrambled to the storefront two doors beyond Lee Harvey. He took two deep breaths and held the last one in for a good long time. Then it was go time.

Jesse's first shot took out the remainder of the glass behind Lee Harvey. Jesse winced in anticipation of Lee Harvey returning fire, but he didn't hesitate and took a second shot at where he had seen Lee Harvey's silhouette. There was a groan and a thud, but Jesse knew the soldier could be playing possum. He dropped down to a knee to make himself less of a target, his legs screaming at him in pain. He peeked through the now glassless storefronts. Lee Harvey was down, pressing a hand to his neck, blood gushing out between his fingers.

Jesse waved to Lundquist to come, and they both rushed the position. Jesse kicked the M4 away from the soldier's side. Lee Harvey had on ceramic-plated body armor, but some of the buckshot had torn through the exposed part of the soldier's neck. As Jesse put his hands over Lee Harvey's to help stanch the blood, Lundquist searched for more weapons.

"Is there a bomb?" Jesse said. "Lee Harvey, is there a bomb? Where is it?"

Lee Harvey smiled and said, "Too late. Tick, tick, tick." He eyes went glassy and his body went limp.

Lundquist got up and started toward the meetinghouse, but before Jesse could stop him, the world exploded and the statie was knocked to the ground by the blast wave. Shards of white clapboard and glass covered the street. Car alarms were set off for blocks around. The blast knocked Jesse off balance and his knees slid out from under him in Lee Harvey's blood. His head bounced off the tiled floor of the store alcove and he fell into darkness.

91

It was dark but for the light of the monitors and because night filled every corner of his room's window. Jesse recognized the sounds and smells of the hospital. He also recognized the pain in his head and the full-body ache. He hoped there were no more pressing emergencies in Paradise, because there wasn't enough adrenaline in the world that could get him out of bed again. He moved his hand along the bed until he found the call button, and when he did, he held it down.

"Chief Stone, is everything all right?" the nurse asked, taking his pulse. "Are you in distress?"

"Other than everything hurting, no. How long have I been here?"

"You were brought in last evening."

"Are any of my officers outside?"

"First, let me get the doctor. Then we'll see about visitors."

Jesse had the impulse but not the strength to argue.

When the doctor was done examining Jesse, he told the nurse that she could send the officer in the waiting room in.

"And, Chief Stone, let's try not to yank the IV out of your arm or leave the hospital this time," the doctor said to Jesse. "You are worse for wear, and brain trauma is nothing to be ignored. I'm not sure how you managed to walk out of here the last time."

"I'm not going anywhere, Doc. Scout's honor. Were there any serious injuries from the explosion?"

"Cuts from flying glass, some tinnitus from the blast, but nothing too serious."

"Was anyone in the meetinghouse —"

"I'll let Officer Crane give you the details. Remember, Chief Stone, no more stunts or I can't promise you won't do permanent damage to yourself."

There might have been times when Jesse was happier to see Molly, but he couldn't recall them at the moment. And when she entered the room, Molly did something very un-Molly-like. She leaned over, kissed Jesse on the forehead, and hugged him as best she could. There were tears in her eyes.

"Just what the hell did you think you were doing?" she said to him as she wiped away the tears. "You could have been killed."

"That's the Molly Crane I know."

"Don't be an ass, Jesse. That was a suicide mission."

"I wanted you to worry about being chief again."

She smiled in spite of herself. "I hate you."

"You love me, Crane."

"That's why I hate you."

"So did Suit get everyone down into the tunnel?"

"Thank goodness for the Underground Railroad. Everyone came out okay — physically, at least. A few of the people were pretty traumatized."

"Suit?"

"He's Suit. He's fine."

"Don't ever tell him this, Molly, but he's a hero. He went back in there even though I told him there was probably a bomb."

"Suit would do anything for you, Jesse. You know that."

"This was different. He's married now. He did it because he's a good cop. How does Pilgrim Cove look?"

Molly laughed. "Like a bomb hit it."

When Jesse laughed, nausea welled up in him and it was all he could do not to be sick. When he collected himself, he asked about the arrests.

"The staties caught Vandercamp at the New York border. He had the gun on him just like James Earl said he would. It was loaded with blanks just like he said on the voice recording, but Lundquist isn't sure there's any way to physically tie it to what happened on Newton Alley."

"Is Vandercamp talking?"

"Claims it's a conspiracy to kill his children and put an end to his attempts to save the country."

"No surprise there. What's Weld say about Alisha?"

Molly smiled. "The DA is withdrawing the charges against her."

"You know I'm still going to have to fire her?"

Molly nodded.

"Drake Daniels?"

"He copped to a lesser charge. Lundquist said you had it about right. The idea was only to rough up Felicity Wileford as part of the scheme to shake up everyone in the area. John Wilkes was in charge, but once Wileford put up a fight, Garrison got carried away and beat her. It was Daniels's idea to try to make it look like a copycat thing. When they searched Garrison's house, they found a private armory, a collection of Nazi paraphernalia, racist literature, and child porn."

"You know you're acting chief again until I get out of here."

"Don't remind me. Is there anything else, Jesse? Anyone you want to see?"

"I need you to get a photo from my room at home and bring it here tomorrow morning. And I'd like to see Suit and Cole Slayton. He's living in my condo and working at Daisy's."

Molly gave Jesse an odd look. "Why is he —"

"I've got my reasons."

"Okay, Jesse." She leaned over him and kissed his forehead again. "Next time you pull something like that, you better get killed. Because if they don't kill you, I will."

"I love you, too, Crane."

92

Cole Slayton and Suit walked into Jesse's room at six p.m. the next day. Jesse wasn't feeling a whole lot better. And the extra day had given his bruises time to mature, so he looked even worse. He'd avoided the mirror all day, but the expression on Suit's face told him he was in bad shape. Even Cole Slayton seemed shocked at the sight of him.

"Cole, could you give Officer Simpson and me a minute?"

The kid shrugged and left the room.

"Holy sh— cow, you all right? You look awful."

Jesse laughed. "I feel worse than I look."

Suit got that goofy smile on his face. "Then I don't know how you're still breathing. I've seen corpses look better than you."

"Come over here, Suit."

When Suit approached the bed, Jesse put out his right hand. As Suit shook it, Jesse said, "I've known a lot of brave people in my life, but none braver than you, Luther Simpson."

"I'm not brave, Jesse, just dumb."

"You can't fool me, Suit. You knew what you were risking and you were scared, but you did it because it was the right thing to do and it was your duty. That's not stupidity. That's courage."

"Elena's not talking to me."

"It won't last."

"I hope not."

"Suit, thank you. You did good. Now do me a favor and send the kid in."

"About him. What's the deal?"

"That's between him and me."

"Okay, Jesse."

When Cole Slayton walked back into the room, Jesse was holding the photograph of Celine in his lap so that it was facing out.

Cole's face reddened. "Hey, who told you you could go through my things? Just because —"

"This is my copy," Jesse said, and then explained about how Connor Cavanaugh had seen the photo in Cole's room at the hotel. "Connor wasn't prying, but he had to pack up your stuff and thought it was weird that you were carrying around a photo with me in it. If you were in his position, you would think so, too."

"I guess."

"Celine was your mom?"

Cole looked angry and pleased all at once. "You remember her name?"

"I remember more than her name. She was great."

"If she was so great, why'd you break up with her?"

Jesse didn't answer directly. "You know there's been a lot going on in town since you got here?"

"I'm not blind. Yeah, I've been paying attention."

"So I've been occupied with that, but I was also wondering why you were carrying around a photo of me and your mom from so long ago. I meant to ask you about it, but you were either sleeping or at work before we could talk."

"You didn't answer me about why you broke up with her."

"That's just it, Cole. I didn't break up with her. She broke up with me."

"Bullshit!"

"No, it's not. Lying here, I've had time to think about it and to remember. We went away for a weekend on Catalina Island and your mom made a big thing about dinner on Saturday night. She booked us at a nice restaurant and got really dressed up. That wasn't usually her style or mine, but it seemed important to her. Things went sour right away because there was a family with young kids at the next table and I guess I said some stuff about never wanting to get married or have kids. She barely spoke during dinner, and when I woke up the next morning she was gone."

"Get outta here."

"When I got home and called her, she said she realized that there was no future for us and that it was stupid for us to continue seeing each other. That's the truth. Believing it or not, that is up to you."

Cole was angry. "You didn't think to ask her why she changed her mind so fast?"

"I took her at her word. She was right. I didn't want to get married and I didn't want kids. Now I realize what that dinner was all about. She was pregnant and she wanted to tell me."

"With me, yeah."

"Why didn't she tell me after you were born? I would have done the right thing."

Cole laughed. "That's funny. That's what Mom always said about you. That you always made a big deal about doing the right thing. And just so you know, she did try to tell you, but you were married by then to some blond woman and she didn't want to screw up your life."

"I'm sorry."

"About me?"

"Never. I want to be your father . . . if you'll let me." Jesse put out his right hand.

"You don't want to take a DNA test and make me prove it?"

Jesse shook his head. "Only if you want one. From what I hear, fathers and sons need to trust each other."

Cole took Jesse's hand and squeezed it with two-decades-plus of longing and anger. For Jesse's part, it was all he could do not to cry.

93

A month later, and much to Molly's relief, Jesse was back at work. All the windows in the Pilgrim Cove area had been replaced, all the glass and debris swept up and forgotten, but the damage had been done and there were some scars that could not be hidden. Mayor Walker and her allies wanted to have the old meetinghouse meticulously reconstructed, while the selectmen thought it might serve a higher purpose to leave it as it was: as a shrine to how far we had come and how far we still had to go.

So it was with no small amount of irony and awkwardness that the mayor showed up at the station as he was in the process of taking Alisha Davis's badge and gun.

"Ask her to wait," Jesse said to Molly.

When Molly closed the door, Jesse turned to Alisha and Dylan Taylor. He looked straight at Alisha. "You were a good cop, Alisha, and I don't regret my decision to hire you for a second."

"Thank you for believing in me, Jesse."

"I still believe in you, but you know how it's got to be. Even though you've been cleared in Vandercamp's death —"

"I know. I'm going now." She shook Jesse's hand and started for the door, Dylan walking behind her.

Jesse called after Dylan, "Can I talk to you for a minute?"

"Go on," Alisha said. "I'll be outside in the car."

Jesse gestured for Dylan to sit.

"When I was in the hospital, I had a lot of time to think about things."

Dylan shrugged. "Things like what?"

"It bothered me almost from the minute I heard Lee Harvey Vandercamp had tried to take out Daniels and Garrison. Then when I heard the slug the staties dug out of Garrison's wall was from a Ruger bolt-action deer rifle . . . You know the staties never found any hunting rifles in his Jeep or in any of the Vandercamps' possession. Besides, long distance wasn't Lee Harvey's MO. He killed close-up and personal, and he didn't usually miss."

Dylan shrugged again. "What about the M4 and the bomb? Those weren't close-up-and-personal weapons."

"Good point. Just the same, I'd lose that Ruger of yours you keep above the fireplace in your cottage."

"Funny you should say that, Jesse. Last time I saw it, it was sinking into the Atlantic."

"What about you and Alisha?"

"I'm driving her home to New York, but I don't think there is a me and Alisha anymore, not really. This thing strained both of us past our breaking points."

"Drive safe. See you when you get back."

It rubbed Jesse hard in the wrong direction that the Vandercamps had gotten even a small victory out of their violence and hatred, but he understood the enormous strain Alisha and Dylan had been under.

Given that he had just taken the badge and gun away from Alisha, Jesse wasn't really much in the mood for dealing with Connie Walker's political gamesmanship. But she had been pretty stout through the recent ordeal and had never retreated from her support of his hiring Alisha.

"What is it, Connie? I hope this isn't about the old meetinghouse. Those decisions are above my pay grade."

"You really can be an ass, can't you, Jesse?"

497

"Uh-huh."

"I'm here because I want to congratulate you."

"For what?"

"For being a father."

Jesse smiled in spite of his best efforts not to. "Thank you."

"You really didn't know Cole was your son?"

"Not a clue."

"How's it going?"

"We've got a lot of catching up to do. Right now I think we're trying not to step on each other's toes."

Then Mayor Walker stood up, came around the desk, and kissed Jesse on the cheek. "You'll be a good dad, Jesse Stone, but if you think this job is hard, just wait."

As the mayor was leaving, Jesse's desk phone rang. It was Lundquist.

"What's up, Brian?"

"Drake Daniels is dead."

"Dead?"

"Hanged himself in his cell. The threats got to him. He knew that even if they kept him in isolation, he was a dead man. With all the white supremacist gangs inside, he knew he was screwed. He figured he'd do it himself and not eat himself alive waiting to get hacked up."

"A guy who would know once told me that if you could assassinate a president, there was no such thing as being a hundred percent secure."

"Here's the best part. He left a note and confessed to murdering Garrison."

Jesse changed subjects. "Why do you think Lee Harvey let me get to him so easily? You know if he wanted to, he could have killed me three times over before I fired that shotgun once."

"Guilt. He did Cain one better. He had a hand in murdering his two brothers."

"He was willing to kill a building full of people and smiled about it as he was dying."

"When you figure humans out, let me know. How are you and your kid doing?"

"Why does everybody ask me that?"

"I think we take pleasure in watching you navigate in unknown waters."

Jesse had gone to several meetings even before he returned to work, and he was no longer keeping his AA visits a secret. He knew it would be unmanageable for him to go to meetings only down in Boston. Bill, the former fence, was officially his sponsor and they had enjoyed their post-meeting coffees since Jesse wasn't always running off to handle emergencies.

"Has Anya been back?" Jesse had asked Bill at that first meeting after he got out of the hospital.

"Haven't seen her and I've been here a lot."

"Too bad."

"That's the way it is, Jesse. It's much easier to fall back down a hole than to climb up."

Three weeks had passed since then, but Jesse was still struggling to make sense of his new life. It wasn't like him to dwell on things. Still, he couldn't stop thinking about how easily Lee Harvey might've killed him and how he might've died without ever knowing he was a father.

When sharing time came, Jesse found himself walking to the front of the room.

"Hi," he said. "My name is Jesse and I'm an alcoholic."

ACKNOWLEDGMENTS

I'd like to thank the estate of Robert B. Parker, Christine Pepe, and Esther Newberg for making my continuation of the series possible.

Special thanks to Tom Schreck for walking me through the potential minefield of AA and sobriety.

As always, I owe the greatest debt to my family. Without the willingness of Rosanne, Kaitlin, and Dylan to make the sacrifices that have allowed me to pursue my passion, none of this would have been possible, nor would it have any meaning. Thank you, guys. I love you more than I could express.

ABOUT THE AUTHOR

Reed Farrel Coleman, called "a hard-boiled poet" by NPR's Maureen Corrigan and the "noir poet laureate" in *The Huffington Post,* is the Edgar-nominated author of twenty-three novels and three novellas, including the critically acclaimed Moe Prager series and the Gus Murphy series. A three-time winner of the Shamus Award, he has also won the Anthony, Macavity, Barry, and Audie awards.

The employees of Thorndike Press hope you have enjoyed this Large Print book. All our Thorndike, Wheeler, and Kennebec Large Print titles are designed for easy reading, and all our books are made to last. Other Thorndike Press Large Print books are available at your library, through selected bookstores, or directly from us.

For information about titles, please call:
  (800) 223-1244

or visit our website at:
  gale.com/thorndike

To share your comments, please write:
  Publisher
  Thorndike Press
  10 Water St., Suite 310
  Waterville, ME 04901